He Without Sin

ED HYDE

Dedication

To my constructive criticizers and,
especially, my patient editor.

Epigraph

But we look for new heavens and a new earth according to his promises, in which justice dwelleth.

Douay-Rheims Bible 2 Peter 3:13

A Question of Guilt

ED HYDE

It's Come to This

I look around the courtroom and see several faces I recognize as former crewmates and associates from the Academy. Some of the crew members are missing; I presume they may be called as witnesses. The ones in the gallery have, like me, no doubt already been deposed as to the matter in question. That's a good thing — I do not want to have to sit in the witness stand.

One former crewmate is absent from the proceedings with an iron-clad excuse—he's dead.

The next trial will be different and not in a good way. I'm not looking forward to it, to say the least. I've already learned I will be called as a witness in that trial, will have to take the stand, and will be grilled about my part leading up to the events that almost took the life of yet another crew member. He is, thankfully, recovering from serious injury and is not present for medical reasons.

Sitting through these interminable proceedings I've had plenty of time to reflect. The places and events I recall seem remote and surreal to me already, so soon after our return. Remote not only because of the great distances we traveled but remote because they lie in the seemingly distant past; surreal in sharp contrast with the mundane courtroom setting.

With this crew I have shared an adventure spanning light-years and seemingly eons, and yet I can scarcely find one who will make eye contact. There is a pleasant exception. I have not seen or spoken to her since our debriefing. I seem to see in her face evidence of the desire for us to resume discussing plans for the future. It may be wishful thinking, but I hope not.

Court proceedings lurch forward in an oddly annoying way. Cryptic terms cloud the reason for endless delay; objections are raised over maddeningly childish topics and then resolved by semantic twisting and juggling; heated arguments arise over outwardly insignificant points that must, one hopes, conceal momentous legal portent—justifications for exasperation are manifold.

The prosecution's opening statement was ominous and disturbing. Paraphrasing, it went something like 'the state will prove the defendant guilty of causing the death of his subordinate through the defendant's inaction and failure to enforce required standard procedures.'

I turn again to look at David and his representative at the defendant's table. David looks different. Not older, but more vulnerable than I remember. His civilian clothes impart an aura of weakness, to my mind. Why did he not wear the uniform and insignia of a veteran commander?

And who is his counsel anyway? Who agreed to let David testify, and why? Sure he can be a charmer—confident, affable and witty, but there is the other side—quick to take offense, to anger, and to answer without filters. No, I would not allow it. It almost came to disaster earlier in the trial with David on the stand. A simple request about the chain of command: 'Please describe, as completely as you can, the chain of command aboard your vessel' or nearly that. I could tell, from long experience looking at the eyes, watching the mouth work, that David was ready to snap out an answer that would be regarded as inappropriate and argumentative. Fortunately, his counsel objected and pointed out that the chain of command listing every member of the crew had previously been submitted to the court as trial evidence.

Compounding the earlier risk, he's been recalled to the witness stand after the most recent delay. The judge calls for order; the bailiff declares the court once again in session.

"If we may, your honor, we will follow up where we left off," begins the attorney for the prosecution. He recaps key points leading up to the discovery of the body, emphasizing the fact that, one, by that stage of the mission all officers should have been aboard ship and, two, that David did not know the whereabouts of his second in command.

David's visage hardens; I wonder if the prosecutor notices?

"Question: Why would your second in command, who you admit was on the surface of the planet without your knowledge and in noncompliance with protocol, ostensibly wander off into a desolate and dangerous mountain pass?"

"I don't know. Maybe he had to take a leak."

The prosecutor reacts only with a smile.

The judge is not amused, pounds the gavel, and announces an immediate recess.

"The defending attorney and your client will please meet with me and the prosecutor in my chambers. Now."

Judge Compton, living up to his no-nonsense reputation, departs the room. David's attorney, clearly stunned by the sharp reaction of Compton, signals David with a movement of his hand and arm to follow him into the judge's chambers. The prosecutor makes a small show of graciously letting them go first, and then follows, still smiling. A low murmur can be heard from the courtroom visitors. No one leaves the room during the few minutes that they are gone. Carol looks at me with her ever calm and composed expression, which I return with an eye roll and shake of my head.

I am surprised to see Dean Carson. To my knowledge, he has never commanded nor crewed on any deep space missions, and yet, obviously, he is receiving longevity treatments. He must have an enlisted family member.

The quartet returns, wordlessly, and each member resumes his former position. Their faces are somber and unreadable. There is the swish of a robe, adjustment of seating and, finally, the pounding of a gavel.

"We are again in session," he says, giving the bailiff a quick signal that he need not trouble to announce it. "Commander Means, I am under the impression that we, you and I, have an understanding of the seriousness of this proceeding. Is that a correct assumption?"

"Yes, your honor, it is."

"And is there that exact same understanding between myself and the honorable members of the bar here representing their respective sides of this case?"

"Yes, your honor," they respond practically in unison. "There is."

"I would like to remind all participants in this case—litigants, witnesses, representatives, interested parties, and visitors—that the defendant is on trial for negligence and dereliction of duty as Commander of a deep space vessel resulting in the death of his second in command, Master Wesley Brachus. The penalties for a guilty verdict are by no means insignificant and may indeed lead to further civil prosecution. Let us proceed keeping the seriousness of this case in mind and act and speak accordingly. I would issue a warning to all of you: Do not make me feel the need to repeat the terms of this understanding."

Part I

ED HYDE

Decision

"I don't recommend it. Have you thought this over? Of all the directions to choose, with your background and ability, why this? You are doing so well!" she says with a mix of pleading, hope and grudging resignation already apparent in her tone.

"I've thought it over. Jared's going," I offer, already knowing that it will not help my case.

"I heard. Jared is a fool. You're not. He is only going because you are."

She may be partially right about Jared. I remember a few years back, when he and I were playing with firecrackers. It was my dumb idea to light them and throw them barehanded. One exploded so quickly that the concussive shock to my hand startled me and scared me out of that plan before I lost any digits. But then we had the idea to blow empty tin cans up into the air. At first, this seemed safer, but it wasn't. We had to place the empty can upside down over the firecracker with just the tip of the fuse sticking out. Now, instead of a hand in danger, a face took its place, as we had to kneel down near the can to light the fuse. There was just a split second between the lighting and the explosive launching of the can in a more or less vertical direction. Jared's contribution to this hazardous occupation was to incorporate the added step (no pun intended) of stomping on the can, after the fuse was lit, to drive it into the ground before it exploded upward. This innovation had three consequences. First, the full force of the explosion was concentrated into the launching of the can—none of the energy leaked out around the rim on the ground—and that was great. But, second, stomping after lighting resulted in a higher state of danger since the fuse was burning while the stomper was stomping leaving very little time indeed to clear the projectile's possible path. Last, an over-enthusiastic stomper might accidentally stomp out the fuse before it can ignite the firecracker. In this case, one of us had to lift the can and inspect the situation. After all, the fuse had clearly been stomped out. Or had it? I am surprised that one of us doesn't have a can-shaped indentation on our forehead.

"Alright, you may have a point. He does say what he thinks and sometimes people don't like to hear it, I'll give you that, but he's no more fool than me. He has some good ideas. He's smart technically and he knows his responsibilities. This job will be good for him as well, but probably in a different way than for me."

"So, why is it good for you?"

"It's a career choice; it's what I want to do."

"There are plenty of things you can do here and still be in your field. Plus there are more career advancement opportunities if you stay home. You know that. Why not continue as you are?"

"First, I disagree. The learning opportunities on missions like these are enormous. We are going to get cross-trained on a whole number of fields—you name it: medical, genetics, psychology, and more. The deep space missions have small crews; everybody has to back up everybody. It will open up plenty of opportunities in the future. I don't want to continue where I'm at now. It's going nowhere, it's boring and it's a dead end. This is the career I want now. When it's over, we'll see then what the opportunities are."

"There's no money in it; talk to Richard."

Richard is one of my old school chums. He's the one that all the parents want their kids to be like when they grow up. 'Oh, Richard got an award for…' or 'Did you hear, Richard got accepted to…' or worse yet, 'Say, why don't you ask Richard to help you with…'

It's really too much. No mention, ever, that Richard is a dull person whose dull life is already planned out for the whole foreseeable dull future. That's not for me.

"That's not right, Mom. There's enough money, and besides, the other benefits more than outweigh any drawbacks."

"Name one, just one!" she quickly counters, sensing an opening.

"Mom, we've gone over this, we've covered this."

"I need refreshing; tell me again."

13

"There's all the training. And I'll be working with top notch people, people who will be able to help me later on. When it's over..."

"Yes, 'when it's over'. How many years is that again?"

"When it's over, I'll have experience that few will ever have; I'll have seen things in many cases that have never been seen before; I'll have connections. When it's over, I'll have my choice of direction," I argue, my volume fading away at the end.

It's not right. The words are wrong. I know what she's saying but really she means 'don't leave me' 'it's dangerous out there' and 'I may never see you again.' I look at her and we are both silent for a few moments.

"I understand mom. It's right for me. I'll be careful. Dad is OK with it—you know that. And besides, you still have Tom here."

"Now, look at Tom. He's got a nice job at a big company. He could get you in there I bet. What's wrong with that?"

"What's wrong...? Mom, ask him, you'll see. He's not as happy there as you think. He'll tell you."

Mom continues fussing about the kitchen moving items on the counter that don't need moving, brushing away crumbs that don't exist, and turns to me. She just looks, then sighs, and finally says quietly, "All right, I give. Be careful. I love you."

———

I spend some time alone arranging my things—a very few items are coming with me, most go into storage. Mementos of growing up bring back memories, each one. I remember the first time I saw these magnets. It was in a third grade class. The teacher didn't give much introduction but simply emptied a box on to her desk. She picked up the items one at a time—a lens, gyroscope, magnets, laser pointer, and more—and talked about them giving a simple demonstration of each. She gave us a couple button magnets each to keep. It was that afternoon that I knew my career path. People have told me many times that it was unusually early for such a decision, but to me it was simple. I didn't know the name of the field, or that it was a 'field' but my interest was piqued and it stayed piqued.

"Is she OK now?"

"Yeah, she's fine. I can see it's not an easy idea to get used to, but she's OK."

"It baffles me how much money is poured into these programs; it's really beyond counting." Dad fidgets a bit, picks up one of my paperweights, and handles it before continuing. "You're going to do great, and have a time I bet. A real time."

"You know, the payback is huge on the work the Academy and others have done out there. New worlds, vast resources…"

"Yeah, I know, I know." And then, "I kinda wish I was going along. Care to trade places?"

It's all settled. I'm leaving. It's still not clear if Jared will be accepted and even less clear if we will be assigned together. No matter, I'm in. There's a bit of a learning curve, they say. I'll be here close to home at the Academy for quite some time learning the ropes. We have to get exposed to specialized equipment and procedures. There'll be medical stuff to cover too.

I'm going to try to keep an electronic version of this diary—my log book, I should say. Once I find out what electronics we'll be using I'll take it up again.

Mom's concerns are misplaced. We sorted some more of that out and she knows that I know that she's being a mom, and it's OK. It is not like I will be a pioneering explorer. Lots of people have gone on missions—ground, space, and deep space—before. Not that it's routine; but it's been done and done plenty. Not to worry.

Dad's excited for me. I know he will want a blow by blow description of it all when I get back home.

Academically Speaking

What could all these people possibly be talking about? I don't get it; I've never gotten it. Small talk is a mystery to me. I find it hard to believe important information is communicated in this way.

It's a big hall and jam-packed. Not surprising—it's the last day of studies and testing for most and all the regular sessions are over. We are waiting only for the wrap-up in the big assembly hall and then … what? Then the last individual team meetings and goodbye to home for a long, long time. I can't say that I'm not looking forward to it. Finally. Let it happen now!

A woman is sobbing. Or rather, one woman, of the type whose laughter sounds like crying, is laughing loudly a few paces away. I have to look at her to be sure and yes, she's laughing, not weeping. One wonders what she sounds like when actually crying.

The dull roar continues. Really, how can anyone hear and follow a single conversation stream here anyway? For me it takes the utmost concentration while focusing on the speaker's lips—then maybe I can follow speech in this environment. What would be a simple and effortless act in other surroundings becomes a monumental task now.

What is going on here then? There's got to be a reward for the effort people expend to engage in this endless and continuous chatter. I heard an explanation once, that many people are insecure about their actuality. They need to get someone to respond to them about anything at all in order to know they exist, in order to prove they exist, in order to be relevant to someone about something even if the topic is meaningless and the interaction short.

I think instead they are insecure about their ideas or, equally likely, about their acceptance into the group. Someone trained in psychology once tried to explain to me the concept of consensual validation. This room may provide a real world example, if I understand the definition correctly.

"Nice day, isn't it?"

"Why, yes, refreshingly cool."

"Do you think so?"

The translation, applying to *both* parties, would go:

> *Whew, I must not be hideous; he didn't startle or move away. I must not reek although he could be hiding his repulsion for now. I must be speaking correctly; I got an appropriate response, perhaps even an opening through which to expand on 'coolness.' Maybe I have found a friend to second my ideas, support me and enhance my value. At the very least he accepts me as a possible equal*

and by extension the possible equal of anyone in this room.

Yes, it has to be something on this order. That's the reward.

How did it happen that I am not like that? Am I missing some valuable ability, need or skill? Chit-chat must sometimes lead to real communication, I would hope. And it sure seems that most people are comfortable with small talk. Where did I miss the boat?

A youngish, clean-cut man is approaching. Small talk test coming right up. I affect the same friendly smile as his and can't help but think he is dressed for an important meeting, not as casual as the rest of us. It sure looks like our stranger—could it be I know this guy?—has business in mind.

"Excuse me, but are you Cadet Shipley?"

"Yes. I'm Jason," I reply and look inquisitively at his clean-shaven face. I don't recall seeing it before…

"I believe I know your brother."

"Really, you know Tom? How did that happen? He lives and works a long way from here."

"Yes. I just saw him a few days ago, before I left to come here. We work together at Ming Data. I'm Jeff Sanders."

"Jeff…? Oh, yes, now I see. Nice haircut. Tom must've

sent a picture or two of you guys."

"Thank you. Yes, it's me. The short hair gets everyone, it seems. I didn't even recognize me at first. I have an interview this evening. At least I hope I do."

I nod and smile, showing what I believe to be the appropriate amount of concern.

"But you know he's leaving? You know he volunteered for one of our customer's testing programs?"

"You've got to be kidding. Who, Tom?" Jeff nods as I digest this surprise. "I had no idea. When did this happen?"

"Just happened."

"I've been stuck with this group all week and will be for at least another few days. Even so, I haven't heard from Tom in a long while. Last I heard he wasn't happy there, but he looked like he was having a good time at the company picnic or whatever it was."

Jeff continues, while scanning the crowd, "He sees this new thing as a real opportunity. Your bro' is something, I'll say that. No, he was not happy. Said he couldn't take much more sitting in a box. Kept going on about limitations and boundary conditions. A real smart guy but no, not happy there. The change of pace will do him good. It's a paid spot too and long term—a few years at least."

We sidle up to the refreshment table and get a couple of

soft drinks before Jeff takes his leave saying, "Hey, I've got to run. I'm going to try to do the impossible and corner Big Brachus alone," nodding in the direction of a knot of men, indicating the tall one with a short military cut to his gray hair, "before he disappears tonight. Truth is, I'm not as Ming-positive as I once was either and would like to see if there's anything else for me out there. I've heard some things about the big boy but I'll try to ignore that." He pauses, smiling, to see if I get the joke before continuing. "He's been around and seems to be a player both in the Academy and in the outside. I hear he was at Ming long ago, before it was even called Ming."

I glance in the direction Jeff indicates and take a good look at "Big" Brachus. I don't know him but have seen him around. He is indeed big. He's tall, but not extremely so, and big boned so that he presents a formidable mass. If you need to plow through a crowd, follow him. I wouldn't say he's out of shape but guess he enjoys his cuisine if you know what I mean. He has a sort of a wobble as he walks as if his spindly legs have a hard time keeping up with the rest of him.

He seems to be having a great time and is in the middle of a small group of men. His round face boasts a big smile as he participates in the give and take of the group. I see him lean in conspiratorially and say something to one person in particular, then lean back and laugh, his grin even bigger than before. Strange, the other person's only reaction is to smile politely. Bad joke?

"Alright, nice meeting you and good luck. I'll tell Tom we

21

met. Say, what program is he going for again?"

"It's the long-term survivability lab or some such thing. Not sure exactly. See ya," as Jeff moves away through the crowd.

Huh, how about that. Real information from small talk—who knew? I'm going to strangle that Tom the next time I see him.

"Excuse me, did you hear the last announcement?" I say in a small-talk sort of way to a random person nearby while trying to re-focus on the evening's agenda. After all, this is the last formal day at the Academy.

"Yes. No. I mean I heard the PA but didn't pay any attention to the announcement," says the non-helpful bystander.

Thanks a lot for responding. Valuable input that. I should thank you no doubt so you can know you are really real. Or not.

Another voice responds, this one familiar. "Relax, I heard it. We are to assemble for the dean's speech. It means we have plenty of time. Where can a guy get a cocktail around here?"

"Hey Mark. Didn't see you."

I had several sessions with Mark Arwyn. Not the introductory ones, but mission-specific ones and the technology seminars. Mark is experienced and has been out at least a couple of times already. He has the facial creases to prove it, although I am beginning to understand that they are mostly laugh lines. He has a slight limp but has never talked about it and I haven't brought it up. Not sure how old he is and of course it's nearly impossible to tell in absolute years, but he shows all the signs of middle age and a little beyond. I wonder if this will be his last mission.

Mark is quite a character. I have been using him as my go-to guy for questions but it hasn't been easy. I mean, he's a bit of a curmudgeon. He comes on that way at first at least. He certainly knows his stuff, and he expects you to know yours. I have to say that I envy the ease with which he interacts with everyone. He seems to know everyone and they him. He's not shy with his opinion on technical matters and is not afraid to contradict or correct anyone, and I mean *anyone*.

"The schedule is way behind, as usual. Did they give a new start time for the speech?"

Mark brushes his thinning red hair across from right to left and speaks at the same time, "No. Because they don't know. Once they herd everyone in, it will begin. They can't start without an audience. Like I said, plenty of time."

"Yeah, ok, but I'm heading in anyway. I'd rather sit where I can hear myself think. See you in there maybe."

Interestingly, as I move away I see this Brachus fellow heading right for me through the crowd, looking right at me. What's up with that? His face has lost its grin but has not been replaced with any other expression that I can read. As soon as he gets to a socially acceptable distance I nod, say hello and pull up to a stop, assuming we are going to greet and make the dreaded small talk. Instead, no response at all. After I stop he shifts his gaze, brushes right past me and moves away. What the...? I turn and see he is grinning and shaking hands with another of the senior men, one that I don't know. Not that I know Brachus. And not sure I want to.

———————

I sit way back in the hall; it is bright and filling up, but at least there is no social pressure to interact. I see I have no messages from Tom and send him a short text. "Dear job hopper. I learn from strangers what you are up to. Details please." We have already received official comms units and I am still learning mine.

I spot that cute young woman with the short brown hair. I'm pretty sure she was looking at me, but not positive. I was in one multi-session course with her. She already had a partner in the lab and we never talked. Unfortunately.

Mark finds me and has a handful of snacks; he sits next to me.

"I'm looking forward to this. Can't wait to see what he has to say," I say.

Mark counters with, "This? You're kidding. 'Rah, rah, blah, blah.' No new information. 'You're the greatest class ever, now get out there and give 'em hell, etc.' Been through this before. I wouldn't even be here if it wasn't mandatory."

"Say, I almost literally ran into that Brachus character a minute ago. Said 'Hi' but he totally blew me off and ignored me. First impression: seems like an ass."

"Hey, don't talk about my new boss that way!"

"Huh, what are you talking about? Your boss?" I look carefully at Mark's face to see the usual hint of mirth but nothing more. There is a small crumb from one of the snacks he is munching on the corner of his mouth.

"Yep, he and a couple of his buds are going to be on our team. We all ship out together. Here, have some." He waves a small bag of something toward me.

"Our team? Is that possible? The leadership mix has been set for ages, hasn't it? Tell me you are kidding."

"I wouldn't kid you," Mark says with a look that says 'Maybe I would and maybe I wouldn't.'

"So much for Team Dynamics, Compatibility Profiling, and all that crap. I don't like it. I didn't like the vibe I got from him—no warm fuzzies at all."

"Relax, maybe I'm wrong. Anyway, I like him. He's great. I was in a session with him." Mark chuckles a bit and adds, "I couldn't pin down exactly what his contribution was, but he looked and sounded great. Shhhh, here we go."

I again wave off his offer of a snack. The lights have dimmed and I have a funny feeling in my stomach. In a low voice I ask, "Where did you hear this? From him?"

"Nope, gabbing out in the hallway. It's the best place to pick up information. Now be quiet and pay attention; this is the part you wanted to hear."

Short introductory comments are followed by the long and boring ritual of naming of all the graduates, their primary area of study, and any special academic honors they may have achieved. Inevitably my mind begins to wander and I begin to think about the future.

This is the end of the beginning and beginning of...an adventure. No, never mind, I am not a poet.

It's the end of training and preparation. Any additional learning will be OJT as they say. This log will serve as my diary and I will add it to my official records of the mission somehow, but in a private manner. The endless introduction of the graduates and their accomplishments is interminable and... Mark is jabbing me with his elbow. Where was I? The real speech begins anon, poetically speaking. Can't record now; more later.

The Devil You Say

As curious and disturbing as Mark's comments about our
team are, the dean's portion of the agenda is on and of
interest to me; my thoughts turn to the proceedings. Many,
I would guess most, of the new Cadets have family
present. I don't. No matter, I will work in a visit with them
before launch. They are lucky to be physically close to the
Academy, except for Tom. Maybe he will be around too.
Apparently I am not privy to his latest activities.

Mark has no one here either but laughs and makes a joke
saying, "If you'd been through this as many times as I
have, you wouldn't be here either." Although that doesn't
make any sense at all, I laugh with him.

Up front, I see Commander David Means, our fearless
leader, pass by the dean and they speak briefly as he
passes.

Dean Carson cuts an impressive figure. He is presidential
in appearance; he should be in politics, where image
counts for as much as, if not more than, substance. Not
that the dean lacks substance, not at all. I have been
impressed with him during my time here. When speaking
in front of a group, he knows what he is about. He has the
cool look of authority and uses it to good advantage. Black
hair, in place. Dark suit, fits perfectly.

David Means is easy to spot; he is one of the few older men with a full head of wavy hair. And not short either—his hair, I mean. Long enough to raise an eyebrow or two when first meeting him but not long enough to create any lasting negative effect. Besides, the salt 'n' pepper coloring gives a sufficient aura of maturity to quell any suspicions.

Several of the team leaders, and I think they are the ones scheduled for departure on the longest expeditions, have a few seconds each with Dean Carson and then:

"Welcome everyone; students, staff, faculty, and, not least, our visitors. We are happy to be able to share this brief time with you all together at the culmination of our current programs. As you visitors no doubt have learned at your orientation seminar, we have, as we normally do, a mixed group of both new graduates as well as veterans.

"Let me first address the vets. If you would please stand, yes, thank you, please stand while I say that you are one of the greatest assets we as an institution could hope to have. No, more than that, one of the greatest assets our society as a whole could hope to have. You are scientists and pioneers, but you are also teachers and leaders. Your presence and contributions bring continuity and richness we would otherwise be without in our quest for a stable, responsible and secure civilization. Whether you are here to prepare for a new mission, or whether you are closing out your career and readying to return, for the first time in many years, to the general populace, we wish you well and again offer our sincere thanks."

The audience acknowledges the standing vets with polite applause and the dean motions for all to be seated once again.

"Speaking of new missions, and certainly not to diminish the importance of shorter term projects, we have with us this evening those special people who have volunteered for some of the longest missions of all; missions that have a significant impact on our future and the future of generations to follow. Would our Deep Survey and Genetic Expansion team leaders please stand? Thank you. These are very special people indeed. We owe a debt of gratitude to these and to all of the teams and their families, past, present and future, for the sacrifices they are making."

More polite applause as the team leaders acknowledge the recognition.

"Finally, we are pleased and proud to present to you the next generation of graduates, men and women whose dedication and performance will no doubt contribute positively to the long and storied tradition of excellence at our institution.

"These are the officers, the leaders, those who will shape the future of our society, some sooner, some later. They are the best we have to offer the world and beyond, to the limits of our civilization.

"We anticipate the accomplishments of this class and enjoy the confidence of knowing they will make us, their predecessors, their peers and their families proud to be among those who can say, 'I know him. He is a good man. We know her. She is a good woman. They are the strong, the trustworthy.' Please join me in congratulating them and wishing them the best of luck in the future."

Dean Carson finishes by scanning slowly over the crowd during a hearty general applause. Afterward, he proceeds with his program by announcing some special service awards and recognition to a few outstanding attendees.

"Told ya. What a load of crap," Mark says in his best dismissive tone when all was done.

"I don't know. I liked it," I replied. "Short and sweet." Was it really that corny? I like that sort of speech. It wraps everything up and pumps you up for the future. All the impact and whatnot. Yee-hah. I guess not everyone feels the same way, in fact I know they don't.

"Did you see your smiling face up there on the screen at the end?"

"What, me?" feigns Mark. "Oh, the ridiculous service award? If you live long enough, they give you an award. I don't trouble myself with that nonsense."

"I saw a couple other faces I recognized. I didn't realize the select company I'm in."

"Yeah, yeah, everybody's a winner. How about that cocktail now? You in?"

"Sure, lead the way."

———

We migrate to a nearby and familiar bar and find a dark, quiet spot to sit. Mark gives specific instructions for his drink. For myself, anything will do, I'm not picky. I have often repeated that the taste doesn't matter, only the effect matters to me. Besides, I've had one of Mark's drinks. It tastes horrible and I've told him so. His enigmatic classic response: 'One is too many, two is just right, three is not enough. Have another.'

"Your drinking preference is unfortunate," he says. "You are missing out. Say, did you notice big Wes B stood up when the dean asked the leaders to stand?"

"What? No. Again, you've got to be kidding! I've barely heard of him and now all of a sudden he is everywhere you look? Team leader too?"

"Not kidding. But I know for sure David is still our head honcho. Maybe Brachus has secured himself another team. That must be it."

I have a hunch that Mark knows damn well that last guess is not true; that's his style.

———

Of all people, I spot Jeff Sanders as we are leaving. "You were in the closing session?"

"No," he says, "just hanging around. I'm heading back to

work tomorrow."

"Did you have any luck cornering Brachus?"

"Yes, I sure did. He was encouraging and said he would certainly try to hook me up before he shoves off. I hope he turns up something for me. Seems unlikely 'cause he's outta here soon, but I'm geeked anyway that he's going to try. Talk to Tom?"

I shake my head. That positive report, however minor, removed a little of the dark cloud hovering over my mood after Mark's comments. I stop myself commenting to Jeff about my annoyance with Tom when I see a pleasant sight.

"Jason?" she asks.

"Yes. Hi. How are you?"

"I'm Carol. Looks like we'll be travelling together," she offers as she extends her hand. I take her hand but she doesn't shake, she just squeezes a little. "Are you leaving?"

Traveling together? Can that be right? I answer her question, "We were, just. I'm here with Mark although it looks like he's disappeared already. Are you here for dinner? Drinks?"

"Sort of. I've ordered food to go and just got the text that it's ready."

We hold each other's gaze for an almost awkward length of time; I try to think of something to say. We move a little to the side to let others pass.

Finally I say, "You were in the medical training," knowing full well that it's not quite the right thing to say.

She just smiles at first and then says, "It's nice to meet you officially. I can't stay. They just released the final crew rosters. I'm on the same team as you and Mark."

"Really? Glad to hear it. I know they're out, but I haven't looked for mine yet. We've known unofficially whose command we'll be under for some time but…" I let a couple more seconds pass in silence. "You have to run?" She nods. "We'll talk more sometime?"

"Of course. 'Bye," she says breezily as she starts to move past me.

"Wait. What… what are you?" I ask as I try to keep our conversation going.

She turns back, looks at me for a second, then says, "I'm a woman."

I smile weakly and blush at my verbal incompetence.

"And an astrophysicist by training. On the team, they're calling me Navigator. Take your pick."

"I see," I say, recovering somewhat. "Well, we need one of those."

"Which one?" she asks. With a wink and the slightest smile

she heads in to pick up her order.

> *Personal log entry number two. I'm getting the hang of this communicator now. It's a universal device; we all have them. It doesn't have the functionality I would pick for my personal use, but it is part of the job and it is the latest communication and computer technology. Gni-M model. Common name: genie. Can't complain.*

> *We've been assigned to man the Hobbe. It's a veteran craft recently refitted with the latest gadgetry. Named after Commander Lillian Hobbe: pioneer, leader, innovator, activist.*

> *I've got to figure a way to link this log with the main archiving system while somehow keeping it private. Dates and sequencing will be all taken care of.*

> *David has scheduled the last meeting before launch with the whole mission team and only the mission team. Compatibility studies are out and rosters too, like Carol said. Looks like Mark was wrong.*

> *I overreacted to Mark's comments, I'm sure. He is a bit of an instigator. Likes to get reactions.*

> *I've got a get-together with the family coming up, and yes, Tom will be there. It's scheduled for right after the last of their visits to the medical engineering center.*

I've now got that Jeff Sander's contact info, and am hopeful to get a last update from him before we are completely cut off. Not a big deal; just curious.

Shakeup

It's all over now but the shouting as they say. So far so
good, and no surprises. Myself, I can't concentrate and am
ready to go. This is my team, my mission family, and the
mood is generally quiet and thoughtful. I do like this Dylan
kid—where did he come from? Clean cut and personable.
He seems a little light on the technical side, but did well in
our sessions together. Already I see us becoming friends.
Plenty of time for that later.

At some point you have to trust the compatibility
algorithms, kind of like an arranged marriage but this way
you get an entire extended family. Speaking of which, I've
got to get out of here and see the real family before they all
have to get back to their normal lives. But that's wrong—it
won't be 'normal' at all anymore. Barring any accidents,
they will be on this journey with me in a way. I can't
imagine how they pulled off these missions long ago with
primitive medical technology. Coming home to strange
people; everyone you knew long gone. Now the mission
members and their families—that's the key, the families—
are all part of the Longevity Medical Program, or LMP.

David is just outside the room, visible by the open door,
talking to someone. I am inside with the rest of the team,
or most of them anyway. I don't like this standing about;
let's get on with it. I am distracted by keeping an eye on

Carol without becoming obvious about it. Where has she got to now?

"Lose somethin' mate?" asks Grigor Bevan. I guess I'm being obvious after all. Grigor is the ship's technician, charged with testing, tuning, maintenance and repair of the various shipboard systems. "You see it too, eh? They've gone missin'."

"Eh? Who? What do you mean?"

"The Steves. They're on the list; they're not here. Somethin's up."

The Steves are not related except by first name, but they look as if they could be father and son. Steve the elder is the leader of the Resources team, and Steve the junior is on that team as one of the subordinates.

David enters and walks to the head table and sits in the center facing us. We take our seats and there is some shuffling and mumbling while we settle in. I'm expecting the 'Let's go, pat on the back, big hurrah, one-two-three break' routine.

I sit and look around discreetly when there's a tap on my left shoulder. It's Carol. She gives me a quick smile and nod. I guess, again, that my efforts to keep tabs on her have been detected. I try to think of something to say but she shushes me and nods toward the front. David is making an announcement.

From the back of the room and up along the right hand

wall walk three people. They join David at the front but do not sit. I get a sinking feeling as I recognize one of them.

"… and Master Wesley Brachus will be leading the Resource team. He brings two of his best people with him, Tracy Cole and Lester Glavin. They each in turn bring a wealth of experience and expertise to the mix. Any questions for me or them?"

Stunned silence, and I'm somewhat relieved by that; it means I'm not the only one in shock. I see Mark grinning at me, apparently pleased as punch at my reaction. David motions and the three take seats beside him.

"I know this is last minute; I know the rosters you have are no longer up to date. Again, any questions or concerns?" Silence again.

"I am sorry to report that we will not be accompanied by the Steves, as you all seem to call them," says David who, noticing some sideways glances, continues with a surprisingly stern countenance, "and we are better off for the change. We are lucky Wesley is available and willing to join us and I expect you all to welcome these three into our group and work closely with them."

There are some additional seconds of silence. I don't know the other two at all; have never seen them before. I wonder if the cool reception indicates that others here get the same bad vibe off Brachus that I do.

"Welcome Master B," says Mark at last, the first to acknowledge the new members. Nodding to the other two new faces, Mark adds, "Looking forward to getting to know you."

I can see the value of David. He has a history as a mission leader. Before that I hear he used his technical training in subordinate roles, starting right at the bottom on entry level, ground-based projects for the Academy. I worked with him here during the last cross-training sessions and, before that, had incidental contact with him around the complex. He is likeable and personable and has a certain aura of leadership and decisiveness. We haven't yet clicked on a bud-to-bud level but, again, there's time for that and then some.

Mark is a given. He knows everyone, and his reputation for competence is widespread. Sure, he's a character and hears a different drummer, but we need a character like that whether on a mission or in life in general. He's a talker too. Should I even say he appears at home in the midst of small talk? I'm not jealous; well, maybe a little. He seems at ease around anyone and in any situation.

The rest of the crew? I've gotten to know most of them over the days and weeks of preparation. I'm comfortable and confident with them.

Besides David and Mark, there's Grigor. He's solid but with an edge. We've gotten along well whenever we've interacted so far, but I don't seek him out socially. He's a bit too aggressive for my taste.

There's Dr. Gleshert and Nurse Vanessa Ward, his

assistant. The doc is a tough read, kinda touchy. He acts all tough too, but I think there's more to him. I have to watch what I say around him though. Now, Vanessa is another story. She is an attractive brunette and a veteran who has crewed with Gleshert before. I've had to go through her for some of the pre-launch regimen. She's competent and I like her. And she is just flirtatious enough to make interactions fun.

Dylan Waters is, I believe, the youngest in the group. I could be wrong. Might be Craig Brown. I don't know much about Dylan's past, but he's got a likeable demeanor. There's a relaxed way about him—not indifferent, but quiet and calm. Dylan is assigned to the Resources team, which means he'll be working under Brachus, but he told me his real interest is people. Craig is not assigned to any one area. He is of the same status as Rick Groth and Chris Seaborn—all three are true floaters; David can task them as needs arise.

Alain Goodwin and Aileen Ireland are nominally with the Resources team as well. Alain and Aileen—I'm not kidding—these are their names. Fortunately they look nothing alike. Alain is rotund and looks self-conscious most of the time; Aileen is small, thin and waif-like. She is the only one I know of who was cross-trained on the Power and Energy systems. I don't think she completed the training though. These two don't talk much, at least not to me. I've not had a single conversation with either of them. On the other hand, I'm not getting any bad vibes from either party. So there's that.

Then there's Porter. Not sure of his first name; I could find it in the records or messages if I had to. Starts with J. Nice guy. Friendly. Easy to talk to. Great to have a drink with. Hard to tell his age. He acts and talks young, but the hairline and glasses say something else. Very unusual to see glasses.

There's Navigator Carol. She's a woman, I am told.

Most of us have had it pounded into us that we will be used in not one, but several capacities, as the situations arise. That's just fine with me. I don't want to be stuck fiddling with electronics for the duration.

There are, however, small subgroups with fixed job descriptions. There are helmsmen Winters and Pearce— one or the other will be at the controls of the ship at all times except when the ship is flying auto. A more demanding position, Power and Energy technician, is shared by three people. As far as I know, they have not been cross-trained on anything and don't interact with anyone but each other. Mark, on the other hand, has received cross-training from them. He's says it's for a high level restricted-access project. Right.

That makes a total of 22. Twenty-two people to cross the universe to another planet and return. Hardly seems enough. And we have to work together smoothly. After years of study, the Academy has developed reliable methods to select the optimum mix of personalities for long missions. Up until today, I have had faith that whatever roster was finally generated, we would get along well. After all, the compatibility study predicts…

"Commander, have the compatibility studies been completed for this new mix? I don't recall any additional…" I try to ask, but am cut off by Brachus before I can finish.

"Most certainly they have," he says with a smile.

With a quick glance at Brachus, David adds, "Look, these new adds are uniquely qualified for their positions within our mission. Our compatibility coefficient has increased with their addition. Increased." He looks steadily and directly at me. "Any other comments?"

So much for trying to verbalize the unasked questions surrounding this last minute move. No more questions from me. Something catches my eye; it's a ring on Lester's right pinky. He is slowly tapping it up and down and it reflects a flash of light each time. Up, down, up, down. Grigor voices a concern, but I am still stinging from the glib response to my question to catch his. I do see Grigor is quieted right away with a seemingly well-practiced quick response followed by another stare-down. This is a new side of David.

The meeting eventually breaks up and we all head in our own directions. I betray just a hint of my doubts to Dylan on the way out. He agrees, but trusts that the bigs know what they are doing. Besides, he said, he, Dylan, is in no position to make waves. What, am I a wave-maker? Didn't David just issue a tsunami? Mark pulls out his usual blithe façade and tells us, "Settle down, it's going to be a great ride."

He's right. This is an important mission and it's what I signed up for. Our actions will significantly influence at least one independent bio system and will help direct the course of future generations of our civilization. Dean Carson had a point yesterday. Settle down indeed.

———

"This is it, folks. I don't have long. Thanks for coming everyone. Uncle Joe, Nancy. Jare, I'm sorry you won't be part of my team. Good luck to you—I know you'll do fine. Tom," I say, and have to pause as Joe shakes my hand, "I hope you know what you are doing. Things were sure to improve for you at Ming if you had stayed. Now I hear you're on some sort of secret project…"

"Top secret," he says. "Don't worry, it's right up my alley, a benefit to mankind, and all that."

"Mom, Dad…" I say. But we've talked it out, there's nothing to add. We finish with the usual terms of endearment and hugs all around.

"Your medical visits went ok?" I ask my parents, and include Tom when I look at them.

"Yes, we told you, everything's fine," says Dad with a firm smile. "Good luck son."

So, this is the last entry before launch. I know I'm supposed to get philosophical and wordy but it's not happening.

You can feel the tension in the crew but I may be misreading. For my part, I am not worried about launch per se, been there done that, but do feel strange in that I have never committed to anything for this long nor have I traveled to anywhere as remote as our destination. Being almost completely cut off from all communication with anyone but team members—now that's something to think about. But, I do have this, my log, my diary. Granted it's one sided communication, but there it is, the last remaining connection with home.

Tom seemed genuinely excited about this testing gig he has lined up. I don't know why but research and testing sounds to me like a good match for him. Way better than working in the data manipulation field, at least for Tom. He never liked to get into a rut. But his description of the testing was vague. I hope it's nothing too dangerous. And why the secrecy?

I did hear back from his co-worker, Jeff, but didn't have time to read the message until just now. Too bad, but it looks like our newest teammate didn't follow up like he said he would. Jeff heard nothing from any of the people or places at which Brachus said he would make introductions. Not only that, Jeff was unable to get in touch with him directly before launch. This does make some sense—it's not a good idea to expect much from anyone when final prep is in full swing; everyone is swamped.

Some of us peons got together briefly after David's announcement. The mood has "settled down" a bit. I still don't like it at all ("it" being not the new team mix, but the way it was presented) but am game to play along as best I can. The workings of the new roster will become evident over time—nothing to do now but wait and see.

One sore point was raised: Surely David knew of this move before our last day. The Steves must've been told about it and been told to keep quiet. I saw both of them at the closing ceremonies and they let on nothing. So why was it kept quiet until the last minute? So many questions!

I hope I haven't forgotten anything important. Final medical coming up real fast; won't be able to log after that until we are well under way.

In Transit

We are ready. The transition from 'all aboard' to 'prepare for launch' is short. It's probably just my perception as we are all quite busy tackling our responsibilities. The orientation went well; I am situated in my quarters now and for the first time since the ship was sealed I have a chance to breathe. But not for long—time for launch is coming quick.

————

Yes, we are on our way. No turning back now! I don't know how the others are managing and haven't had the time to talk to anyone but Vanessa during my routine check-up after launch. It's interesting to see this crew at work, really, for the first time. Those who are directly responsible for the running of the ship are totally focused; no small talk at all. Nice.

We are still in communication with the ground. That's part of my job, keeping the signals going and fixing it when they stop. So far, it's been all routine. The normally expected glitches responding to the standard fixes. Very good, let's keep it that way. I have to set everything on auto before they knock us out for the main leg of the trip.

I'm a little nervous about the gravity wave business. Thankfully, there isn't much time to be worried.

"You're next. Where do you want it?" Vanessa says straight-faced.

"Pardon? It's up to me?"

"Never mind. It's an old doctor joke. You feeling all right? Anything unusual? Anything?"

I shake my head.

"Good. Now, be a good boy and let me do you… I mean let me take care of you…" she teases while looking for a reaction from me.

"Van, have you gone through this part before?"

She gives me a serious look and then says, "Oh sure, don't worry, you won't know what hit you."

———

I can see my hands. I know I am dreaming and yet I am conscious of the fact that I can see my hands. I only remember doing this a couple times in my life. A clear thought arises: What would I see if I faced a mirror in my dreams? I am helping a neighbor outside of her place near where we used to live. The ground is torn up around the stump of a large bush. I am over the tangle of roots and using a hand axe to hack at one, then another, and another, with slow success. Someone, it must be the neighbor, calls out something about wood chips flying. I deliberately feel the edge of the axe; it is dull. Somehow I go to my little home shop and sharpen the axe, although no time seems to pass, and return to the roots. As I get down and begin to chop again, I realize that the root I am working on has already been cut free; they all have. I can see their whitish cut ends, wet with sap, in sharp contrast to the dark and dirt encrusted exterior of the roots. I am left puzzled by how this has happened as my waking mind slowly but surely takes hold. Groggy, I can feel the normal mechanisms of my consciousness resuming control.

Well, the downtime portion of the voyage was certainly interesting if not a little disconcerting. It was not exactly what I was expecting either. A touch of reality can "explain" or "describe" what words cannot. Hmm… how would one verbally describe what just happened to someone else? Mental sticky note to self: Get down and talk to medical about downtime. The vets could help too, no doubt.

According to the ship's clock, that was a long night's sleep if there ever was one. I feel more-or-less normal now except for the impression that I'm inside a large transparent pillow. It's strangely pleasant to move about. I could get used to this feeling.

Ha, there's the note I put up before I went under, per Vanessa's instruction. Ok, self, I will be careful! Set timer, relax. What did Tom mean about the lab work he volunteered for? Not sure about his long term direction. And why so cryptic? I remember…

We used to have a wagon. On the nearby street there was a hill. How many times did I roll down that hill? Tom would watch for traffic, but there was little to none most days.

Where was the traffic? It's hard to understand. We wouldn't last a minute out there now.

Boy, you had to be careful turning the wagon. It would go two-wheels and over on you in a heartbeat if you weren't careful!

Tom found an empty box. Not a big one, not small either, just big enough for him to scrunch into. I didn't understand but helped him up the hill and held the wagon. Whatcha doin' bud? And there goes Tom careening wildly down the hill in the wagon, in the box. He is in the fetal position, not looking out, not steering, the flaps of the box only revealing momentary glimpses of his back. Of course the wagon veers off the straight downhill line and eventually the speed and arc of his path send him tumbling, box and all, over the curb and finally to rest on a lawn. Mom is going to kill me and him, if he's not already dead. I run down. He's not moving but has come to rest on his back outside the box. His eyes are closed; he is smiling. He opens his eyes but remains quiet and still for a few moments more and then says, "Yes." That was it. Yes.

He went again and again. The box was torn and battered to shreds before he was done. How he wasn't maimed or run over I'll never know. I'll always wonder. But one thing's for sure, he has always had some weird ideas about confinement and space. Back to the womb issues? I wonder about that too.

I feel more human now. Time to do a run-through of the comms systems and logs. There's not much for me to log aboard ship, really. The ship takes care of herself. If there were any minor problems during the voyage so far, they would be automatically recorded in the issues files or taken care of by the self-healing systems. If there were any major malfunctions, no worries, we would already be scattered atoms across a broad swath of the galaxy or perhaps frozen chunks spiraling into the nearest star.

———

I feel a little unsteady but am able to make my way out of my quarters and through the narrow passageway.
"Hey Grigor. What do you know?"

Grigor is the stocky and muscular tech who takes care of many of the systems aboard. He will have ground duties as well—as will most of us—and will be needed on the surface to set up and maintain a functioning base camp. He is, as we all are to some degree, a jack of all trades. There are not enough of us to have many specialists. Grigor is only approaching mid-life but his blond hair is already disappearing.

His rugged demeanor is matched by his facial appearance. Unlike so many who have opted for a sedentary existence, Grigor is a man who welcomes physical sports and rough play. The rougher the better as evidenced by a broken tooth and one or two other facial scars. The cut on his lower lip must have been painful.

"Hey J-man. Anything to report?"

"Nope. Waking up and checking status. You alright?

Anything I should know?"

"All quiet. I was sick as a dog earlier but it passed like a summer shower. See you in the exercise room."

Exercise room? A puzzled look from me as I try to think what he means.

"You know, the meeting room wherein our superiors will exercise their jaws," Grigor explains with the help of an unflattering facial caricature.

Everyone's a comic.

"Hey, check in with me later, I want to make sure everyone's data links and logins are up to speed. Bring your genie."

"Eh? What's that? Bring what?"

I hold up my new comms device. "Model Gni—genie."

"You got it, mate. It's with me ever 'n' always."

I'm feeling more sure of myself now—steadier on my feet. I move along, toward the next work station.

Here's the one I want to spend more time with. She is a professional, make no mistake, but there is something else too. There is a softness and depth that I would like to understand better.

"Would you like to take a look?" It's really a clear image;

the optics are spectacular."

"Oh, hi Carol. You sound chipper. I'm still a bit shaky. What do you see out there? Anything interesting?"

"It's all interesting, Jason, to me anyway. And you have here a chance to look using some of the best equipment I've ever run across." I hesitate to answer, only because I've seen plenty of deep space before, as have most people. "You're not interrupting me," she adds. "I've already done my checks and verifications."

"Sure. Thanks."

She is right about the optics. The flat console screen is small and doesn't hold a candle to the view through the binocular telescope. I get a little vertigo tingle in the first seconds of viewing. "What am I looking at, exactly?"

"It's trained on one of my verification objects, but you can move it wherever. I'll be right back."

I look and slowly but surely become accustomed to the image before me. The image is captivating and I am temporarily lost in the universe. I am entranced by the incredible dynamic range of vision in space. From 100% saturation when looking at unfiltered starlight—not generally done by the way, but it looks like Carol has opted for an unfiltered view—to absolute zero input when peering into the vast blackness in between. High sensitivity instruments can detect even single photons but the eye cannot. For us, the "empty" space is truly visibly empty and the blackest of black. And yet it has depth and volume. Empty space seems to me to be *something*. Something like a cloudy crystal with tiny imperfections scattered throughout. It must be that the brain, tuned by evolution for survival and procreation, must try to fit sensory input to an internal map of reality as a first-pass processing step. It is then up to the intellect to test and accept or challenge and modify the mapping. The interaction between the evolutionary and intellectual assessment is likely the source of my fascination.

But it is more than this. It is the sheer volume of space that is imputed by the brain when this raw perception is processed. It is the unfathomable and unending depth of the universe that so mesmerizes me. At times like this I feel the urge to look deep, and deeper, trying to grasp the immensity, to feel part of it, to feel at home.

"Jason, you OK?"

"Huh? Yeah, I'm fine," I say as I move away from the telescope rubbing my eyes.

"You were absolutely motionless. I thought maybe you weren't quite with the living yet."

"No I'm fine. You are right about the optics. I got a little lost in there."

"Do you have a minute? Try the mag function and tell me what you think. Wait; let me get you pointed in a safe direction."

She moves close and leans in front of me making a quick

54

adjustment while eyeing the small screen. She smells good. Another something to get lost in? Maybe. Love the hair. She keeps it sort of short, but it's full and wavy. It's the kind that looks messy, but you know it's not. It's a "look" and I like it.

"There, that should be safe. Take a look and don't touch anything. Tell me what you see."

I look. "What am I looking for exactly?"

"Nothing in particular. Just look and tell me what you see."

"Stars and nothing. This thing really brings out the colors of the stars."

"Some of the objects aren't stars, but never mind. And forget the colors, but try to remember the image as best you can. OK, close your eyes a second." I do. She adjusts something. "Look and tell me again."

"Is this a test? All right, it looks like you moved the scope. I don't see the same *objects*," I pause as I make the air quotes gesture while still looking through the instrument, "as before."

"What about the density of stars in your field of view? Do you notice anything?"

"Density? Looks about the same to me."

"Close 'em again." I feel her move in and make another

adjustment. "Last time—take a third look. Note and describe the density."

"Well, it looks like you moved the scope to another new position. Star density looks roughly the same. But who's counting?"

"Jason, sit back now. No, it's not a test. But, your conclusions are both right and wrong. The direction of the scope did not change at all for any of the three views, but the magnification did." She enabled a grid overlay on the screen. "You were first looking at the view that you can see here now on the full screen. For the second view you were looking at the smaller field here," pointing at the central square of the grid overlay. "And the third time you were looking at the central field of the second view. So each time you were looking in the same direction but at a higher and higher magnification."

"No kidding. Nice system, but what are you getting at with the density?"

"Here, look at the first view again on the screen. Look at the central area. It looks mostly black and empty with these few visible objects, yes?" I nod and she flips to the second view. "Doesn't look empty anymore, does it? In fact, you described the object density," she makes the air quotes, winking, "as basically the same as the first view. The same relationship holds for the central area of the second view as well—basically empty until we look closer as we did in the third view."

"Yes, very interesting." A moment of silence extends to a few seconds. "Is there anything else I am missing?"

She laughs and smiles, "No, no, nothing you are missing. It's just me. Maybe I need to get away from this thing for a while, but I think the fractal nature of the views is incredible. It doesn't mean anything else. The closer you look, the basic view doesn't change. Visible object density, at least for our limited equipment, is insensitive to scale. Isn't that something?"

"Ok, I think I see what you mean. Very nice. Let me think about it a while."

I don't want to stay on a technical subject, but can't seem to think of any way to segue into to a non-work topic.

"I do have a question, although you may be the wrong person to ask. We learned that artificial gravity is created by spinning the ship along its axis. How come the image in the scope is stable?"

Carol smiles gently, "You are still groggy. The scope can compensate for spin but that's not what's happening. You also learned, or should have, that shipboard gravity is maintained using a hybrid system—we are not rotating but are either accelerating or decelerating at a constant rate. I'm embarrassed to say I don't know which at the moment. Probably decelerating."

 "Right. Hybrid. Thanks," I said. She's right, I am still groggy. "We are decelerating, by the way. What happens when we are surfing?"

"Surfing? Oh, you mean riding gravity waves. That's the longest part of the trip in distance, but we are all under during that portion of the journey anyway so… Nothing."

"Nothing?"

"Nothing. No artificial gravity is required or even makes sense, if I understand the physics of it."

"Right. Sounds correct. I really should know these things but there is just too much to learn it seems. At some point you have to deal with the details that you must, and let the rest go." I better bail out of this before I really say something stupid. "I should be getting along. See you at the meeting?"

Her eyes narrow and her demeanor cools a bit as she answers yes.

"Thanks for the demo Carol, I really did like it and am interested in that sort of thing. If you ever want to get bored, I'll show you what I do sometime. How I ended up in that department I'll never know. Please be ready later to verify your links and logins with me," I said as I leave her area to continue my rounds.

> *Too busy to log anything in here until now; all the official logs are initiated. No glitches from launch through now. The first of the ship's accumulated data successfully archived, all the automatic dumps worked without a hitch. The system is working. A couple hundred packets out of tens of thousands had retries, but eventually all made it through.*

Don't know what that was about, probably a normal amount of redundancy failure due to noise.

The official records of the meetings so far are part of mission history but I haven't had a moment to put any comments in my notes until now. David welcomed everyone aboard and discussed the mission again—mostly review. He emphasized the primary goals which I can summarize and paraphrase as:

- *Safely travel to our assigned planetary destination*
- *Gather detailed information about it and its star system from orbit*
- *Establish a presence on the surface for the purpose of acquiring necessary raw materials to ensure a safe return home*
- *Sample and document the extant environment and biota as completely as possible concurrent with the above procurement activities*
- *Evaluate the findings from the above steps and determine the correlation factor with the desired evolutionary development vis-à-vis the status and predictions from the previous visit(s), if any*
- *Depending on the correlation value, intervention may be indicated, the degree of which is left to the discretion of the Commander, within the guidelines specified by the Academy*

- *Safely return ship and crew to origin*

There were some questions about ground based duties, mainly from the women—and Grigor. We were assured that at some point everyone, and he is making the assumption for now that there will be no surprises regarding habitability, would be assigned to ground duties, excepting the power and helm teams, and that individual flexibility would be key; he is not prepared to make assignments until later. I could sense Grigor's irritation at possibly having to work at something outside his comfort zone. Too soon to worry, I say. For myself, I am looking forward to ground duty. It can't get much more interesting than this—a new world to explore!

I find it distasteful that Brachus seems to cozy up to David much of the time; in meetings he seems to make a point of sitting right next to him. And his constant nodding and grinning when David makes statements—it's all getting to me. I'm not sure why it bothers me so much, but shouldn't he be trying to become more integrated with the rest of the crew, not just with his cronies and his boss? Maybe he is, and it's me that's on the outside. Could be. But the nodding—I watched and David takes no notice of it, so it must be directed at the rest of us saying 'Look at me, David and I are in agreement' or some such childish notion.

Then there was wave downtime. Whew! The techs back home really should set up a simulator for that one; there are no words. Strange dreams. Feeling of being lost, not in space, but in time. Ha, and that's appropriate for sure. From a conscious perceptual point of view it's the shortest leg of the journey; from a distance point of view it's the longest; from a time point of view, it's a poser! It's hard to explain downtime.

Did a quick physical tour after waking, once I had my wits about me again. David says his transmissions are successful; he is happy. That's all good for me, less to do in this phase of the outbound journey. Vanessa says Doc's data is archiving OK too.

Prepped everyone for linking up their genies and biometrics. Would like to stay ahead of the game if possible.

Shipboard

Dr. Gleshert looks at me steadily and without expression. "Shut up and be still." I shut up and am still. There is no fooling around with Gleshert. He is a smallish man and solidly built. There is a permanent cowlick on the crown of his head. Seems like he could do something about it, but *I'm* not going to be the one to bring it up. Rumor has it that Grigor coined the Doc's nickname, GlassHeart, aptly reflecting his brittle personality, at least when he is working. "Don't mess up these tests; you're not getting out of here until I am happy."

"Could be a while then," I foolishly say, knowing immediately it was a mistake. I suffer through another silent stare during which he doesn't move until, I assume, he feels certain that I am not going to speak again. Behind him, Nurse Vanessa is busy with something. She apparently knows what's going on because she looks right at me with a slight smile and shakes her head. I saw her wear some flashy jewelry back at the Academy, but there is no trace of it now. No rings, nothing.

"I meant to tell you earlier that I saw your family not long ago," he says while continuing to check me over, performing routine tests as he does for the entire crew periodically. "You are very lucky. I have no family to speak of, only an ex and we won't speak of her either."

I see a spark of fire in his eyes—torch or dagger?

Doc continues, "I cannot tell you about their individual results but I think it would be safe and proper to say that there were no glitches; they are now part of the same longevity plan that you are."

I smile and nod, silently thanking him for sharing that information.

"You know that, even though they are on the same program, there can be no guarantees?" I nod yes. "We can do a lot, but we can't do everything. It's always been that way and will always be that way."

I just listen as he continues, "In the case of serious trauma resulting from an accident, for example, there is a limited window. Within that window, we can do miracles but…"

He stops speaking and moving and looks at me steadily again. "You may speak now," he says, with a tight little smile and a bemused shake of his head.

"Why are you telling me this? About the accidents and trauma; is there something I need to know?"

"Nothing you need to know. I am simply managing expectations. I will go over this same topic with everyone who has family in the program. There will be a general meeting at the end of the mission where you will hear it again. Not to mention at mission debriefing. It's important."

"So how does it all work Doc? I mean chemically or genetically or whatever? I know we enjoy incredibly long life spans compared to the untreated, but what is really going on?" I ask as I get back into my clothes.

"Every single person in the program gets telomeric treatments. Crews on these long and deep missions get additional consideration. You might call it a hybrid treatment program in which we do everything possible to minimize the effects of aging. It can't be stopped altogether, but we can sure stretch it out."

"Hybrid." I say, mostly to myself.

"Yes, hybrid. Is there a problem?"

"No, not at all. It's just that 'hybrid' seems to be a popular concept lately. So besides the telomeric part of it, what else?"

Gleshert looks at me pityingly and says, "We don't have the time for any more of this right now. I am a busy man."

"You can just say if you don't know," I say, making the mistake that he would understand that I was joking around. He didn't.

"You're done, for now. Get out and take your questions with you."

"One last thing. Grigor says we are all in danger from high energy photons and particles out here. He says it's common knowledge that they are damaging our health no matter what the Academy says. Is that…"

"Grigor needs to stick to what he knows," interrupts the doc. "You're done. Goodbye."

"Don't make him mad. I have to work here," says Vanessa playfully as I am leaving. Tracy brushes past me, entering as I leave. She looks me over and then I notice that she and Vanessa share some sort of look. What was that all about?

———

I return to my quarters. Up 'til now I have been struggling with the exact procedure to adopt to archive my personal records. Meeting transcripts, digital messages, status reports and the like, both open and encrypted, are included automatically in the archive, and I want to be able to add information of my own. I know enough about the ship's systems now that a decision is easy. I will use the required protocol for all official data and will add a separate private channel. Let's just call it a hybrid system and get with the program. That's funny stuff. It's somehow satisfying to be self-amused, no? With this setup I'll have a way to indulge myself with a personal log or diary, as well as a way to send private messages. Who will read the personal stuff besides me, perhaps, someday? I don't know. That doesn't matter. The writing helps me collect my thoughts and clear my thinking for the next day or task.

The ship's communication is primarily one-way, depending on the length of the voyage. In our case, we have planned for no incoming data packets from home for the bulk of the mission. It may be possible to communicate with ships or outposts during the mission depending on their distance, but as far as I know, we are not expecting to be near enough to any to even think about it.

For outgoing communication, we do continuously send routine data toward home. The stream is highly redundant and for sure will eventually arrive, but at our planned distance it's a long time in transit. One transmission from the field before we head back will be different. All the accumulated data up to that point is archived and encapsulated in a pod. The pod is then accelerated using the exact same system that will be used on the ship itself. The acceleration is sufficient that the pod and, later, the ship too, can use gravity waves to reduce transit time. The pod will make it home only just before we do, assuming that neither of us runs into any major problems along the way. If one is lost, the other contains the data. If both are lost, well…

It's true, the on-board QEQ entanglement transceiver is distance-independent and instantaneous but it is for very short messages indeed. It is generally used in emergency situations only to send out an SOS or maybe an SOS with location, although adding the location data means the message length is at or near the upper limit of today's technology.

The archive scheduler software is set to accumulate, store, and transmit data from the ship as well as all the other inputs periodically. Doc has his own system for medical records but even his makes it to the scheduler, encoded.

I'm using both my genie and the console in my quarters to run a performance test for all sources and formats.

David surprised me earlier when I asked about genetic broadcast seeding, an area of interest to me and one of the automated functions of the ship itself.

"Already done," he said. "The carriers' release is triggered by the ship's position. The only way we know about it is if something goes wrong, or if we deliberately pull the ship's data. The target systems are already chosen and the mixes are preloaded. There may be a couple still to go, but I believe most have already been sent on their way."

I try not to look at David's mouth. He has a habit of working his tongue and pushing out his lower lip, then sort of pursing his lips as a kind of reset action before the cycle repeats. It's evident he doesn't know he's doing it when he's listening or thinking.

I ask, "Isn't seeding this way a giant waste of resources? It seems to me that the vast majority of the specimens will be lost or frozen or burnt up."

"Yes and no. This method has been shown to be a very effective way to seed arable tracts. How in the world could it otherwise be done that would be more cost effective? Yes, the bulk of the seed material is lost but any that does reach an environment that is or will soon become appropriate has a high likelihood of surviving."

He adds, "The mixes are released and scattered spherically if and when each of the carriers reaches a star system. We know from past results that if there is a planet orbiting and if it is even remotely suited for life, a portion of the seeds will end up safely on the surface, be it liquid, solid or gas. And if the conditions are suitable, then the basic genetic template will be in place and the rest, as they say, is history. Literally."

David smiled at this last comment, apparently amusing himself. I'm not the only one self-amused.

My silence signaled my interest and he continued, "The target systems will be periodically scanned using remote sensing to see if and when a significant signature of life is detected on any of the planets. The most promising ones then become destinations for missions like ours. But you know all this already, or should."

"No, not really," I reply. David's expression changed to one of puzzlement. "I mean, it's one thing to hear about it, but another thing to live it. I suspect that training will prove to be no substitute for the real thing. Look at surfing—I mean downtime. Nothing prepped me for that, really."

David gives me a look that suggests I said something important. "Yes Jason, you are quite right about that. By the end of this mission you will be an expert on this business. We all will."

That was one of the few conversations I've had with David not counting abortive, largely meaningless and uncomfortable small talk. Other than occasional

encounters in passing, I haven't seen him since the
Welcome Aboard meeting before launch when he gave the
brief "Our Mission" speech. He has been generally genial
and polite, aside from the infrequent sharp retort, but I am
still not getting any positive person-to-person connection
with him. He must be focused on big issues and his other
direct reports. It still surprises me though, as we seem to
have similar interests and he does have a technical
background. One has to take what one can get, I guess,
and even that is one step at a time; we will see if our
relationship develops further. What he says about past
missions intrigues me. I need to dig through our database
for those old mission summaries.

I still can't wrap my head around the timing of messages
and events as they relate to the family back home. Mark
tells me to forget it—you have no chance to figure it out at
all during acceleration and deceleration, and when we are
ground-based we'll be too busy to worry about it.

"Treat the mission like a separate history from the folks
back home," he says. "They will have a history during the
time you are gone; you will have lived through the mission
history. But if you try to line them up and figure out what
they were doing at a certain time in your history, forget it.
I'm not sure if it even makes sense to think about that sort
of thing."

> *Mark answered Grigor's concern about damage
> from being out here in space, but Grigor didn't buy
> it. I hope he, Grigor, is wrong about this one. Mark
> says, in his grouchy way, that we are not out in
> space, we are inside this ship. And that's the*

difference. He went into some gobbledygook about how the needle shape coupled with our high speed through the interstellar medium combine to protect the interior from any charged particles, and that the skin of the ship itself is active and takes care of the neutral particles and high energy photons. They all provide energy that we can harness, apparently. 'Kind of a hybrid system,' I say, smirking, but nobody gets me. Grigor said it doesn't work, it can't. But Mark wouldn't budge and said it does work but it doesn't work perfectly; we are getting no more dangerous exposure than we would back home on solid ground. Grigor responded with a sigh and his 'people believe what they want to believe' eye roll. I said that the explanation sounds logical and besides didn't we learn that the doc could detect damage and take measures to reverse it?

I've had a chance to corner Gleshert when he wasn't busy. What a difference—seems like another guy entirely, not GlassHeart at all. He let me know the answer to my earlier question. I appreciate that he didn't forget me. He says the additional treatment for deep mission members slows the metabolism in two stages. One is a light stage where we can still function and the second is a more profound depression of functionality for downtime. I made a simplistic analogy but he's says call it what you want, the effect is to keep us from operating at a high metabolic rate when none is necessary.

I'm very curious about the return launch system and Mark seems to know but he put me off for now. Note to self: Corner him before this is all over.

First Look

"Ok, if you can stay with me here I've just got a few points and I need to get through them quickly. My memory's good, but it's short." Groans from the crew. Mark continues, "We've gathered all the data we can from up here. You've all had a peek out—inviting-looking, isn't it? There is just the one moon, relatively large compared to planet diameter, similar to home, and no doubt will be an impressive sight from the ground. We've dropped several probes after making some initial observations, which I will cover in a minute. The environment is actually perfect. Well, let's not say perfect, but it's as good as anywhere I've seen and about as good as anyone could hope to expect this far from home.

"First, livability. Atmosphere, clean and rich. Whatever that plant life is, it's doing its job. No toxins detected at significant levels. It'll take some getting used to the pressure and density, but I don't think anyone will have a serious problem. Water, tons of it. This means accessible hydrogen. Lots of water in the atmosphere too. And because it's a rocky world with a G main sequence star, we have confirmed the overall makeup of the crust is what we expected and closely matches the data from our predecessors' records. Here's a treat, we've got silicon galore and right on the surface—thank you, water and weather. Metals and other rarer elements will need to be mined and processed. But there is no shortage. None at all. Carbon galore too, in many of the usual natural forms. Easy pickins.

"Gravity. Again nothing dramatic but it will take some getting used to.

"Temperature. Pick your poison. As expected there is a whole range. I think we will primarily all be working in the equatorial regions except when we have to go after some specific resources that are less accessible.

"Next, fauna…"

Brachus interrupts, "Mark, what about processing? Any progress in that area?"

"I'm getting there, I'm getting there. That's covered in the next round if you can hold out." Mark's comments are received with a chuckle by most, but not Brachus.

"What about the processing of special compounds and alloys? Can you report on the availability of resources to make the specials?"

Mark now responds to Brachus without the addition of a humorous affect, "Look, everything we need is here. We will be able to set up a fabrication facility and a processing facility. Your team will have to feed in the resources, I'll handle the processing."

"Can we move on please," David says, indicating that Mark return to his prepared agenda. I notice Carol looking at me. There is no discernible expression on her face. She turns her attention back to the front.

"Sure. Now, where was I? Oh yes, we don't have good solid indications of land-based life other than plants, but the presence of a large amount of carbonates says that something is going on in the ocean."

Mark flips through several graphics summarizing the data acquired to date.

"I think I spotted evidence of migratory behavior on land. Not really my field. Our image recognition algorithms flagged one or two areas that look suspicious. Possibly some interesting land-based animal life there and David may have something more to say about that later," Mark says, pausing, looking at David for feedback. He gets none and continues.

"For sure the environment is suitable for land and sea populations. I may want to stay here myself when this is all over." Mark briefly puts up a goofy graphic of himself lounging in an exotic location, drink in hand, and a flower in his straw hat. "And last, we find no trace whatsoever of electromagnetic signaling in any part of the spectrum."

Brachus looks at his genie communicator, gets up and walks out of the meeting without a word. David apparently thinks nothing of it and indicates this is a good time for a short break if anyone needs one. I use these few minutes to lean over to Carol and ask what's up.

"What do you mean?" she asks back.

"You know, the look you gave me."

"I gave no 'look' but was wondering if you noticed Wesley's odd questions. As if he wasn't following Mark at all."

"He probably wasn't following. He's a ground guy; probably can't wait to get to work," I say, although I don't know why I ought to make excuses for him.

"He's got something up his sleeve. I don't trust him."

Mark runs a sequence of surface images while people shuffle about. David signals his desire to get things moving; the members of the crew turn their attention back to the front of the room and Mark starts in again.

"Alright. Here is where we are going to call home for quite a stretch. If you look at this mountainous region," as he circles an area on the current image, "and we zoom in a bit, you can see this area that is enclosed in sort of a triangle."

"Huh? Hold up Mark. Triangle?" says David.

"You may have to squint a bit and have a good imagination like me, but if I trace three lines here through these valleys you can see they form a triangle. There are plenty of spots inside here that we can use. First and foremost, we will be exquisitely isolated from whatever populations," again with a meaningful look at David, "may or may not be down there. Secondly, as you can see if I zoom out a bit, we will have nearby access to practically unlimited water and silicon, not to mention the other mineral resources that will be found in the mountains themselves—several outcroppings have already been identified. There are numerous other sites around the globe to pick up the other needed elements, minerals and compounds.

"David, I will leave it up to you to review possible locations for the bio work; I sent you the obvious potentials. There are any number of options, and we have good ground images to go by. Or I will be happy to go over them with you if you'd prefer."

"Yes, I want to go over that part together, but not here, not now. We'll reserve final judgment on those until after on-site inspections. I will get with you separately. But we do need to talk about another issue right now. If there are no questions for Mark…? Thanks Mark."

This is as good a time as any for me to ask, "David if I may just ask the group…" and I get a nod to go ahead. "Thanks. Most of you have already responded to my comms link request and to those who have—thank you. I've returned a verification packet to each of you just before we sat down here. However, there are a couple null responses that need to be cleared up before any landing."

"Who?" asks David.

"There's Grigor, for one…"

"Check again, mate. You'll find you're wrong about that," interjects Grigor, without any hesitation and bristling slightly, looking at me, then David.

I do a quick refresh on my communicator and confirm his statement. "Ok, you are right—thanks. Verification on its way."

"No worries, J-man."

"Then, there are a couple from the ground team that I have not heard from," I continue, nodding towards both Tracy and Lester. Brachus has still not returned to the meeting, and I see Tracy making a few short keystrokes.

David again chimes in, "How many and who? You mean the whole team?"

"No, just the three. I mean, both Lester and Tracy, along with Wesley. They were included on the general request, but nothing yet. I'm sure there are a lot of preparations before landing, but this is one thing that's got to be done."

Tracy says, to David, "I can't speak for the others, but I'm not sure I received any link or login request. Jason said it was coming, but I haven't seen it." David nods and looks at me but does not speak. I see his mouth working, repeating the same movements over and over. "And I think Wes has some reservations about having to link anyway," she adds.

"The request and instructions went out to everyone at the same time," I counter, adding, "but I will be happy to re-send to you three." I resist the temptation to add anything else. I know damn well everyone received my verbal and my electronic requests. The instructions are crystal clear and in any case, mission directives make compliance a requirement.

David begins to speak just as Brachus returns to the meeting, sitting again next to his two teammates. "Wes, do you have any issues with Jason's request for his communication data linkup? He's still looking for a few responses."

"Not at all," he responds. "Is this a mandatory hookup?"

"Yes," I say.

"Why do you ask? Is there a problem?" asks David.

"Not at all. There's a lot to do and the window for preparation is now short, that's all," Brachus responds as he grins genially.

David accepts this and closes the discussion by saying, "Ok, I will leave it to you to look into it and make it happen."

"Most certainly," agrees Brachus. His interest is now on another topic, judging from his expression. I look at him for any sort of connection or closure, maybe just a smile or nod, but get nothing.

David finishes up with a few more comments—nothing major. He says all hands must appear at a follow-up meeting, time TBA shortly.

Push the damn button you ape. Wait, I can't let this clown get to me. Requests re-sent. If no response, bingo—it's David's problem.

Ha, the above comment I added via hand-held during the last part of the meeting, but it accurately reflects my mood at the time. No response yet, from any of the delinquents, and I am not surprised.

I took some time to go over my responsibility checklist and reviewed each item one at a time carefully. I don't want to find out later, and especially not in a meeting, that I have failed to do my part.

I enjoyed Mark's presentation, even the corny stuff. At least he has a personality. I've seen way too many presenters that don't have a clue about how to hold an audience's interest. For my part, some research is in order about the "expected" distribution, as he called it, of elements in a planetary system around this type of star and at this distance from it. He's right of course but a refresher won't hurt.

My thoughts have been turning more and more to the near future and what it will hold. Carol has given me some scope time and the view is just spectacular. It's a new world all right—bright and shiny. Crust tectonics are at work and the atmosphere supports some very active weather both of which explain the bewildering variety of landforms.

At the next meeting there is again nothing on the agenda for me to present—nice!

Findings

David stands up and addresses the group first by looking around the meeting room until there is silence, then by saying, "I have reviewed the image recognition hits gathered during the surface scan Mark alluded to earlier."

Again, he slowly examines our faces before continuing. "There is without question at least one intelligent population down there."

There are more than a few sideways glances during David's pause. Mark on the other hand is smiling a little and slightly nodding to no one in particular. He knew it already.

"There are small but clear patterns in the images, widely scattered in the more temperate zones. Obviously, at this stage, we don't have an idea of the total population or even the number and distribution of intelligent species, but the evidence we see is convincing. We are quite sure their development is primitive and limited."

"David, what is the evidence? Can we have a look?" asks Dylan.

"Sure. Mark, do we have those images right now to show?"

Mark answers, "Not immediately, but I can make them ready if you want to wait. Better would be to come and see me individually or have a quick follow-up meeting later when I've had a chance to prepare."

"Right, ok. Later then. Don't worry about it now Mark," says David.

"I can tell you the image recognition software looks for patterns based on previous experience, and it's very reliable," David continues. "For example, we have three strong indicators in one small area that's located pretty close to the base site Mark pointed out earlier. First, we have images of some sort of structures laid out in loose geometrical patterns. At the scale of these images, when you start to see regular geometry, something's up. The structures themselves are small but we can make out that their shapes are sometimes geometric – rectangular and circular. Hard by these images we see what look to be signs of primitive agriculture including what are almost positively small sets of irrigation ditches. Last, there are more than one of these 'settlements'—let's call them settlements for now—and between them are what may be trails or primitive roads. Taken all together, the conclusion is clear; although I have to emphasize that nothing is certain from up here.

"As I started to say before, until we know more, we cannot predict exactly what we'll find, but our best guess right now is that there is or recently was some form of intelligent life at an apparently low population density living quite near our projected base camp. ImRec also picked up a handful other potential sites scattered across the globe."

"What does this mean for our mission?" asks Mark. "I mean, isn't this what we expect to find?"

David takes a moment to work his unconscious mouth habit before answering, "Last question first: Yes, this is what we, the royal 'we,' are hoping for in the big picture. Although ours is not the first mission to this site, it's very difficult to predict the paths that evolution will take. So we can never predict exactly what we'll find. The basic building blocks are there, and the last mission reported no unusual or potentially dead-end scenarios.

"As to your first question, it simply means that we have a lot of work to do. The bio area will be interesting, and I myself expect to be hands-on in there. Mark, your ground-based responsibility changes very little. We are going to be here for quite some time to repair, refit and replenish—I know you've heard those words before—with or without this confirmation. Some contact with the natives will likely be required for the mission, of course, to collect the data we need, but beyond that, we will have to wait and see what we find. The thing to keep in mind is this: Go by the book if there are any doubts. Please review the guidelines that all of you have received."

Grigor apparently cannot resist saying, "Let me get this straight; seeding has worked so we are for sure farmers here to tend the crops, evidence shows some kind of aquatic and probable terrestrial animal life…"

Mark throws in, "Yes, by the way, some of the supposed trails or lanes that are not connected to those so-called settlements are very likely migration pathways for terrestrial herds."

Grigor continues, "Ok then, farmers first and we are shepherds as well, tending to the flocks. And now I hear we are to be baby sitters for some primitive population. Let me do a quick inventory of my hats to see if I have enough."

Sometimes it's hard to separate humor from sarcasm with Grigor and this is one of those cases. David looks at Grigor for a few seconds but declines to comment. He takes a few more questions, but the team is generally satisfied that all is as it should be and the meeting breaks up. A few, including myself and Dylan, hang with Mark to see the ImRec hits.

————

"So. What do you think?" I ask, directing my question to no one person but to both Mark and Carol.

Dylan overhears and says, "I think it's fantastic. I am really looking forward to this. I know we'll be busy but what else are we going to do out here? I for one can't wait to see what the natives are like."

"Yeah, I bet they can't wait to bash your head in, mate," is Grigor's reaction, as he is also within earshot.

"I don't know," I say, "I've still got reservations about 'the big picture' as he put it. Should we be messing with intelligent life? Or any life, really."

"Oh dear, you should have been weeded out of the program long ago with thoughts like those, eh J-man?" gibes Grigor.

"I think the big picture directives are correct," says Carol. "Although it's an almost totally independent biosphere, it's still arable land; it's still a fertile environment. Think of it this way: It's a good spot for a garden that just happens to be isolated and a long way from home. One has to tend a garden to produce anything beautiful or useful," she adds, parroting the accepted line, "and this is one of our many gardens to tend. The results in other cases have proven excellent beyond doubt. You've all been to the Academy Outpost, yes?"

"Yes, nice spot indeed, the outpost," says Grigor. "But do you really believe the Outpost started out like this place, doll?" I try to understand his implication, but dismiss it as another 'Grigor moment.'

"What are we looking at for ground transportation, Mark?" Dylan asks.

"Assuming we get the go ahead and are set up on the surface, we will make do with two for starters; one is a small runabout, the other is a little bigger. It's a workhorse and big enough to be called a transport unit. You've all no doubt trained in or at least have seen similar models before. It's up to David and Wesley if we need to do anything more in the way of fabrication. Speaking of the devil..."

"Mark, I need to get with you about the ground images and what you've found. Can we do it now?" asks Brachus after approaching the small group discussion.

"Absolutely. Getting ready to go exploring?"

Brachus chuckles and says, "Yeah, that's right."

I still don't have any warm feelings for this guy. I always get the sense he's hiding something. David seems OK with him, so he must have some value, something positive to contribute, right? Whatever it is, I'm not impressed. Neither he nor his two underlings have bothered to comply with my request regarding their comms linkup and channel verification. We'll see how that works out for them when they have no communication or data path on the ground.

———

In orbit, the ship has a different feel than it did before. It must be due to the way artificial gravity is handled. The famous hybrid system. Also I believe there are certain correction thrusts periodically. I say I can feel them, but Carol thinks it's my imagination.

That Tracy woman sticks like glue to Brachus. I bet they've opted out of the 'medical relief' procedure as Grigor says, jokingly. Ha. Could be some truth to that. When I try to contact Master Brachus, it's hard to corner him without going through her. I think it's an intentional firewall.

No response from the Resource team triumvirate. Time's up and now the ball is back in my court. My plan is to make one last attempt to talk directly to him or his whole team without having to involve David. I can't work out what the problem is. It's not a big deal; just do it! Is it possible he is a technophobe? Hardly seems likely but in that case I will bite the bullet and do it all myself. Funny, it's not the amount of labor—that's negligible—it's the idea of not conforming to the rules and crew expectations that bugs me.

I like Grigor; he's a good one to cut through the crap and get to the point. He questions everything and gets me to thinking. Something he said earlier triggered an idea that I've had before: How is it, really, that our little mission is here to document and help guide the evolution and development of an entire planet? Talk about improbable. The same sort of feeling of awe occurs to me when contemplating many modern devices or systems. Just think of this ship as an end product. How in the world did people, regular people like us, create such a device? It's just mind-boggling all of the steps, the trial and error, the sacrifices, the insights and creativity that had to occur and be brought together to make it happen. Not to mention the incredible complexity of the myriad support systems.

Conflict

"I don't have to take this shit anymore…" Master Brachus says to no one in particular as he gets up and walks out of his own quarters.

Stunned, I look at Dylan and Tracy, then at Lester, and they in turn look at me. "What the hell just happened? Is he coming back?" I ask, although I know he's not. Dylan has a sober look on his face but Lester has a smarmy smile. So far I've had little interaction with him, meaning Lester, and I'm beginning to think I won't enjoy having any in the future. "Do we wait?"

Tracy doesn't show any reaction, but that in itself is a reaction, to my mind, when your boss acts immaturely. She and Aileen remain silent. I saw them share a quick glance, however. I don't know why Aileen was asked to this meeting. Alain's not. Both she and he complied with my request and neither needs to be here. I look at Lester.

"I don't think it'll be productive," says Lester, still smiling. "Waiting, I mean. He doesn't like the way ground communication is set up." He uses his right hand fingers like a comb to slowly and deliberately rake his longish stringy hair straight back on his head. And again, raking front to back.

"Doesn't like it? Doesn't like what? It's not set up yet. Is he not capable of explaining the problem? Or is this his solution—to stomp out?"

"No, I'm sure he's got something in mind," explains Lester.

"You've got to be kidding. Would you care to share it?" I say, at this point not caring to hear the explanation at all.

After waiting for but receiving no answer other than the permanent smirk, I stand. Dylan glances at me, and then looks away and down, apparently unable or unwilling to comment as I leave the meeting to find a place to cool down.

————

I pass by Carol on my way back to my station. "You won't believe what just happened."

"Try me," she says.

I remind her of the issue I brought up in David's earlier meeting and begin to describe the Brachus meltdown, but, before I can get through that, I see David waving me over into the meeting room. As I approach I see Brachus is sitting in the room. "Yes?"

"About ground communication for the Resources team…" he begins, motioning me to take a seat.

"Yes. It will take only a few seconds to set up, as you yourself know, once I get the required responses. Is there a problem?"

"There is. It's a division of responsibilities problem," David suggests.

"A division of… Ok, I'm lost. What is needed? The instructions are dead simple and apparently clear enough for everyone…" I respond, confused and reaching for an idea.

"It's an IT function," says Brachus.

"It's what? All you do is push a couple buttons." I say to him, and then look at David for support that I expect, but find none.

"He's right, Jason. Please find the time to setup and test their systems for both comms and data, including their GNI units. You call them genies," he needlessly adds, pointing casually to his device lying on the meeting room table.

Stung by David's siding with Wes, I say, "Impossible without their passwords," and look back to Brachus. He remains close-mouthed and expressionless.

David answers for both of them, "No, you can use an admin or master sequence to set up and test. Individual private codes can be entered later." David pauses and looks away. "And one more thing…"

What now? This is getting ridiculous. I don't respond, but instead wait to be informed.

"Please enable a secondary channel just for Wes' ground team. Make it a private channel and test it as well when you do the other business."

I look at David to see if I can catch any glimpse of emotion or other telltale sign. The lower lip bulges out, the pucker resets it. Nothing. Brachus is fooling with his communicator.

"Sorry David, but Wes, we've got the..." Tracy says, appearing at the door.

"Oops, gotta go, David," Brachus says displaying his biggest, most genial grin while standing up.

"All right, thanks, both of you," concludes David. He gets up and leaves right after the Resource team leader without saying another word.

I remain sitting for a few minutes stewing, tapping my fingers slowly on the table. We all have things to do I guess, some more distasteful than the rest. I finally get up and go about my usual business in an effort to settle my mind.

———

"He looks normal, but he's not. I mean, he could visually pass for a mature adult but his actions remind me of a spiteful rude child," I say to Carol when we are alone. "It's incredible. I can't imagine what hold he has over David. He ran right to David to get his way *and David listened.* It's stunning."

Carol leans in and speaks carefully, "Not just David. You remember how he was shoehorned into the mission at almost literally the last second? He must have pull that goes above and beyond David."

She has a point. And of course she's right. But what is his game? And how high do you have to go to get this kind of pull? It seems evident that the compatibility matrix was not rechecked. If it was, there is no possible way the index remained the same let alone went up. I got along great with Big Steve and although I never had dealings with Steve the younger, he couldn't have been worse than the greasy grinning Lester.

To Carol I confide, "It's a shame how the Steves were booted out for this lot. With all we've got going on, we don't need issues amongst the crew added to the mix. I am definitely keeping a record of this in my log; in my personal one at least."

Carol nods thoughtfully but doesn't respond otherwise. We both have a lot to do before landing, and agree to try to not let any of the recent events get in our way.

————

It's a busy time. Tiring but exciting. Tomorrow will be the first trip to the surface! We are going down in stages as the base camp is set up and begins to be able to support us. David has been adjusting the day–night schedule aboard ship to match what we will find down below.

The darkness in my tiny quarters is, as always, refreshing.

There are new sounds in the ship; no, not so much sounds as vibrations and small jolts. But, yes, sounds too. When you close your eyes and relax other senses seem enhanced.

I need to rest; the real meat of the mission begins soon. Got the last Gleshert treatment and warnings from Vanessa today. David and Mark don't seem worried; Dylan's positively enthusiastic. Stepping out onto a strange world will begin the next phase in our adventure among the stars.

I am relaxing now but still awake in the darkness on my bunk. With my eyes closed I see again the faint deep blue light that I've seen before. I open my eyes to see if there is an external cause. No. Nothing. And I knew there wouldn't be. There never is. Close again and there it is, faint but there. I can see it mostly at the edge of the right side of my right visual field. That is, it emanates from the edge but dims rapidly as it shines outward. It appears on the left edge too but much dimmer. When I look to the edge to see it, it doesn't move with my eyes. It seems a fixed phenomenon. In spite of the dimness, the blue is not pale or washed out; it is a vibrant steady deep color. Is it an artifact of the visual apparatus? Perhaps the retina, in the darkness, as it regularly rejuvenates itself for another day, has this subtle but noticeable side effect. But why doesn't it follow with eye movement? Or—can it be?—is the light really there? Yes. And what is it from? What is close to but behind the eyes? I have wondered—does the brain itself glow? Can it be that the activity of billions of neurons, endlessly processing, receiving, sending, storing, living, utilizes enough energy that some is lost through light as well as heat? This is what I must conclude: At the edges of the eye socket, a tiny bit of light leaks out from the vast assemblage of active living cells glowing like the core of an organic reactor.

I don't feel well. Carol says it's nerves. Mark says I need a cocktail. Grigor says it's too much work and pressure. Dylan says to see the doc, who says it's a minor reaction to the treatments we've all received, those of us who are part of the first ground crew. He says rest, read, write, sleep; whatever relaxes and calms you. Porter says, in his unique way, to get to work. He's right.

Doing inventory helps. All my gear is in order. Really there's not that much to carry on my person; a little more to set up my ground quarters work area. But even so, what's forgotten can be ordered for the next trip down. We are told that Mark's 'fab lab' equipment will be set up as soon as possible. And then needed items can be made right there on the surface.

One last sweep of the ship's systems; current states and codes all logged and archived. I can monitor these from the surface too.

Sleep helped. A nap can be a wonderful thing. I had an odd vivid dream about drowning. I was in shallow water near a shore. There were waves but not large ones. I was doubled over, face down; I could touch bottom easily, and if I tried I could stand up and breathe. But the strange part was

97

that I was OK not breathing. I had no desire to stand nor was I in distress. Not OK with drowning mind you, but OK with the current state—like I said, odd. Then the second strange thing: Someone waded into the water, grabbed my arms and / or shirt and hoisted me up and onto my feet. I turned to see who it was and saw...me. Told you—weird dream.

Part II

Surface

Another deep breath; the air is thick and rich. The red-orange glow of bright daylight through eyelids is glorious. The heat of the sun on my face—it's been a long time. The occasional gust of wind has a bite to it but no matter. After the monotony of the uniform and unchanging shipboard climate the heat and cold both bring the pleasure of sensation, of being part of a real world again. It's exhilarating.

"Snap out of it and give me a hand, will you?" Mark is smiling as he asks, and tilting his head upward takes a deep breath as well, and another. The contrast in environments between the sterile confines of the ship and this fresh organic world cannot be larger. "I smell flowers somewhere."

"It's probably me," I joke. Looking around at his chosen base site, I see barren rock. A jagged and rough location with little to no sign of vegetation. There are no flowers and not likely to be any nearby. "This is the spot, eh? It's isolated all right and no flowers."

"There's something for sure on the wind, coming from the lower elevations no doubt, but it's there. I need to get around and see what's what but not until all this is up and running." Mark is referring to his fabrication and processing facility. Using the natural formations in several cases, he has created a number of closely situated enclosures, one of which is my tiny home on this world.

"They seem pretty flimsy for any kind of longevity," I say already knowing that they will suffice for whatever work needs to be done. I don't mean to insult. I just want to keep the conversation going.

Mark gives me a look but doesn't speak right away, as if asking himself, "Is he kidding?"

"Although, our quarters are sturdy enough for our purposes," I add as a palliative. "How in the world did we get all of this equipment and material in the ship?" I ask, now more serious.

"We didn't," he answers as we walk toward what he earlier called his command cave. "You'd be surprised how complex a structure can be built from just a few simple components, if you have enough of them. We carry with us a couple of small fabricators for the purpose of making what we need on-site out of local materials with local energy sources."

Now in his work area, he says, "Look here at these four little items: I can make these now at will. They are what all this is made of," he says, pointing around and overhead and then hands me the pieces. I look. They are light structural components, simple in design.

I look back at Mark, "All this? Where are these pieces used?"

"Look around again, they are everywhere. They can be made in to a door, a wall, a table. What do you want?" He walks to the door, takes back the handful, and shows how pieces of the same design are part of the frame construction. "See? They are the same pieces. It's just a matter of adjusting the dimensions to suit. Longer, shorter, different connections. You add this sheeting component to span the large areas and there you have it. Boom—that's a door. There's a door. The sheeting is really the same material, but thin and plain with no edge treatment, and can be lapped over itself to make any size panel. Cool huh?"

Oh, he's in his element now. "Yes, cool. Doors, walls and…everything?"

"Look, we carry digital models for every component we can foresee needing, and can modify existing design for those we can't. One fab unit can make repair parts for another unit should one fail, or it can make parts for the runabouts or lander; it's really a tight system. While I can make inorganic parts to suit, Doc has a similar but different gizmo to put you or me back together as well if need be."

"Speaking of that, did you receive the want list from the Hobbe? David wants to know."

 "Yes, priority one. As soon as we are completely set up, the needs of the ship are first on the schedule. We have to make sure we can get out of here and get home. Although…" Mark leaves an opening that I don't follow and choose to ignore, for now, while we step outside to see the source of an overhead sound.

The thrill of being out of doors, the expanse of it all, dominates my attention. It's still there but I hardly notice Mark's limp anymore. It sure doesn't slow him down any. We walk toward a sheer rock face and sit on a boulder seemingly conveniently located for that purpose as the vehicle arrives. I see it's the larger of the two models, the transport, and David's not in it. "Wait, David took the small one? What's up with that?"

"He had to; I need the carrying capacity to bring in resources on the transport. Priority one—I told you. He is off somewhere with the other unit scoping out the bio camp parameters and location. I'll be able to divert some, but not many, of my resources to his work to keep him happy. In any case, we are going to be here a long, long time, by my reckoning, even if there are no glitches. Plenty of time."

"Perfect. I mean the progress so far, not the long stay," as I get up. Why did I say that? I don't care about the length of the stay, within reason. As long as we make it out someday, I'm good. I check my genie for the runabout, the one that David has and get a quick status from it; all systems good. I have no reason to contact David directly at this time although I am curious as to what he is finding out about the natives. It might be too soon. "These guys been reporting any interesting native contacts yet?" I ask, referring with a nod to the transporter crew.

"All kinds," says Mark and adds, "mostly plants and simpler life—the place is teeming with it. Until David's OK we are under a strict hands-off policy."

"That's not what I mean."

"Oh, you mean the other…" Mark pauses for effect and then adds, "Oh, they're out there all right."

Pre-landing analysis showed a safe environment in general, but there is still reason for caution. The areas we'll be working in need to be checked carefully. We need to know what 'unexpected problems to expect' as most of us heard during a short speech from Master Brachus before we landed. Brilliant.

I am startled to hear, "Hey, where are the portable assay units?" from off to the side and behind us a bit, which I thought was solid rock wall. Mark doesn't blink and silently indicates his work shop.

"Relax, why so jumpy? We are safe here," he says to me. "I've made sure that there are no easy ways into this area. He's one of us!"

"Yes, but why sneak up on us like that? And where the hell did he come from?" I answer, annoyed. I've taken a look around our site and see that the raw rocky site has more than a few spots where a person on foot could come or go. And there are nooks, crannies and crevices galore, including one just off to our left.

"Craig's probably still checking nearby for any useful

outcroppings."

We see him, Craig Brown, now looking back towards us with his palms open and a questioning expression on his boyish face. He has to be older than he looks, because otherwise he wouldn't be eligible to enlist. The freckles and mop top only accentuate the impression.

"I told him they were there but didn't tell him I have the only access. Hee. The fun never ends. Later."

"Wait, didn't you need help with something?"

"Nah, I'm good. Forget it."

Mark gets up and casually walks toward Craig, who shakes his head when he no doubt senses Mark's amusement at his expense.

> *My official data logging and archiving functions are primarily automatic. If there are any flags, I have to manually resolve the issue, but that's that. What I've found through experience is that there are a large number of possible problems with a complex system, not restricted to networked data systems like ours, but any complex system. The distribution of problem types is such that they lend themselves very well to analysis. Once you understand the high frequency problems, know how to address them and, hopefully, prevent them, you are left to deal with lower and lower frequency problems. End result: manual intervention is required rarely. Once*

problems start to repeat and you recognize them, things start getting easier right away.

The field reports are coming in, formats are good, and nothing more needs to be done by me. I've looked at a few. The freeform parts of the resource team's submissions are pretty bland. Not much there. Realistically, most of their data comes through from their instruments, so what's there for them to add? Dylan is the exception; he notices things and likes to comment. Wes' comments seem like so much gibberish to me, but I may be biased. It's hard to believe he has any standing at all, but there he is. Mark's reports are professional, to the point, and regular. He's a good writer.

I do follow David's reports—these reports I am mentioning are all public record by the way. His reports are interesting. He likes to comment too. He's called me down at next light to see what he's set up for his bio work. He's made contact.

Bio Camp

"I'm going to ask Mark to put together another flyer. You Ok?" David asks.

"Whew! Yes. Man, the air is really thick and sweet down here!" This is my first trip to the lower elevations. We're at roughly 3 East and 27 North. It's not far from base—which we are using as zero longitude—but what a change! The higher density of the atmosphere coupled with the humidity make for a marked difference from base camp conditions.

After a quick orientation inside we have made our way out of the concealed landing and camp area and stand now in the midst of an alien and yet somehow familiar world. It's overwhelming and I am disoriented at first.

"You've checked this all out?" I ask, gesturing vaguely at the greenery all around us and probably betraying some anxiety.

David looks at me, and then looks around with me as if he perhaps remembers when he saw it all for the first time.

"Yes and no. This area has been explored and cleared for our use by me personally, along with help from Groth and Seaborn. But, it's a foreign world; don't go sticking your hand into the underbrush or random holes." He looks at me again as if silently evaluating my potential for getting into trouble.

"Where is your test area?"

"We are standing in the middle of it. You saw the central camp and lab where we landed. But out here, this is the main part."

I take my time and do another visual scan of our surroundings. "I'll be careful." I see now that the landing spot and small work area are indeed well-hidden. As a start, we circumnavigate the entire hidden central area and then I follow David's lead as we move out and into the wild.

"When here, or at any field site really, take care. I haven't run into a large predator, but we've seen evidence enough to know they exist. This test area has been isolated and a reasonably secure perimeter is established but it's a large expanse; we may have missed something or some creature may find its way in without our knowing. Don't wander around out here without protection. Speaking of that, you are using the spray on any exposed skin I hope?"

I nod. The occasional breeze signals its approach via the rustling of leaves and branches long before we feel the effect, if any, here at ground level. The temperature is warm but not unpleasant. We can hear the sounds of myriad creatures, some near, some far. Some fly and flit from branch to branch, others leap. I haven't yet seen any ground dwellers, nothing larger than a bird, but David assures me I will. Some of the plants are incredibly like home, and catch my eye. Others are unlike anything I've seen before.

"We are evaluating the possibility that at least some of the fruit is edible," says David as we emerge into a more open area. He stops and turns to me. "What I meant before is that your protection is the number one priority. Do not hesitate to disable or kill if you get attacked. Having said that, our primary bio mission here on the surface centers around the hominids." I raise my eyebrows in question, but nod to show that I heard. "Yes, we've made contact. More than that—I've done some preliminary testing."

"Really. So soon?"

"I've given the order for the resource guys to bring in samples of plants and animals whenever they can safely do so while not interfering with Mark's needs. Not entire organisms, mind you, but samples from which we can pull DNA and start the process of recording. It's a big long job, and it's started." We are walking further away from the center now, approaching a small stream. I spot something on the ground, stop and look, and wait for David to acknowledge.

"What made that?" I ask when he looks back at me.

"Well, there you go. That's one of the pieces of evidence that I mentioned."

"No claw marks."

111

"Retractable? Could be. Anyway, it's a big quadruped," he says as he sees me fumble at my weapon as I make sure it's at the ready. "Discreet samples have also begun to be collected from the natives, over a surprisingly large area by the way, and these have been evaluated for genetic configuration and drift since the previous mission. It turns out that here, right where we are standing, is nearly the perfect spot for our purposes. The genetic makeup is as close to the ideal mix as we could have hoped to find. Not perfect, you understand, but getting there."

"When you say discreet samples—how do you mean? How is it done?"

"Well, look, we need to get back so I can get to work so let's walk and talk and I'll cover as much as I can. You already know the basic starting chemistry for life on this planet was provided by a seeding program similar to the one we use now and have used on the Hobbe. So we know that life here uses the same basic strategy, the building blocks if you will, at its core as ours. Barring any unforeseen events, the natural progression of life will, given enough time, transform a suitable planet into a lush, arable and hospitable world with plants and animals. It boggles my mind how well a system, and I mean a whole planet as a single system, can self-regulate into a stable, hospitable environment.

"Now, one cannot predict the vagaries of evolution. On one hand, a basic pattern of strategies for survival and procreation appears time and time again. On the other, sometimes it is necessary to intervene and nudge the biota in one direction or another; sometimes, when things go awry, it's necessary to take more drastic steps. In the end the results all tend to be similar. Not in the detail, but in the general. Similar but different. You've noticed this already no doubt. I saw you looking at some of the plants." David pauses here to look for a response or nod from me. "If you squint and tilt your head and look around you could almost believe you were home. Remember our overarching societal goal is to expand and unify—we are treating barren worlds as potential gardens as well as potential homes."

We move back inside the well-camouflaged central area and sit in the small camp near the landing zone. David leans way back and points up to a large soaring bird. We both follow its movement until it swoops behind the arboreal canopy.

"Now, during direct contact like ours we can collect samples at will but … when you deal with intelligent beings—no matter how primitive—you have to be careful. In all cases, they will fit you into their world view any way they can and how they do it may have an important effect. So, when I say discreet, I mean in such a way as to minimize the shock not just to their bodies but to their minds as well."

David seems done talking, but I sense he wants to say more. He looks around and begins to fidget with some of the equipment on the work surface to his left. "But," I say, eager to hear more, "how do you do that? The sampling. How is it actually done?"

David returns his attention and gaze to me. "Depends on the quality of the sample required. Jason, let's pick this up another time. If you don't feel your questions are being answered by my notes and reports, try the database. I know there are at least a few descriptions of similar work in there. We can talk again soon, too."

"You mentioned that this area is the ideal location for our purposes. Our purpose is to sample and record the existing organisms' DNA. Can't we do that from anywhere? Why is this spot better than anywhere else?" I ask.

David doesn't answer or respond right away. I think maybe he is preoccupied with other thoughts and didn't hear me, but he does finally say, "What I meant to say was the population of natives that has the highest correlation to the ideal, the ones most like us in other words, is centered here. Right here. We have to leave it at that for the moment."

"Alright, no problem. Thanks for the info. You're staying out here, I presume?"

"I am staying here. Urge Mark to work on that second runabout; I will be here a lot and don't like to be stranded. Tell him to have Porter return with this one as soon as the supplies I ordered are ready."

That reminds me of my job and I have a quick look at David's electronics. He turns his attention to what must be samples and analysis equipment.

"I saw where you reported that you made your first direct

114

contact with natives," I say as a way to see if he wants to talk about it some more. "The notes don't mention any issues. I presume all contact so far has been uneventful?"

"No. Eventful, but in a good way. As I said, we have actually pulled in a good set of samples. We are in the right place. I've already targeted an individual for more extensive work." In a quieter tone, almost as if to himself, he continues, "We were wrong about the interpretation of some of the images—development is not very advanced. We are talking stone age here, maybe a little beyond," and then added, looking my way, "but not much."

I continue about my business and let David do the same. I set up advanced syncing parameters and do a quick manual read of a couple local report files. One is from Brachus; I guess it makes sense he has been here with David while the rest of the Resources team does the actual work of his department. I shouldn't complain. Look at me—I have spare time too as long as things continue to work smoothly, electronically speaking.

"So, have you worked with Wesley before on a mission?" I ask as I wrap up what I need to do.

"We have worked together over the years and go way back as acquaintances even longer. This is the first time we've been on a deep space mission together." David pauses to work his lower lip as usual; I try to ignore it as usual. I hardly notice it any more, really. It's like Mark's limp. "He led his own mission not that long ago, you know."

"I didn't know. In fact I hardly know more than what I've learned since we met before launch, and that's not much. I am surprised he is in such a high position seeing as how he was the last member to be brought on." Oops, I can see right away this is a mistake to mention.

David's demeanor at once turns cold as he replies, "What should I have done, punish him for coming to the team late?"

I decline to answer, wisely, I believe, sensing that there is no right answer and no answer is in fact wanted or expected. David offers no follow up comment and we both work in silence for my last few minutes at his bio camp.

Even after such a short time, we have learned a lot about the native populations relative to their environment. First, from our point of view, the days and years are incredibly short. It takes a little time, but we all seem to be getting used to it. Carol just joined the ground crew and although she thinks the place is beautiful she's still disoriented.

Maybe it's tied to the short daily and yearly cycle but, if you can believe his reports, the natives David wants to study have very short life spans. In local years, the average is between 20 and 30 maxing out at maybe 50. Even compared to the general untreated populace back home, this is really short. We are going to be here for many of their generations. The magnitude of the life span difference brings home the major advances in medicine and healthy living that I tend to take for granted.

Strange, back at my ground terminal at base camp, I read the same report that I scanned at the bio station, Brachus' report, and it's different! Not sure what is happening there. Maybe I am mis-remembering what I read, or is it possible he edited the report later? No, the time stamp says it couldn't be. Like I said, I'm not sure what's going on there. But the reason I mention it is when I tried to contact him on his communicator, I got Tracy. He's jacked around with the addresses and redirect settings so that Tracy gets his calls and messages while she continues to get her own as well. Why am I not surprised? I may go to David but I can already guess that he thinks I am overreacting to the Brachus business.

I'll tell you what though, the evolutionary convergence that David started to talk about is really something. I see it mostly in local plants, although I suspect this is because I don't have a background in plants and couldn't identify differences without more study. Someone who actually knows plant structure may have something else to say. The few animals I've seen look familiar but only when viewed from a distance. Markings and coloration let you know right away that you are not anywhere near home!

I have seen the relief map of the bio camp area. It's in a moderately small valley with only one narrow natural way in and out. I see why David likes it: it's easy to control and isolate. The central camp is right in the middle of the widest part of the valley near the one small meandering stream.

I took a little time to pull up and review the database for information on previous similar missions. I found a couple but won't have time to extract details until I get back from a trip to Dylan's current field location. Should be a fun visit; I'm looking forward to it.

Dex

"What reservation?"

"Are you kidding me? I'm heading out to one of the mineral outcroppings today."

Mark comes right back with, "Which one?"

"Which one? Does it matter? What do you mean which one?" At this point I am starting to get peeved; this excursion has been set up for some time. I see Dylan approaching and give him a nod.

"All set?" he asks. "Let's go. It's not far. You're gonna like it out there."

"Oh, why didn't you say it was Dylan's reservation? You are set to go. Don't forget me while you're out there; I gave you the signature you are looking for. Bring in at least the minimum amount specified and I will be a happy guy."

"Not funny, Mark. You knew this was Dylan's."

"What? You didn't say that," he says with a smile, brushing his red hair away from his forehead. Yes, he knew all right, I'm sure, but again with the games.

As we take off I see what looks like Grigor down in the camp. I didn't know he's down here. We haven't talked in a while and will have to get together soon.

Dylan and I are quiet as we travel to our destination. Coming out of the mountains Dylan maintains a high altitude. It's unlikely any native would spot us at that height. We know they have no technology to speak of. No way to enhance their vision. But why would it matter? No sense creating a scene, I guess. Up here we are just another bird, albeit an odd looking one. Landing is more problematic outside base camp. For sure we are visible and noisy as we approach and leave the surface. Observation is unavoidable.

The views we get from orbit really don't offer a good 3D feel for the topography. The view from up here in the transport sure does! From the rugged, mountainous base camp and surrounds to the distant expanses of water, the shapes and textures, bright and colorful, are incredibly fascinating. Intense blue and white in the sky, the desolate areas of barren brown surrounded by lush shades of green plant life—all of this punctuated by jagged mountains of varying height with striking, sharp delineation between light and dark areas. If that's not enough, the sparkling deep blue-gray expanses of water set the rest off dramatically. It would be a pleasure to spend some time just exploring. I wonder how Carol's schedule is looking.

"I'm going to take a spin around before we land. That's

where we are going, right there," Dylan points to a rough-looking spot where vegetation is spotty. It's one of several jagged brown uprisings surrounded by lush green overgrowth. No more talking as he takes us on a precipitous drop to a landing.

"You've been here before?" I ask in such a way as to hopefully not show any apprehension.

"Yep, a couple times," Dylan responds glancing at me. "Don't worry. The natives are friendly." He smiles calmly.

We exit the transport and Dylan quietly follows me as I tentatively walk to the edge of the rocky outcropping where there is a view of a lower-lying expanse.

"I like this spot," he says as I look around. "Mark gave us several sites located from orbit. This one is very rich in something we need." He waits a few seconds before continuing, I guess waiting for a comment. "Don't ask me what it is. I don't know and haven't bothered to check into it. I've got a specific spectro signature, and when I get a close match on my sensor here, that's it. Probably it's a good mixture of more than one thing anyway. Mark is very picky because the richer the samples are, the less processing needs to be done. As he says, 'Why settle for rotgut, when a good martini is sitting right out there on the table?' Or some such corn. All I know is that he seems happy with what we bring him. I'm working a place right over here on this cleft face and already have about half a load going. Help me undock the mining cart. We can load it up and then have some free time if you want to look around some more."

I have heard about these units. They dock directly to a flyer and are used for transporting raw materials or anything really. I can see where Dylan has been working this site. We muscle the ore cart to a pile of previously broken rock and begin loading the easily manageable pieces. I like this work. I can see that Dylan could handle it alone, and probably has done so many times at various sites during our stay. Even though we don't speak much I think Dylan enjoys the company.

The right hand rule is, of course, applied to all new worlds to establish a uniform reference for north. Latitude is straightforward. Longitude is based on a stake dropped into a hopefully stable and prominent land mass upon first mapping. Sometimes this works for eons but other times upheavals on a planet's surface will obliterate the stake. In that case, a new one is planted at the next visit. For missions like ours, base camp center is the local zero for the duration of our stay and it is offset to the stake location in the official records. It's a best attempt at continuity over time. This system places us at about 7 W and 34 N.

There are clouds moving in from the northwest, but not threatening ones. The way the sun and shadow play on the lower elevations within our view is beautiful. Dylan points and we see the distant sea, far off to the southwest.

"This sure seems inefficient, carting these small loads back and forth across the planet," I say as we continue to manually load. "Is any of this stuff radioactive?"

"It's not as bad as you might think. We only go after the richest deposits in the easiest locations to access. The yields that Mark gets are high. And he purposely chose base camp close to the items he needs the most of. He's a smart cookie… although I don't think he likes me. As far as radioactive material, that's not what we are loading here. I mean, there could be some percentage but it's not the main resource. Just be sure to check in with Doc when you get back and you will be alright."

He smiles at my concern and looks away, toward the vegetation to the west, the side of the outcropping that begins to slope downward steadily.

"Oh Mark likes you alright, he just comes on gruff. Did the same to me. Still does. He gets a kick out of it. Say, how is Brachus working out for you guys?"

"Hold on," says Dylan and he gives a sharp whistle while continuing to look in the same westerly direction. "He doesn't know what to make of you. Stay here. Take this," he says as he hands me a small pouch and heads away.

I tense at the mention of 'he' and try to follow Dylan's gaze. There is something there at the edge of the clearing, but what? I stand erect now, listening and looking intently. What the…? Out of the brush comes a dog. I mean to say, it looks for all the world like a kind of dog! It's got a somewhat odd shape, especially around the head, and looks like it could fend for itself no problem. And the mannerisms definitely say 'dog.'

"Dylan, what the heck have you got going here? Be careful with that thing. If he attacks, I'm taking off, you're on your own," I say, only half-joking. I have fumbled for and pulled out my weapon, but Dylan looks back, sees me, and waves his hand as if to say 'not to worry'.

"Put that away. Toss one of the pieces of the food I brought over here. I want you to meet Dex."

"Yeah, that's ok. You keep him right there; I'll toss the food."

I do not take my eyes off 'Dex' while trying to figure out what to do next. Wait, what happened to the pouch? I see I dropped it when Dex first appeared. Still holding my weapon, I shuffle to the pouch and pick it up.

"Did you say he wants to meet me, or eat me?" I ask in an effort to disguise my concern. Dex looks like he might be about a quarter of my weight, and if he took a running leap could easily knock me down. I'll keep the weapon out, thank you. Those two seem to be getting along OK but I swear the dog is watching me as closely as I am watching him, or her, or whatever it is.

"He lives down the hill. He heard us. He came up the last couple times I was here. Jason, ease up and come here. Toss him something. He's not here to stalk or attack, he's curious and friendly."

"Ok, sure, whatever you say. I'll be right there," I lie,

having no intention of leaving the relative safety of my position at the ore cart. I toss a bit of food toward Dex as Dylan, realizing, I guess, that I'm not coming any closer, begins to walk my way. Dex warily watches my toss, then turns his attention to the food, likes what he smells and eats it up. He follows Dylan but stops short, well back from me. It seems we are on the same wavelength there. It's a standoff of toleration for the moment as Dex actually sits down on his haunches and assumes a more relaxed but alert posture, ears erect and gaze steady.

"Ok, you two. Have it your way. At least he has seen you. Next time you will be old friends."

I suggest we get back to work, secretly hoping Dex will skedaddle back to his cave or wherever. "Man, that was a shock. I mean, how did you get him so tame? It's almost like he's been with people before."

Dylan looks at Dex, then at me and says calmly, "He has."

I am getting used to the short days now. It's beginning to seem normal whereas just a little while ago I had a sort of dizzy feeling as they whizzed past. This has to be a brief entry. I am logging this from the field at Dylan's mining location. I'm still not over the double whammy of, first, Dex and, second, Dylan's admission of native contact. This kid is a wonder and apparently fearless. We finished loading all the prepped ore, cracked out some more, and tomorrow will locate and prepare even more for a future visit. If we are lucky, he says, he may be able to introduce me to one of the locals. As incredible as it seems, Dylan says he has started a rudimentary communication with them. I say he is playing with fire as any native will find us not just as an outsider in his territory, but a way outsider, and may therefore feel threatened and become aggressive. If they find the transport or ore cart, they will not be able to reconcile these things with their experience, period. The results are unpredictable, and I told him so. I know he heard me, but made no reply.

Burnin' Fire

Sleep is impossible. After learning that Dylan has made contact, and knowing that we are in an exposed area, I can't help but stay alert. And of course now I clearly hear and ascribe every night sound to prowlers, murderers and savage beasts.

Dylan is immobile and out to the world, deep asleep by all signs. The perimeter alarm is set and we are in his little temporary dome. 'That's enough for us,' he says, 'they have no lights or real weapons to speak of, we are safe, especially at night' he says. Bull. I just heard pawing and snuffling right outside the dome.

Sleep comes, dreams come. I am standing alone in our back yard, in the dark, facing the rear of the house where I grew up. I have lost the dream-thread that led me to here but no matter. My attention is drawn to the sound of children playing. I listen without turning, for the sound comes from behind me, for several moments. It gets louder. I turn without haste and see, through a chain link fence, a scene as if on a large, well-lit stage. The fence separates me from the stage; the setting is a schoolyard. The schoolyard is filled with youngsters out for recess and they are in various phases of activity, on and around playground equipment. The sound of their high-pitched voices, laughing and shouting, changes character slowly

127

and for some length of time I am puzzled. It is at this moment of awakening that I realize the vision is a dream but the sound persists! In the dark, I turn my head and see Dylan, sound asleep, in the little camp dome. The sound from my dream continues, but it is not children, it is a pack of baying animals in the night, and not too far away either. Their yipping and howling combine and separate, rise and fall, and then stop altogether. Could it be Dex and his kind? No, not Dex, the sounds are too high-pitched for him. The night passes into silence and sleep eventually returns.

Notwithstanding this restless night, I am getting used to these incredibly short sleep/wake cycles. A good long rest at base camp is in order however, as soon as I get back.

We finish doing what we can on this visit, re-dock the ore cart and return to base without further incident. Mark is nowhere to be found. Porter helps us deliver the ore and is scheduled to take off with the transport next. Dylan thanks me for the help. He hopes I enjoyed being out in the 'real world' and heads off on some other business.

Porter asks me, "Do you want to come with? I have to run out and swap an empty tub for a full. It's a great ride, over an ocean and all." He waits patiently while I think how to answer, unsure if I want another adventure so soon. "How about a cup of burnin' fire while we wait for Mark to return and empty the tub?" he offers with a grin. "It's the latest discovery—here, I'll get us both one. You've got to try it."

I follow this eager and friendly young 'kid' to the mess hall and sit. I say 'young kid' but it's only in response to his demeanor. I suspect he is a bit older than me. He prepares and brings a couple cups of a steaming brown liquid, his cup having a lid for travel. "Doc approved and David blessed. Careful, it's hot." His curly hair and near-constant smile add to my positive image of him. Porter is one of the very few people who have opted for external vision correction and his glasses, wire framed and slightly askew, fit his personality exactly.

"Burnin' fire, eh?" I say, as I tentatively take a sip. I notice I have several messages and need to address them; one is from David. "Who do you work for? Mark?" I ask.

"Everybody. What do you need?" he responds happily. "I have several bosses and like it that way. They can fight out for their priorities and let me know who wins. No sweat, no strain. Right now, Mark wins and I have to git." He takes another sip, heads for the flyer, shouts something to Craig across the way, and departs.

David's message is an ambiguous query. Something about a separate private and personal channel, but linked into Brachus' group. Great, another one. I check via my genie that he is free at the moment and contact him; he picks up. "Private channel, linked to the Resource Group?" I begin.

"Yes, please, as soon as you can get around to it. Wesley is working with me down here and I need to be able to communicate with him directly but not publicly with both voice and data." I can see the Academy's 'open and clear communication' mantra is going to take another hit.

"Alright. I can do it, should have it ready by tomorrow. You'll receive a message from me with your access ID and instructions on how to initiate and make it your own."

"One more thing…"

"Yes?" I ask, after a few moments of silence.

"I want a separate way to keep notes for myself only—not public or official or shared in any way." I don't need to hear the reason for this, after all, he is the boss, but he offers one anyway. "A lot my documentation will be indecipherable to anyone but me. I need a way to make quick entries without taking the time to formulate and clarify them. I will go back later and enter the relevant info into the official record. It will make more sense than the raw notes will. You follow me?"

Oh, I follow. I don't like it, but I follow.

"Yes, sir. I can set this up and send you a second message with everything you need."

We disconnect. This request is not a big deal technically; after all, the last part of it is essentially the same thing I have done for my little diary. But he is the commander, and, as he said, he wants to keep his raw notes private and off the official record until he can massage and enter them. What the heck is he doing down there? Isn't the sequencing and logging of the genome and variants a straightforward task? Can this be about the 'more extensive work' he referred to on my visit to the bio site?

———————

Dylan never answered my question about working for Wes. I wonder what he can tell me? Porter—he has the right idea. Mind your own business. Get a task, work on it. Get another one, work on it. Certainly less stressful that way. He seems happy, this Porter.

I'm off to Gleshert to see if I did any damage to myself out there at the mining site, and I better ask what this stuff is I'm drinking while I'm at it.

"Sorry, mate, just leavin'. How are ya keepin'?" says Grigor as I make my way into the med reception area. I get the expected wink from Vanessa.

"Grigor! No problem. I am good. You?"

"The GlassMan says I'll live to fight another day." He shows me a nasty abrasion on his right arm. "It's a lucky thing I have two of these." Meaning his arms.

"What happened? What do you have on it?"

"Just a scratch, just a scratch. Doc has some new goo that he used to cover and heal. Touch it."

I decline. "You get this down here? I saw you when I took off with Dylan. When was that—today? No, the other day. I've been losing track of time lately."

"Yes, I hear you there. I did some mountain climbing; my

own fault. Well, no worries, I'll leave you to more important business. See ya Doc. See ya doll."

"Hey, wait, and you too Doc, what is this concoction I just had over at the kitchen? It's coffee-like. You've had it? It's a little bitter but what is it? Actually, I don't care what it is. Is it safe, is the question."

"It's a Weasely Brachus thing. I won't touch it and you shouldn't either," says Grigor as he pauses momentarily before heading out.

"Doc, what do you say? Have you tried it or tested it?"

"Come in and sit down. You've been out at one of the remote sites?" I nod as he looks me over and begins what seems to me to be a routine checkout. "Give me your card." He takes it, inserts the card, mumbles to himself, and then turns to me. His cowlick is still right where it's always been. "Drink the stuff if you like it. One of the Resource team found animals eating some berries. They were bitter and inedible to him, but someone in his party, in their apparently abundant spare time," he added with obvious distaste, "figured out they can make an interesting beverage if boiled or processed somehow with water. I don't know the details. I believe Aileen could tell you more of how it's done." Distracted from this train of thought for a moment by the results from my card reading he says, "The card shows negative, same for the other tests. You are clear until your next t-session." Meaning the telomere treatment with which we have all grown so familiar.

"So, it's safe?"

"I told you, drink it if you want. It produces mild physiological effects but no serious long term concerns that I can detect." With this, the doc indicates clearly but non-verbally that it's time for me to go, and turns to other business in his small, ground-based lab.

I take a stab and say, "I haven't seen David around base much lately. He's doing OK as far as you know?"

Gleshert nods without turning. "Oh, he's around. He was here recently and practically cleaned me out of reagents."

Time is passing quickly now that I'm into a routine. The local years are flying by, it seems. I've visited a few more of the remote sites. Some are truly spectacular to behold. We see less and less of David and Wesley. Both seem to have dug in for the long haul—Brachus somewhere out in the field, and David splitting his time between the bio camp and sequestered in his makeshift lab in his quarters here at base. Brachus is occasionally seen teetering about base camp on his spindly legs with a big grin on his face. I heard from Craig (confirmed by Porter) that he's fashioned—Brachus, that is—his own "headquarters" out in the wild somewhere mostly out of native materials along with some construction and connection pieces from Mark. He uses the transport unit to cart the pieces to the site and then when the flyer returns, it is loaded with ore or whatever other raw materials he has located for Mark. Ok, I have to hand it to him, that is a clever arrangement.

I try to spend as much time as I can with Carol. Her setup for linking to the astrophysics equipment up top, on the Hobbe, is very cool indeed. I make excuses to visit her as much as possible and pretend to adjust and tweak the electronics. She's on to me of course. The good news is, she doesn't seem to mind at all. She is really good to talk to and I found out she has a background in botany of all things. Who knew? Well, this must be a paradise for studying new and exotic plants. This entire planet would be the textbook definition of 'new and exotic' wouldn't it? I keep vowing to collect and bring her some that look especially interesting.

I know there is something Carol is holding back about Brachus, but I have been making an effort lately to concentrate on other things. Everyone has their own responsibilities and I have mine; so be it. I don't like the private channel business, but I keep getting periodic official reports submitted by him and his team (their reports are filtered through Brachus, which I also don't like, but nobody cares what I like) and that's enough.

I also have been spending some time with David. He's reviewed my background and he quizzes me about it and my other interests. You can never predict his mood though. As Grigor quipped, you don't know if you are going to get David or Mr.

Means from one moment to the next so it's like walking on eggs around him.

He's been working on his "specimens" now for some time and I get the feeling that something is not right but he hasn't opened up enough for me to confirm it. I confided to him that the idea of treating the natives like lab animals doesn't sit well with me but he countered with the notion that they are already in essence being tested in their natural environment and evaluated for survival by evolution; we are just trying to speed things up a little and make sure we nudge the process in the right direction. That was the word he used, nudge. I guess by comparison Dylan's interaction with the natives is mild and benign.

The Big Picture

The team has been on the ground for more than 50 local years. I should just say plain old 'years' and get used to it. The native animal and most plant populations are on a very high metabolic rate, compared to us. Dex is long gone, but Dex's descendants are around and Dylan continues to interact with them and the natives. He thinks more highly of their current state of development than does David. He, Dylan, has learned the basic languages for the areas he routinely visits.

Carol and I have opted out of the 'medical relief program' (yes, that's right!) and now spend more time together than ever before. This is going to be a good trip, no matter what else happens!

I had a big flurry of activity recently after a major solar storm impinged on this world. Carol had warning via her shipboard sensors but it still caused havoc. I had to return to orbit and look after my responsibilities there, not to mention a short list of items to check for every crew member. Everything is restored now. The good news is that a repeat is unlikely. A direct hit like that from a solar storm is a low probability event.

The flurry over, I collect my thoughts. I am surprised at how the ship seems to me now. It is sterile, but not

entirely lifeless; it lives the 'life' of a complex, life-
sustaining machine, constantly humming and occasionally
clicking and clacking. It has a sound and feel and smell all
its own. There is some comfort of security in its close
surroundings; my work and bunk area, with its sprinkling
of personal artifacts, evinces a feeling of calm and
familiarity. But compared to the world below… There *is*
no comparison to the fresh expanses of a brand new
world.

I return to base camp and to Carol to hear the troubling
news that David has indeed begun experimentation with
his selected subjects. Not just documenting, but
experimenting. Gleshert has reluctantly admitted that one
native in particular has been deemed 'the right one' by
David and has been receiving t-session treatments. David's
reasoning: if we prolong the reproductive stage, the more
offspring there will be; the more offspring, the wider the
distribution of the selected genetics. By inference, I assume
he believes that the descendants of his starting stock will
become the dominant variant on the planet.

"They've got too much time on their hands. We all do." I
know who Carol means when she says 'they.' She means
David and Wesley. "Idle hands and all that," she
continues. We're sitting at our favorite table in the mess
hall. "You saw the timeline. We have barely begun our
stay. Mark laid it all out. It's a complicated process to refit
for our departure. You should talk to him, by the way. I
can tell he's not happy about something but as usual, he's
being Mark about it."

"What do you think about the overall mission now, the big picture again? Should we be here, and elsewhere, interfering not with just bio systems, but with intelligent beings like we are doing? What I mean is this: do you buy into the whole program of expansion and survivability? I know that you said you were OK with it before, but now, in the middle of the actuality, do you still agree with it?"

"Jason, I do. Maybe I spend too much time looking out into space and the vastness of it, but in the *really* big picture we are small potatoes. Sure, we've visited and affected any number of worlds but there are, without any possibility of doubt, many many more that we haven't visited or affected. Those worlds will, if conditions are right, and, again, there can be no doubt that conditions *will* be right on some percentage of them, develop life on their own. And let's say intelligent life. And let's say aggressive intelligent life. And let's say these beings are very successful and begin their own campaign of expansion. Now, even if we assume that the basic building blocks, the amino acids for example, are much the same as ours, we must assume that the genetic code is not. That is, the letters that form the language of inheritance must almost certainly be different from ours, since they are, at the core, a random assignment. And what if they are incompatible? What if, upon the meeting of our two civilizations, this alternate structure and composition is fatal to one or both? What if a basic incompatibility—it doesn't matter what it is: virus, germ, protein—exists?"

"That's a stretch, Carol," I respond. "I know you are right in your chain of thought, and I know it agrees with what we were taught, but it's still a stretch. May never happen. Probably won't happen."

"But should we risk an entire civilization along with its history and achievements when we have the technology to try to prevent it? Even though we are a very small part of the universe as a whole…"

"Small potatoes as you say…"

"… yes, it's true. But even so, our civilization as a whole has amounted to *something*. All the achievements, discoveries, inventions, ideas… These, I believe, are bigger than us. I think they're worth trying to save and protect. And if that means saving and protecting our civilization as a whole, I'm in."

"Ok, let's go with that, just as you describe. Why not be satisfied with simple seeding? Why go to the extent that we do? We seed the possible planets with compatible starter materials, ensure that basic code is the same, and let it be?"

"That plan would work only up to a point. It works only for those worlds that are barren when seeded. And sometimes things go awry even with successful seeding. You told me you are researching histories of previous missions. Evolution is unpredictable in its details. Sometimes a planet becomes dominated by a non-intelligent species and in such a way that an intelligent one is never likely to arise, at least not in the foreseeable future. In a case like that, it's best to start over, unless we just give up and write that one off as a loss."

"But David—what he is doing—what do you think about that?" I ask, having earlier confided in her about my qualms regarding his searching for and finding an 'ideal specimen' and what I think that means. "Can't we just leave these people alone? Let's finish with our business and move along."

"Alright, but are you sure you really know what he's doing down there? I mean, it's just rumor."

"Good point. But I hear the source is Doc and he's not one to spread unfounded rumors. Something is happening beyond just recording data."

"Ok, maybe so then. That's tougher for me to take as well but look at it this way: we've already been here. What you see around you is partly our doing. We're already deeply in the game. You do like it here, right?"

"Alright, that's a good point, we're already in deep. But it just pushes the question farther back to the previous intervention, and so on, back to the first step of the program."

"Ah, but wait, now I have you!" she says with a sparkle in her eye. "I keep coming back to my garden example. Let's say you paddle out into the ocean back home and find an unknown uninhabited island. It's teeming with plants and animals, some poisonous and dangerous. What do you do? Assume you are going to be stuck there for a while—years—maybe forever."

"I would order in some food on my new genie model Gni-

M and scout out a place to camp right near the beach."

"You goof. You know what I mean; no communication devices," she says, taking a breath. "Here's what a *normal* person would do. Once you'd figured out that you will survive—the food and water problem solved—you would begin eliminating the poisonous plants and dangerous animals. You know you would. Over the years, not as some evil and dastardly scheme, but as the normal course of events, you would change your environment to be more and more compatible with yourself and your survival. It's normal; it's what you would do. Start with a small garden and expand it to cover the entire island if necessary."

I see where she's going, but simply nod and keep quiet.

"Well, there you go. Here we are. This is the island. This planet. The modification of the biota is exactly the same process here as on our imaginary island. No difference in concept. None."

"Yes… ok, but there are no people on that island…" I start to say, and then notice that Grigor has joined us, standing nearby, and has evidently heard the last part of our conversation. "There are no people…"

"If there were people, it would nice if they too were compatible, yes? If they were of the same mindset, in the broadest sense, people that you could communicate with, work with, live with…"

"If not, we should wipe them out and start over, eh doll?" interjects Grigor. "That's the human thing to do, is it not?"

"Hold on a minute…" I start to say.

"It's ok. Grigor, I'm sure has a point. He's a smart guy," says Carol.

"Tendin' the plants 'n' animals is one thing, but if it can talk—leave it alone," says Grigor. "It's not our business."

"What about our mission here? Recording the genetics, monitoring the evolution. You know there's been some genetic manipulation already…"

"I know it, but I don't have to like it. And certainly don't agree with it. We don't have a clue what we are doing. Manipulation…" Grigor makes a sound of disgust instead of finishing his thought.

"But David's had training, and many others before..."

"Trainin'? Don't make me laugh. It's like me teachin' you two how to use my tool belt here and sending you up to work on the ship… It's like me decidin' today that I'm a brain surgeon. Here Jason, lay your noggin on the table. Porter," he shouts. "Hey Porter… Rick… hey Rick, toss me a butter knife. Today I'm a surgeon. I'm going to operate on poor backward J-man here and fix 'im up good. Maybe a fork too, he needs a tune up—sputterin' bad."

"Oh no, don't tell me," I say to Grigor. "You belong to one of hands-off groups back home…"

"I do, and you should too. Look, it's enough already. They're on their way, let's leave 'em alone." We are all three silent for a moment. "And, sayin' that folks, I'm on me way too." He looks each of us right in the eye before turning to go. "Think about it," he says as he heads out of the mess hall.

"Whew, he's somethin' alright. And he thinks *I* should have been weeded out of the program... You ok?" I ask Carol after Grigor is gone.

"Doll. He calls me 'doll'," she says.

"He calls everyone by his pet names. You *are* a doll, too, you know," I add.

"Oh good grief. From you I like it; from him, it's irritating. But I like to hear his ideas if I can make it through the bluster. He comes on strong, but underneath there is always a point. I disagree with him though. I would apply the same logic as in my island with the plants and animals to the people here. Same logic."

"Really? The same?"

"These people are nearly savages. It will take them millennia to physically and culturally mature. The members of the vast majority of these populations will lead a rough and crude and short life. Think of the hunger, the cold, the constant dangers they encounter and the horrible deaths they may face. We, on the other hand, have and can implement a known good solution. It puts them on the fast track for a relatively low cost, in terms of sacrifice.

"Another aspect," she continues, "and this is a pet peeve

144

of mine when speaking of letting 'nature take care of its own', or of letting 'nature run its course', aren't *we* part of nature? Can't *we* be considered a tool of evolution and nature? Of course we can and are. So yes, I can justify what we are doing and what David may be trying to do."

Like I said, she's good to talk to.

> *Right after my return from flare damage control, I found Mark and Grigor at base camp. They now are charged with organizing the first small steps in the refit of the Hobbe. I requested that one or both of them help me to understand the acceleration system we will use on the outbound leg. This interruption in their train of thought resulted in blank stares from both of them followed by overlapping responses to the effect that "...it's too soon..." and "...years and years away..." and "...can't think about that right now..." and so forth. That's all right; there's time.*

> *I ran into Mark, grumpier than ever, a few days later. He shared a concern with me, but was too vague about it for me to help. Something about bosses making up their minds and about having to divert time from his primary job. "It's a goldmine down here," he says, which explains nothing and he neglected to explain how this relates to his complaints. I think it's clear he's being pulled in too many directions, but he's a big boy and can handle himself I'm sure. I wish I could think quicker on my feet; as I walked away I realized I should have given him his own advice—'Relax!'*

I did have a chance to pull some data during the last few weeks. There's interesting information about our ship's namesake, Ms. Hobbe. Commander Hobbe. I've saved that along with a few mission histories for later. Love how easy it is to capture documents on the genie and then display them later on whatever screen I'm near.

David seemed in a good mood for my entire visit to bio camp last time. We observed a couple natives from our hidden location. He wants me back there soon and I am anxious to go. I've got an itch to know more about what he's doing and how it all relates to my recent discussion with Carol. I just hope he doesn't call right away; I've been up to my ears in work.

I had to negotiate a really sticky problem the last few days. Communication was messed up in one direction only, from ship to ground, and for certain devices only. Very hard to resolve. Had to dig through some equipment specs and put on my troubleshooting hat. Turns out, at long last, that some code got corrupted up top and then the bad sequences migrated to some of our other devices during routine updates. Don't know how it happened—cosmic rays hitting the chips or organics maybe? And why didn't the healing algorithms catch it? Doesn't look like it was related to the solar flare but... you never know. I had to knuckle down and think hard about the code and how to fix it without causing more damage.

I notice I am driven to add to this personal log less and less frequently. Suffice it to say I am really beginning to enjoy the world we have here. There are some spectacular sites out there. The never predictable results of the forces of nature can create wonders to behold. Ha, 'wonders to behold'—where did I come up with that?

Modifications

"Get down here right away," David says on a genie-to-genie call, "and plan on staying for a while. Oh, Jacob has put together some supplies. Bring them."

"Jacob?"

"Gleshert," he clarifies. I had never heard Doc's first name out loud before. Saw it in print, never heard it.

"He's up top at the moment so it'll be a while before…"

"Yes, yes, so he is. Just get the supplies when he lands and come down as soon as you can."

Just like that. Grigor was right; we need plenty of hats out here. I do check with 'Jacob,' but he will not be hurried. He transfers the supplies David wants to me after he arrives on the surface in his own good time.

When I finally arrive down at bio camp, days after David's call, neither Porter nor Craig make a move to exit the craft. "Coming?" I ask, to both of them.

"Nope. Like I said, we've got an important date," says Porter.

"Oh? But I thought you meant…"

"Ah, but the date is not here, it's somewhere else. Where are we going, Craigster?"

"32 East and 37 North or thereabouts."

"32 East and 37 North. We are just doing a drop off and a pick up here," Porter echoes with a smile.

"But I'm staying here."

"That we know. That you said."

"Right. Thanks for the ride. I'll just grab these…"

———

I set my load down near where I see David and have a look around the small enclosed camp area; things have changed. David greets me.

"I see you've enlarged the work area."

"You bet. It's a must. Spending a lot of time here. Think I'm onto something. Make yourself at home; you're going to help me."

He doesn't notice my look of concern and for the moment I choose not to say anything more than, "So how can I help?"

"Plenty of time, make yourself at home, I'll be right back. Sorry, I'm right in the middle of something."

150

He checks the exterior surroundings via cams and then exits the carefully camouflaged bio camp work area. I see that one part of the expansion includes a more extensive lab area. It's with a shock that I notice in the lab area what is clearly a patient examination table. There is no doubt in my mind now that David has had his work subjects inside here. For what purpose—sequencing and documenting their genetics? From what I know, getting a sample shouldn't require this equipment.

David returns while I am still looking over the changes.

"Damn, they are at it again," he says, shaking his head. I don't respond but I see that he sees me looking at the table. His hair is longer than I remember it and he's neglected to shave in a while. "Cloning," he says simply. "You're wondering about the lab. Look, I found ideal specimens here. They were right where the most optimistic predictions said they would be, genetically speaking."

"Ok…"

"I picked a few really prime examples, found the purest and made a decision. My background is technical—you know this?—and is specifically in genetics—theory and applied. We know where this genome should end up…"

"Hey," I say, not meaning to interrupt, when I notice there is someone else in the camp with us. It's Brachus. I can feel the tension rise in me, but I'm not sure why it should be so. I've had little interaction with him for a while, only what's absolutely required. I've known from almost the first moment that we will not get along personally and I believe he feels the same. His official data and reports come in regularly, and that's enough for me.

"Hey yourself. How's it goin'?" Brachus says with his big, toothy grin.

"Good, good. David asked me in for a while. You here too?"

"Yeah, that's right," he says, chuckling a bit and his eyes sparkling. Why does this guy irritate me so much? But he does. Turning to David he says, "Natives restless again?"

"Prowling around our perimeter. Again. They know we are in here, or they know something is in here and they won't let it go." His face shows puzzlement, then concern. "The package?"

It takes me a second or two to realize he is talking to me, and is referring to the medical supplies. "Over here," I say and I move to grab the supplies I got from Gleshert. David helps and we put the cases on the lab's open shelving unit. I pick up my personal effects and throw a questioning glance to David. He points to the bunk that will be mine. As those two begin to talk, I take a few moments to relax on the bunk and close my eyes. It seems like seconds later but it must have been longer when I hear the runabout leave.

"Wesley?" I ask, getting up.

"It's just you and me now, bud," says David.

"David, what's going on? What can I do?"

David works his lower lip and looks toward me and then away as if trying to think where to begin. I take a long look at his outfit, which, while standard garb, it is not in the best of condition. In fact, it looks to me as if he has been doing a bit of prowling around himself.

"You mentioned cloning…"

"Yes, yes, cloning. Well… modified cloning… let's say that."

"Ok…"

David moves to the shelving, transfers the new supplies to the table and I join him as we open and unpack the contents. Working side by side, David begins again. "I need your help. Here's where we are. You've heard the first part of the story. Using our genome template we gathered initial samples from the people, the natives. Short version: I identified what I call a nearly ideal population— really close to the optimum predicted in our mission folio."

Occasional eye contact whilst sorting and storing the medical supplies helps me to judge David's state of mind. I get the feeling that he's leveling with me, or just about to.

He continues, "And that's fine as far as it goes. We could continue the documentation process for the people and include the major species of plant and animals. There are endless opportunities to document, but…"

153

"And have we gathered enough data to satisfy our minimum requirements?"

David stops for a moment with his arms in midair after putting an empty case up on the top shelf. "Bare minimum, yes. Suggested minimum, no. The analyzer takes a bit of time to sort and classify sequences; then makes suggestions for additional samples."

"Makes suggestions?"

"Yes. All the samples are tagged and entered with location information. Once the system has a handle on the global variants, it can suggest where to look for intermediate populations if it thinks there should be one. It's still making periodic requests."

"Oh, and Wesley and his team are no doubt able to pick up the remote samples." David nods agreement. "But what's the problem?" I ask.

"Hold up. Let me continue," says David. "First, Mark's timeline says we are here for quite some time yet, maybe a total of 4,000 local years, so I believe there is a real opportunity for this mission to shine."

"How so?"

"Look, I've gone ahead and selected an ideal specimen some time ago. Also, I decided to begin telomeric treatments on him," David says quietly, looking at me as we move to the central clearing in the bio camp and sit. He leans back and looks up while holding his head with both hands and stretching his legs out.

"I had heard something of that."

"Well, it's true and the reasoning is that…"

"More offspring equals more good genes."

"Exactly. If we could just get a good population going I'm sure we… I could make a few adjustments to really bring these people along. After all, we know where the end line is…" David smiles and trails off a bit. By 'end line' he means 'us', I'm certain.

He shakes off his momentary silence and continues, "But, it's not working. My hero is mixing with other natives who may or may not share all or even most of the positive traits we are hoping will dominate in the end. Dilution. It's not going to work. The best thing would be to have a controlled population beginning with a mating pair both of whom have the desired traits. So…" David sits up more or less straight, feet flat on the ground now. "That's where the cloning came in."

He seems to me now to be talking mostly to convince himself. Or maybe this is a rehearsed logic that he needs to say to solidify it. If he can get me to agree then… After all, the more buy-in one gets—the consensual validation concept again—the surer one feels about one's ideas.

"But…"

"*Modified* cloning. I told you, I have some experience, I

155

know what I am doing, and I have all the equipment I need here. I took a viable sample from my—I call him Alpha but already Wes and others are calling him Al—from his bone marrow and created, not a true clone, but a mate." I remain silent and nod, looking down now and not making eye contact. "It's a bit tricky but it can be done. The hard part is making sure the mate, Bee, develops normally and in a proper environment with native upbringing."

"Don't tell me. Bee—for Beta. Al and Bee." He nods. I want to make a crack about their kids, but stifle it.

"You were saying Bee and a native environment… Wait, you are talking about native parents for the clo… for Bee? I mean, and having her raised among the natives?" The look I get from David tells me the answer is yes. As this sinks in, I say, "I guess we should start calling you Doc now too," without smiling and without expecting a smile from David. He does not disappoint. "So, is it working? I mean, where are we in this?"

"Oh, it's working all right. Born and raised. She is a young adult already, and healthy. She has been brought into the valley and now we have them both isolated in the study area surrounding this camp."

"Wow, so you have been busy out here. How long has she been here? I mean, any results yet?

"No."

"Nothing?"

156

"Nothing, and there won't be any, at least for the moment."

David looks at me but I fail to understand. "You mean…?" I begin but David interrupts.

"Temporary sterility. I want a little more time with these two before enabling reproduction."

Now I am really confused. "Why? It makes no difference genetically. Let them go."

"No. First, I am going to add Bee to the t-sessions."

"And…"

"And, that's where you come in."

> These few notes are made on my genie in my bunk at bio camp with David. He has requested not to use, for the time being, open channels for any of the data or records of incidents that fall outside of basic mission directives. He left me understanding that once he is sure of some significant progress his records will be added in toto. I don't like it; the objectives do say something about 'discretionary intervention' so why hide it? My guess is he's not as confident as he acts about what he's doing.
>
> Dylan has been in several times to teach us as much as he can of the local native language. He's become reasonably fluent with each of the populations with which he has had contact during

his field trips. It's easy for me to pick up the basics. Gestures are a part of it as well.

Dylan has confided in me that his work under Brachus is less than fulfilling; he, Dylan, finds that the relationships he has formed with the natives at the remote sites, now spanning several generations, capture the bulk of his interest. It fills what must be for him, in my opinion, a familial need. I should ask him about his past sometime. He says that he learned from the local group here their word for this planet—Amara. Nice, I like it. Amara.

David wants to use me for direct contact with Al and Bee on a regular basis.

He filled me in on what he's trying to achieve. Although the native populations are essentially on the right track, some better, some worse, he thinks he sees a way to make a significant change for the better with just a few tweaks in their code. As he told me, Alpha is actually the offspring of modified parents. The modifications targeted brain function and capacity primarily, if I understood him right. Specifically, he altered code to match the template more closely as regards the related functions of speech, cognitive ability, and memory.

Now, each of these assets blossoms through use and I have been tasked to mentally exercise Al and Bee as much as possible during the next years (due to their treatments, they will be around for several hundred years, barring accidents) and verify the coding has taken, so to speak. If it pans out as expected, David plans to let them procreate and build up a population that will eventually dominate.

I am not comfortable at all with this plan, for any number of reasons.

As far as the larger picture goes, David swears he only made small careful tweaks and that the result was verified by the analyzer as being closer to ideal. I need to talk to Carol about this. Doc would have strong opinions too. I already know what Grigor would say.

Damage

"I can't do it," I say to David. I can tell he's shocked at such a black and white statement, especially from me. I have thought about his idea of working directly with Al and Bee—it's not for me.

"Alright, what's the problem? What do you mean?" he replies. He puts down his genie and I can see the map app on the screen. Grigor or someone up at the ship has finally successfully deployed a handful of transceivers. It means any of us can now know precisely where we are on the planet and David can plot the locations of everybody on the ground. Should have been done long ago. David sits and kicks the other nearby chair over to me.

I am little apprehensive since I fear triggering his 'Mr. Means' side, but somehow I don't think it will pop up this time. I sit. The screen over this part of the bio camp work area is transparent, or nearly so. The blue sky is clear—it's a beautiful day.

"It's just not me. I don't have the training for it. My background…"

"Yes, I know. Physics. The poetry of nature, as you once called it back at the Academy. Electronics is your primary field." David closes his eyes and stretches his neck side to side, back and forth. "Jason, you were cross-trained on a number of disciplines for just this sort of reason. Was it not clear from the beginning that everyone would be asked to stretch their comfort zone?"

"I don't mind stretching; I just don't want to stretch too far. You want and need real results. There must be someone else in the crew who can do this right. Look at Dylan…"

"No, no, no. First, Dylan's fine. Love 'im. He can help you out, ok, that's fine. He really is a genius with the language, but I am not going to dedicate him to this more than part time. You've got to be able to tell me you're willing to at least stick your toe into this, and then tell me if it's going to work for you."

David stops talking. We sit for the next few seconds in silence. I'm a team player. "Ok. Alright. I'll think it through; I'll get through it," I say finally.

————

"Say, that Carol is something special. I like her a lot."

"You are correct sir; she's a doll!" Dylan is right about her, and I can see that his comments are both genuine and innocent. "What made you think of her out here?"

We are just finishing what I call a patrol of the bio area outside of the central landing and work area. We are now walking towards the valley entrance, generally following the stream down. One of our A/V units has crapped out and I need to locate it for repair or replacement.

"Oh, I don't know. We disagree on that 'big picture' business but she does have a sincere empathy for the people here. She doesn't see them as simply specimens, or gene carriers, or, worse, as insignificant precursors to 'real' people; no, she thinks of them as 'real' enough already. I like that. She's right too."

"But you agree with Grigor—hands off?"

"No, not totally. I say look around—it's beautiful. Talk to the people—they're human. We're done. We did a good job. Let's go. Amara's done. Next planet."

"You did a good job back there, by the way. You've got a real skill with language," I say, referring to the impromptu meeting we had with David's subjects a few minutes ago on our patrol.

At one point, we were about to make one of our stream crossings and there, right across, I saw Al looking at us. I froze, but Dylan took it in stride. He made a hand gesture, which was returned. I did the same, but got nothing—I'm the new guy. Al looked to his left, upstream, and I knew that Bee was around but never caught a glimpse.

I am good enough now to catch the gist of the language and heard Dylan basically say 'Hi. You look good. This is Jay,' pointing at me. One syllable names are easier, he says. No response from the other side except Al looked me over some more. He, Al, sort of nodded towards us, gave another hand signal and was gone.

"You know you don't need your weapon at the ready like

that. They are scared of us and really don't know what to make of us being here," he says, giving a nod to my open holster. "I know you see how they react to us, even just now. They were quite subdued and willing to humor us. Respectful."

I don't respond but continue to walk to the nominal position of the camera. I can only think that Dylan's stance on this issue is foolish. We see these natives that look so much like us; we want to believe they think like us. I'm not so sure, at least not yet. The fact that they do treat us differently than they would another of their own is proof that we can't let our guard down, in my mind. Besides, there are no doubt other reasons we may be thankful for having ready protection out here.

I stop and point, waiting for Dylan to see what I see.

"What the...?" he says.

We found the unit alright. It is lying on the ground in the open, case broken.

I pick up the components; some may be salvageable.

"This didn't fall and get this much damage, it was thrown or crushed deliberately," I opine out loud but mostly to myself, and the thought reminds me immediately of the possible danger of getting too friendly or close to the natives. I scan carefully around to try to locate the sensor mount in order to know if that has been broken as well. It takes a few moments, and we both spot the marked tree and mount at almost the same time.

164

"There it is. It's bent, but attached."

"I see it. I'm going up," I say as I begin to ascend. This unit was not hidden well enough. The location is easily spotted and accessible. The small power module is part of the base and still shows life. I obviously can't install the new cam in the same location and so remove the mount and secure it before descending.

"Hey!" comes a shout from higher up in the tree.

I almost lose my footing, startled at the voice above my head.

"Hey! Get out of here!" it says again.

Try as I might, I see no one above. But then, I see it. Someone has already installed a new unit about a body length higher and more well-hidden than the broken one.

"Yes, you!" and there is some not-so-well-muffled laughter as well.

I climb down and drop next to Dylan. "Some jackass is playing games. Not funny; I could've broken my neck."

"I know the voice. It's Lester," Dylan replies, keeping his voice low and his back to the cam.

Without thinking further, I immediately try to reach Lester on my genie. It picks up on his side, but there is no sound. I don't wait for him to say anything. "What the hell are you trying to pull?" I ask bluntly.

165

"You should see your face! We got a great shot of you. What did you think—a man eater about to jump on your head? Look up and gimme that face again, will ya?" More laughter.

I'm very tempted to use my weapon, for the first time on the planet, on the cam but think better of it; David needs these cams for his work down here. Besides, it's not the equipment at fault.

"I could've broken my neck because of your stupid stunt." And I disconnect without further comment. At this point, I know I'd better cool down before I do or say something I shouldn't.

"Thanks a lot, Dyl," Lester says accusingly through the unit's speaker.

We head back to bio camp.

———

"Now, what exactly happened out there I wonder," I say to Dylan, curious to know what he knows.

"What do you mean? Lester is just like that, he thinks he's funny. See what I have to put up with?"

"No, not that. I mean what happened to the original cam, and who installed the new one? Why and how is Lester on one of them? I thought David had all these links down here on a private channel."

"Wesley has a private channel too, you know."

I stop at these words and Dylan stops too. Of course I know Brachus has his own private channel; I set it up. But what is going on? Why would Brachus want to have a separate cam unit in David's bio area?

"Yes, you are right. He has his own channel, yes…" I concur tentatively and pause.

"Look, I'm not on the 'inside' with these guys, Wesley and Lester I mean. Or even Tracy. Neither is Aileen or the rest. They are their own little group. I mind my own business as much as possible," he says, evidently sensing that I want more information. "Wesley spends a lot of time down here with David, helping David, but I don't know what he's up to, really, any more than you do." He pauses as we continue walking and I try to puzzle it out. "I do know he spends as much time with the others as he does with David's new project—you know—Al and Bee."

"Wait. Others? What others? Do you mean other natives, like those you talk to?"

"Yes and no. I mean others from David's program here."

I stop again and wait for Dylan to turn and face me. "I thought there were only the two. He wants to test them, and educate them I guess, to see if they are learning and remembering and then let them go ahead and populate the planet; isn't that what you understand?"

"That's what I know too, but there were others. Al's parents—he had those two in. Didn't he tell you all this? Those two were the best of the bunch, but there were others."

"Yes, you're right. He told me. And Bee is from Al himself... Say, speaking of that: Isn't that just wrong? Assuming they start to reproduce. It's like mating with yourself. Won't that cause a lot of undesirable characteristics, genetically speaking?"

"I know what you mean, but I think there are techniques... Actually I don't know, but David thinks all is OK. Talk to him about it, or somebody who knows more than I do. I do know he is wrong about one thing though."

I wait for the explanation but it doesn't come. "Yes?" I prompt, but still nothing. "Anyway, you were saying there were or are others..."

"Are."

"Others that David has worked with? But I've only heard about the two. What's happening with them, where are they?"

"They are not here in the bio enclosure. They were sterilized and released. Put out. Only..."

"Only... what?"

"Only they *are* reproducing. I've seen the results."

> *Dylan, modified natives released, David, Lester, what else? Almost too much.*

Dylan confessed to me that he thinks David's attempt to improve native stock is misguided. Not only misguided but doomed to fail.

First, he says, at least some of the rejects—the supposedly sterile natives who were used by David in the early part of his testing and experimentation—are in fact reproducing. And not all of the results are benign. He, Dylan, has personally witnessed a strain of very large aggressive adults, about 25 to 30% physically larger than the average adult that we have recorded so far. They do not mix well with the untouched population and he has seen the gory results of one of their clashes.

In the second place, again according to Dylan's theory, David's attempts are already doomed since Al and Bee have not begun to propagate, yet the others, the rejects, are, and are doing so at the normal high rate. This means David can say goodbye to a pristine gene set; it will never happen. The others will outnumber A&B (Al and Bee) and their offspring right from the start and by a large factor.

He does acknowledge that only A&B are being given the t-treatments, and so will have a much longer time to reproduce than any other of the planet's inhabitants but he doesn't think it will matter. He thinks the head start of the others, and the fact that their supposedly inferior gene set will taint the pool going forward, will combine to ensure that David's work is reduced to a waste of time. I tend to agree with Dylan on this point but I reminded both him and myself that David's background is in this field and ours is not.

Dylan's last comments strike me as important and insightful. He says that the natives, before any of this current manipulation, are at a higher level of development than David or any of the team has given them credit for. He has seen their use of tools and has noted in some cases their rapid advance, culturally, during just the time that we have been here. He thinks, and here I agree completely, that there is no way to force cultural maturity, it has to develop on its own. David's attempt to bring their genetic development along is one thing but to believe he can "manipulate" them into being civilized and mature is another.

ABCs

I casually ask, "David, are you aware of the broken cam and A/V transponder?"

"Electronics fail occasionally and need to be fixed. Which one are you talking about?"

"No, this one didn't fail; it was smashed on the ground." I began to see fire come into his eyes.

"Alright, then the cams are not hidden well enough. It can't be that difficult…"

I interrupt him by showing him the mount that I had taken off the tree. "Look," I said, "the cam unit wasn't broken off the mount. See? It's bent but you can see it was unscrewed. With the proper tool." I don't mention about the other cam being installed and, interestingly, neither does David. Why?

———

Lester is in the bio enclosure on some errand for Brachus. I confront him about the incident out by the broken cam unit.

"Quit screwing around. Somebody's going to get hurt," I say. I mean me almost falling out of the tree but hope he will interpret it differently.

"Get over it, it was a joke," he says. But he doesn't move away.

"I know one of you took the cam unit off the mount."

"Yeah? You don't know anything," he says and clams up. He crosses his arms and I get a good look at his pinky ring. It has the image of a face or skull set into the silver with deep red stones. He stands silent.

"You can't knock out one of David's cams and replace it with one of your own, especially one that we can't access since it's on a private channel."

He looks at me with his slight sneer, rakes his hair straight back, and says, "Wrong. I can do whatever I want." And he turns and walks away.

————

I am in my bunk area trying one of the newly-approved fruits from our little orchard right outside the bio camp. Delicious. Really good. I have been preoccupied with Greg's request and my determination to comply, but my comfort level is decreasing, not increasing. I do have some ideas about how to test for the cognitive functions of interest to David, but am dreading the actual implementation.

I look up and see two of the crew approaching. It takes me a second to realize they are coming to see me.

"At your service boss," says Craig. I stand and discard the juicy remnants of my snack, wiping my hands dry. I'm still impressed by how young he looks. Aileen is with him. She looks tan and not as thin as I remember her.

"Hi. What's up?"

"The Commander sent us to you. He said you'll fill us in and put us to work."

I look at Aileen for confirmation; she nods, smiles, and says, "We hear you have a project. What can we do?"

———

What a relief! I tell you, when David has his head on straight, he's all right. It turns out that Aileen has experience in teaching, especially with the young. And Craig is willing to do whatever is needed. This is a huge burden off my mind. We discuss how to handle the natives and agree that for safety's sake they both will always work together. We arrange to receive language training from Dylan.

It's cramped down here relative to base camp but I set them both up in our bare-bones 'visitors quarters' and they stow what few supplies they have brought with them. They walk through a brief orientation—Craig has been here, but not so Aileen—and then we head out, taking the usual precaution of first scanning the outside area. I stress the importance of being careful not to betray the location of the hidden door.

"This area will work. We'll set it up right here." I take a

look above and around. There's a fine spot for a hidden cam. "You guys will be out here always together. I'll monitor the cam should anything happen." This spot is very near our small garden and can be reached from the camp in seconds if need be. "No matter, always carry your standard protection, just like out in the field." I look at them both. "You both were out in the field, right?" I search their faces for signs of concern. None. Is it just me that feels exposed and vulnerable out here? I look around one more time, judging carefully how secure from surprise this position is.

"Do you think this will take long? I mean the whole project—do you think it'll take, what, days? ...years?" asks Aileen.

"It's only results he wants. Certainly more than days, less than years. Most important is to see if you can document any improvement over the baseline... Dylan says he's already talked to you..."

They both nod, and Aileen answers, saying, "We are good there. Dylan will take us out to see first-hand how they talk and act. Plus, he's got a lot of contact experience already. He's going to take that and work it into language training. You've got to jump right in, he says."

"But what about this 'baseline'?" asks Craig. "Where do we get that?"

"The baseline is where they are now. It's a little fuzzy, but you are to look for a change from what they can do now."

Nods only.

"Perfect. Perfect. It's a go then just as soon as the cam is set and running." I pull the cam hardware from my pack and give Craig tools and instructions on how to mount it. He is able, after some struggling, to reach the spot I had eyed earlier, to attach the hardware and activate it.

———————

It's really turning out well. The set-up I mean. It's too soon to tell if there are any meaningful results. Aileen says it is going to be difficult in any case to say without doubt that our little family is above a baseline. I agree with her and can understand.

I'm happy with the safety aspect. Craig is always there and someone is always monitoring the cam. So far so good. The initial meeting, set up with and by Dylan, was a hoot to watch. Al is more cautious than Bee, and you could see that they both trust Dylan. He started with introductions. Aileen becomes just Ay, and that was easy. Craig's name, on the other hand was more difficult to convey. A couple others were watching and listening to the cam feed with me, and we nearly wet ourselves laughing. I made quite sure we were on mute. Anyway, his name ended up something like Cray-gah. That's the first two-syllable name I've heard any native use.

For the life of me I cannot figure out how Aileen maintains the natives' interest. She is able to set them at ease and they keep coming back for more. And strange to say, Al and Bee have 'selected' the time. Our clearing has become one of their regular stops during their day it seems.

She uses Craig to set up something for the day, like maybe items of differing colors, or sizes, say, and uses them to test or expand vocabulary. She works with extremely basic math skills by repeatedly counting objects, and later asking 'how many' when there are one, two or more, and also asking 'how many' when there are none, just to see how they handle that.

I am watching a session and see her point to objects— these are objects not normally found in the native environment, but still made out of natural materials—and see if Al or Bee can remember what they were called during a previous one.

"Box."

"Correct."

"Plate."

"Correct."

"Ton."

"No. Not ton."

"Not ton."

"No."

Silence. Craig brings the object to Aileen.

"Tube. This is a tube," she says while holding it to her eye and looking through it at her subjects.

———————

It's frustrating and curious that the sessions have taken on the character of three steps forward, two steps back. While most of the time Al and Bee seem to be advancing in terms of comprehension and conversation (don't get me wrong, they converse only about the most basics things—weather, injuries, food, and such—and in the simplest terms) sometimes they show a dogged determination not to cooperate during the very next visit. It's at these times that I get the most nervous. Craig says he gets nervous too, and that can't help the situation since I'm sure the natives can sense it. If the back-and-forth between the four continues, all is fine; when there is silence and staring, it's something else again.

Which brings me to David's pet peeve: Al, and presumably Bee, simply will not stay clear of the central bio camp enclosure. I have to admit it is carefully concealed behind a wall of dense native vegetation and it is large enough not to betray its presence by having an easily distinguishable shape or visible top, but they surely know it's there and continue to circumnavigate the camp periodically and to poke and peek at the border. I have stood quietly outside and can hear absolutely no sounds from within but there's not much we can do about the flyers' sounds and certainly nothing we can do about their being occasionally spotted. The foliage blocks most of the view, but someone in the right place at the right time could spot them. It's also likely that someone has been seen passing through the hidden entrance even though we try to scan the area to locate anyone nearby before using it.

David's annoyance with their persistent curiosity, however, seems to me to be incommensurate with the undesirable behavior, if you catch my drift. He's overreacting.

"No, that won't work. Think about it: if you tell someone 'Don't go there' where do they immediately want to go?" I say, after he asks me to have Craig or Aileen warn them to stay away. I know it is risky to question his order. As I've found out, I never know ahead of time if I will get the calm and reasonable David or the angry and defensive Mr. Means.

"We must not let the presence of the bio camp disturb the testing of their abilities. We want them to behave as naturally as possible while spending exactly zero time thinking about any of our other activities, installations, or comings and goings," he says calmly and reasonably.

I just don't see this as a realistic wish. "David, whatever you do, don't think of Vanessa up at base camp. Especially don't think of her red fingernails when we were all back at the Academy."

He looks puzzled for a second, working his mouth habit, but then smiles and says, "I see. You got me." And then, "Move the testing area out farther. Get them away from here."

Aileen came up with a fascinating activity for Al and Bee. She's showed them how to weave these long thin dried leaves from common local plants nearby into sheets. The sheets can be folded or curled into shapes—like a basket, or hat, or a rope—and fixed into those shapes by weaving or tying more leaves to hold them. Craig pulled tough fibers from some plant (not sure which) long enough for tying too. It's a limited technology, but technology for sure.

We three went out to find a new location to continue "Ay" and "Cray-gah's" work. Our decision was to rotate from clearing to clearing, always near one of the hidden cams, on a regular basis instead of setting up a permanent site. I'm not thrilled with them being farther away in case of danger, but it seems to be working so far. Aileen has been using a bell sound to begin and end their sessions. It's curious to watch the reactions as the ending bell is anticipated, and then rings.

David seems pleased with the reports he's getting. Brachus needs to pull Aileen and Craig out for a few days, and that's a good thing, a break is in order. She tried to explain to Al and Bee they would be gone. Not sure if it took. Craig cleared off the flat surface of a big rock at one of the clearings so that marks could be made. Aileen had a series of marks made and then, each day, crossed one out— like a calendar. She had Al begin crossing them out eventually, at the end of each session when the bell rang.

She had Craig make slightly different marks to stand for the days they would be gone, with another special mark for the day when they are to come back. This way, maybe Al will mark off the days on his own and be able to anticipate their return.

It was of some special interest to all when it was noticed that Al made his own special mark, like a dot or tiny circle, right under the previous day's crossed-off mark. We had a discussion of the significance, if any, of this mark but got nowhere fast. It was finally David himself that said, "Full moon. It was a full moon last night."

Change of Plan

"Have you heard about Mark's latest toy?"

"If you mean the solo flyer, not only have I heard about it, I've taken it up. It's wonderful."

"No kidding? You've taken it up?"

"Through the mountains near base camp. Just for fun. He says it's a snap here for a unit like that since the atmosphere is so thick, and it's even more so down here I notice. 'Here' being at sea level, or nearly."

"Let me get this straight. You flew his new toy up over base camp?"

"Yes. What's the problem?"

"Nothing." She's something.

Carol and I have taken some time to be alone and explore for a few days. At the moment we are at 31 West and 9 South on a small dune at the base of a tall bluff right where one of the planet's continents meets the ocean. Majestic. The bluff is one of several that extend as far as the eye can see north and south of us. Our view of the western horizon is clear and magnificent. In the far north the horizon is obscured by clouds or mist or rain.

"It's something here, isn't it." She says as a statement, not as a question. I nod, not knowing if she sees me nod, but knowing that she is aware that I agree. We both look at the sky, the sea, the birds. Way out in the water, some kind of animal surfaces briefly, then again, and again, and is gone. We are facing west, toward the sea and the setting sun.

"Yes, it is," I say. She looks at me with a slight but discernible questioning expression. "Something," I say, "It's something." She laughs in that way that I like and for a few moments I watch as the onshore breeze plays with her hair. She is looking back at the water.

"It's called Amara."

"It is? You mean…"

"Here; the planet. Amara."

"Amara. Nice. I like it."

I notice the way the sun is approaching the horizon and how the reflection of the sun plays off the myriad swells, waves, and wavelets. I fix now on that reflection and see the intense contrast between the dark ocean and the momentary sparkles of the reflected sun. The effect is mesmerizing as each part of the surface of the ocean, in its turn, is lifted or descends, tilts backward or forward, right or left, and for an instant, perhaps, is at exactly the right angle to reflect the sun to my eyes.

"You ok?"

"I'm ok. You?" And we somehow both know that we are. "Shall we sleep out again this evening? We are totally remote. There is no danger. Or we could set up the dome tent here or maybe back a little closer to the bluff. I'm good either way. I want to be able to hear the surf though; that's a must."

She doesn't answer, but hooks her arm into mine and inches a little closer.

I am tending to ignore my communicator, at least not jump when it buzzes, during this time alone with Carol. Nothing can be that important. And a little time off is something that I… we have been looking forward to for a long time. But I do look now and notice 'Gleshert' flashing in the ID window and decide to pick up. It's a text: DAVID HURT. WANTS YOU TO COME NOW. Good grief. David's hurt? But he's OK enough to ask for me? Why me? Too late to ignore; Doc knows I received it. I show Carol the message and then type a response: WHERE? I don't see any other option so I begin to pack up. Carol doesn't say anything but joins in the packing in her careful and deliberate way. BASE CAMP, the reply comes back. I arrange for a pickup as soon as possible.

———

"Shut it down! Shut the damn thing down!"

"Take it easy, Commander, quit yelling, and lay back," advises Doc.

David does not look good but I imagine it looks a lot worse under the bandages on his left arm and on the left side of his face. His salt'n'pepper hair is sticking out in crazy directions. "Shut down... You mean the bio camp?" I ask tentatively.

"Yes, I mean the bio camp. The camp, the surrounds, the whole thing. Shut it down. Now. Brachus, you organize it. Shipley, you assist. Arwyn, prepare to transport equipment and materials out; salvage what you can." David closes his eyes for a moment, evidently trying to maintain composure. Mark, Brachus and I are the only visitors, aside from Doc.

Gleshert insists, "Take it easy David, it's not that urgent. You said so yourself not so long ago. Don't move." Vanessa has entered and she administers what I presume must be a calming agent. No flirting this time—all business.

"I said it but I changed my mind. That's why I called you all here. I want the site dismantled. They are probably inside right now getting into who knows what." And David looks at each of us in turn.

"We are all right David. I've got Lester and Alain there right now. Chris too. They are tightening everything down. Nobody's in and nobody's gettin' in."

"Damn it man, make sure they somehow secure above. The bastard came over the wall and almost fell right on me. He hit the cover, ripped it and came right through."

"Yes sir," says Brachus, "I'm on it. The intruder Alpha is out and he and his mate have been escorted out of the area. They have no serious injuries. Roof closure has been resealed and nothing is coming in that way unless we open it."

David relaxes somewhat and the tension in his demeanor recedes as he lays back and closes his eyes. He does not look at any of us but does say something too quietly to make out.

"Sir?" says Brachus as we in attendance glance questioningly at each other.

"I said, don't hurt him. Them. Don't hurt them." David angles his head toward us as if to say something more. Instead, he turns back and closes his eyes again.

I was right about Vanessa and the sedative; he's resting. We file out and try to understand what happened.

Doc comes out with us and short-circuits any questions by saying, "Here's what I know. David has a nasty facial laceration and a broken left forearm. Other damage too minor to mention. None of this is major; he will be back to normal soon. Physically.

"Now, here's what I've been told. Mr. Alpha (I guess you call him) simply would not mind his own biscuits and somehow scaled the wall of David's little secret lair down there. David was alone inside and was apparently in just the right spot to receive the visitor—on his head. It was at this point that the side of David's face was damaged by the raw edges of the broken cover and supports. The cover material must've broken his fall because Alpha stumbled to his feet and started to look around at the equipment, the lights, the screens. You know, bewildered. David thinks that he was so stunned that he didn't know he fell on David at all, since he didn't even seem to see or notice him in the first moments of looking around. There were a couple changes of clothing hanging by the bunk area and for a moment Alpha advanced toward them, probably mistaking them for people. At about this time, he turned and for sure saw David but was too disoriented— frightened, says David—to know what to do. I imagine David was a sight; there must've been a lot of blood from the wound to his face. It was then that aggressiveness took over from fear, or because of fear, and Alpha grabbed something and came at David and swung. David still doesn't know what hit him. Literally. Fortunately he was able to operate his weapon and disable Alpha before anything more happened."

"How did we not know he was climbing the enclosure, or even know that he was in the area?"

"Surely you are not asking me?" says Doc, "I've told you everything I know. Physically David will be fine. I believe he will take longer to heal emotionally. He's disappointed at the collapse of his little project." With this last comment he excuses himself.

"Mark, can you shuttle me down there?" asks Brachus. "I need to see how the boys are doing. I'll get them to open the landing area just before we touch down."

"Absolutely," replies Mark, and then to his genie comms unit, "Porter? You there buddy? Pick up, Jimmy."

"No Mark, I want you to do it," counters Brachus.

I detect a brief flash of irritation crossing Mark's face before he begins to answer. "Not a problem, not a problem."

"Here. What's up?" says Porter's voice through the tiny speaker.

"Forget it. False alarm. Wait, what's the status over there? Transport in?"

"We don't need the large one," suggests Brachus.

"Yes we do," says Mark. "I do. Doesn't make sense to go there and not bring back a load of salvage in tow. We're taking the transport."

"Room for me too?" I ask, looking only at Mark for a response.

"Sure. The more the merrier. Pile on in. OK by you?" Mark asks, giving a look towards Brachus.

Porter's voice interjects, "It's out now but should on its way in in a couple days. Won't take long to unload."

"Most certainly," agrees Brachus in answer to Mark's question.

Mark nods to the one and to the other says, "Nope, contact them please and say it must be here tomorrow. Any static, let me know."

While waiting, I am able to catch up on the work that has been piling up since I took off with Carol on our aborted vacation. Who drops their brand new genie off a cliff? Pearce from the helm was down for a visit, was exploring in the mountains around base camp. 'What happened?' says I. 'Bad footing, slipped on the sand and gravel', says he. Several other minor issues were in my inbox. Nothing major to contend with though.

Another of the bio area cams has blinked out and I may be able to look at it when we go down.

———

Mark is on an interesting project, as always. He's putting together the first pieces of the homeward bound launch boost system—the so-called double L system. It's quite a sight, consisting of a swivel mount and a dangerous looking beamer. It's big, but still seems to me to be way too small compared to the Hobbe. Mark says the power it can transmit is enormous and is delivered via repeating impulses.

"We will all be able to see it in action when we send off the mission history pod near the end of our stay. Should be a good show," he says while smiling and working on some hardware on his table. His red hair seems thinner and longer than I remember and he has to brush it back when he looks up. "You ready?"

"Sure, fire it up," I say, ready to see a demo.

"No, this thing would blow the roof off if it we fired it up in here. I mean ready to go down to the crater."

"Hah?"

"The crater—David's bio camp; our Commander's late project. The transport is ready to take us down and see what we can salvage. Let's go see if I still know how to fly it."

We head out to the flyer; Brachus is there waiting for us. He looks at me but does not nod or otherwise greet me. Instead he climbs into the transport. I get an alert and 'Bevan' shows up on my genie ID with an urgent flag. "Hold up guys, let me get this."

"Hey J, I'm comin' to base camp to see you, mate."

"No can do, I am leaving right now and don't know when I will be back. Out a few days, more than likely."

"Belay that. Orders from the top. Need your undivided attention. On my way down. See you in a bit."

And he's gone, just like that. I am not sure what this means but hesitate to take off and instead say, "Guys, I just got an urgent message from Grigor. He's on his way down from the ship right now. Don't know what it's about, but he says he needs to see me."

Mark answers, "No problem. Wesley has to go; I'll take

him now. Between the four or five of us down there, I'll load up as much salvageable material as I can. You can take the next flight out if you want. I'll set it up. Porter's your man."

I'm telling you, I sometimes think Mark should be running the show. He knows how to make a decision and it sounds like the right one to me. I head from the landing area back to the camp proper, get a cup of Porter's 'burnin' fire' from the mess hall, and head over to Mark's work area waiting for Grigor. There is always something interesting to see there. I've learned it's best not to touch anything.

———

"Hey, Cap'n! There you are. Permission to come aboard granted!" I hear when entering the crowded workshop. It serves as a sort of control center for production and fab, as an inventory storehouse, and as the primary work area for Mark. There is a wide array of parts, assemblies, tools, and test equipment on the several workbenches.

"Oh, Hi. I didn't realize…" I start, taken aback at finding the shop occupied. "Is that Goodwin? Sorry, hello…"

"Al is fine, just fine. The wizard is out. You are Jay. It's a bit rough in here. How are your sea legs?"

"Sea…?" I notice Alain is weaving somewhat as he speaks. And he's carrying a beat up cup. "I am good Alain… Al. How are you?"

"Oh, that Mark's a wizard and I am fine, just fine. A sip for you?" he asks, indicating the cup. And then, "Ah, you

needs yer own mug. Yer own mug fer sher. Yer own…
Here we go. Be right back Cap'n!" He says merrily,
weaving his way farther into the shop.

I can guess what sort of 'production' Mark has branched
out into now. When Goodwin returns I take a sniff and
small sip. At least it's not the horrible concoction that
Mark makes for himself.

"Here's to you and to me and all the ships at sea in this
godforsaken ocean of stars!" We drink, my sip and his
gulp.

"What are you doing here?"

"Emergency, emergency. Brought the ore tram in. Big
rush. Heard Davy got jumped by Al. Not me, the other
Al." Alain finds this comment amusing and chuckles a
moment. "I am fittingly paid for my troubles
howsomever." Another gulp. "Have a seat," he continues
and begins to push clear an area on the bench nearest him.

"I wouldn't…" I start, but then decide to keep quiet.

"Ho, neither would I if I were me!" he says, as he sits with
his rear end half on the bench. "That fixes it. Now, there's
a seat for you. The waves are rogue t'day." I sit in an
adjacent chair and we face each other. Another sip for me.

"Not bad. Not bad at all."

"I say again – that's a wizard you've got here. To Mister
Mark!" he shouts. "Me on the other hand…" and he has

another drink.

"How's it going out there?"

"Out there? Oh! It goes. It goes all right. It goes." His face and neck are flushed red. "I'll tell ya, it's wine, women, and song. That's what it is. Ha!"

"Is that right?"

"Oh, it's right all right. It's right…" he says, trailing off at the end but looking steadily at me. "That's what it is." Suddenly serious, he adds quietly and firmly, "You've got yer wizard and me… We… we've got our bastard."

I don't respond. Alain takes another drink and continues, louder now, returning to his earlier mood, "Ah but should the sea toss me about roughly t'day, I shall hold and hold on 'til tomorrow! Pipe me ashore Cap'n as I seek shelter before we break deep and take water."

"But…"

"I must go. I may have tripped over the line."

"You mean…"

"I mean the line that ev'ry seaman must learn the hard way. It's drawn at the bottom of yer mug there. Shall you take more?"

I shake my head. He drains his cup and carries it with him as he leaves.

———————

"Hey mate, how you keepin'?"

"Not bad Grigor, not bad at all. You found me! What can I do for you?"

"The question is, what can you do for me?" Grigor replies as he puts his communicator and other key portable electronics on the worktable in Mark's area.

"What, are you quitting?" I joke. "Give me your card and archive then," I say, hand out, smiling. No smiles from Grigor.

"Not kidding. Rumor says my connections and links are crossed and wrong. Data lost, data corrupt, audio garbled. All of it ready for the dustbin."

I see that he is *not* kidding and start over. "Rumor? What rumor? What are you talking about?" We walk over to my quarters, bringing his equipment with us.

"Direct order from the former Master Manipulator: he says to get with you to get my comms straightened out ASAP. You should know."

I begin basic inspection and tests while absorbing this information.

"Master…? Oh, David you mean. Is he involved? What do you mean, 'I should know'? What sort of problem did he have? Was he trying to reach you? Where is he anyway?

I'm in the dark here."

"Easy big fella, easy. One at a time. He came down with me, but has gone who knows where. He's been holed up up there staring at his readout doing fuck-all since he became one of the walking wounded. He's all depressed. Remember what we talked about? Remember? See where it got him?" Grigor sits and watches me closely as I run unit-to-unit checks: memory, error logs—all the usual. "Don't *even* erase the memory on that device or anywhere else of mine."

"Might have to but I will warn you first. We'll back it all up."

"So he says that you talked to the Weasel, Weasely talks to him, fearless leader talks to me, and here we are. Fix it."

All of a sudden I get it and stop working. I reset his devices to normal operation and hand them back.

"There is nothing wrong, you are good to go."

"Are you sure, mate? The Weasel told David he couldn't reach me, was getting crosstalk, everything all messed up. I sent him test messages right after, no response."

"You are fine. I never talked to Brachus about you, your equipment, or anything like this. He's lying and I know it but I don't know why." Grigor grumbles and is not happy but I remind him that the "wanker," as he says, is Brachus, not me. He, Brachus, wanted to get Mark alone for some reason and he's done it. "If it makes you feel any better he never responds to me either," I say.

David says tear it down; Brachus says leave it up. At least part of it. He wants the central area and perimeter secure, but most of the testing hardware out. And where is David now? Not a word. He's been spending his time up and down between his ship and base camp quarters. I mentioned his two personalities before; now there's another one— sullen and withdrawn. I hear he spent a lot of time at first with Doc right after the "accident" as he now calls it. He's been spotted in the med lab with Doc discussing genetics again during his recovery exercises. Once, in his quarters here at base camp, I caught him deep in thought while poring over what looked like endless code on his screen. He didn't seem to hear my attempts to get his attention until maybe the third or fourth try. I don't like it. I'd rather have mercurial David than sullen David. We talked some.

We talked a bit about the bio camp and he seems happy with what he's heard about the changes. He's not countermanding any of it. Salvage and tear-down are complete. Al and his girl are booted out. Brachus has set up, in the valley near the natural entrance to the area, along with existing cams and detectors, a combination of lights and speakers to frighten off any would-be visitors of the hominid variety. The outer perimeter and the central camp wall have both been beefed up. The garden and orchard have been expanded.

David has not given up on his experiment, believe it or not. He has faith that the genome of Alpha and Beta will supply enough of a pool of desired traits if only they can reproduce enough. He says he had Dylan go and talk to them before the final goodbye and explain that they are on their own, with a stern warning not to return to the test area. He administered, via shared food, the necessary chemicals to enable reproduction. With their long life spans he, David, thinks it will all work out in the end; that he will have engineered a significant step forward for this planet's population.

My visits to the old bio camp, now Brachus' resort villa, it seems, have been uneventful. I see some of the medical equipment is staying. Oh, the cams and remote units haven't been going on the fritz as I first thought. No, of course not. They are being reconfigured to their private channel. What's the big secret? I have a feeling it's just me Brachus wants to keep in the dark. I haven't confronted David about this.

One thing that has worked out, since I am not spending nearly as much time as before away from base, is that Carol and I have had a lot more time together. She's been working her shipboard equipment remotely and has been mapping the planet in detail for many variables while recording global metrics. She and Mark are working together to pinpoint more sites rich with materials we need.

Part III

Opinions

"I told him it doesn't work like that," Dylan says, recounting his recent conversation with David, "after he told me Al and Bee had no reason not to be content with the way things were."

"'They had it made; they blew it', he said," Dylan continues. "I told David 'No, they didn't blow it. They were acting normally. Wouldn't *you* try to see what was going on behind the wall if you were them?' I asked."

We are outside the central camouflaged wall heading toward the perimeter of the bio area, down along the stream. Dylan lowers his voice and continues, "He was getting upset so I didn't even try to tell him the rest."

I see he wants to continue, but I decide against prompting him.

"I didn't tell him he was up against more than just natural curiosity. Someone was working against him," he continues

"No way!"

"Yes way. I suspected something and saw a little bit, but it was Trace that let it out. Confirmed it. While you were having Craig and Aileen do the teaching sessions, Wes was sending his own messages to them. He was egging them on in a different direction. Not in person, but through his remote speakers and cams. I don't believe he has any respect for these people."

"These people? From what I know and what you are saying, he doesn't respect *anyone* and that includes David. But it does explain why he wants his activities kept private."

"But it's over. They're gone. No more Aileen, Craig, or you—at least not on a regular basis. Me, I wonder how and if they think of the time they spent here, what sort of lasting impact it will have. If any at all."

We walk on, heading to the end of the valley, where it narrows and the stream exits. To what is now called the gate. Beyond is the wild, wide open world—the ever more densely populated native environment.

"Are you upset about the electronics?" he asks.

"Which?"

"You know, what used to be David's," Dylan indicates with head movement up towards one of the camouflaged cam installations. He continues, but more quietly, "Now that Lester, I mean Wesley, has taken them over? You can't access them anymore, right?"

"I don't give him or them or any of it a thought any more if I can help it. David's basically left him in charge; they're

200

his cams and he can do what he wants with them. Although I have a suggestion if he's looking for one." When I get neither a smile nor further comment I add, "David seems OK with the current situation. He feels there is still a good chance that his original work will be significant and says that even if he turns out to be wrong, if what he tried doesn't pan out, that our basic mission objectives will nevertheless be met. Either way it's a success."

"I hear things a little differently," Dylan replies. "The word in the Resources group is that David has left fingerprints. That the changes he made were unauthorized and will be eventually discovered. They will of course be traced back to our time here during this mission. Wesley thinks this is why David's depressed. He thinks that rather than receiving praise, David will be criticized, or worse, for his meddling, especially if the changes prove harmful or detrimental in some way."

"Huh. Interesting. I don't know though. Brachus has such obscure motives; I wouldn't be surprised if this theory isn't somehow self-serving."

"No, he's simple. He's out for himself. Period. He judges everyone else by how much they augment his power and control." He adds with a shy smile, "That's why I'm not a favorite. And you're not either."

"Ha, this I know and I'm good with it. About me I mean. And the feeling's mutual."

We come upon an area where the stream has cut into its bank, exposing a small jumble of rocks. I pull out a couple of the native fruits I brought along from our very productive orchard and offer one to Dylan. These have a unique and delicious flavor and we decide to stop and sit for a moment. I notice that Dylan sits right down, where I take my time and scan the area carefully first.

"You know, what you say would explain something I've thought about for a while. It seemed to me some time ago that Brachus was not on board with David's plan. I don't want to say he was actively working against him, just not trying to help more than he had to."

"You're partially right. I think what he was doing during Aileen's testing could be called actively disruptive."

"But why? What's he trying to do?"

"My opinion? I think it's just him screwing around for fun. He couldn't care less about training or testing. But what I don't think you know is that he continues to sample the descendants and…"

"Oh…?" I interrupt.

"*And*," interrupting my interruption, "he continues the telomere treatments for selected individuals. That's what I don't get."

"Is that right? Monitor I get—probably requested by the boss to track the line—but t-sessions? If that's true, it has to be by David's order."

202

We finish the fruit in silence and then continue our trek to the perimeter. We arrive and turn and begin to follow the border back, partway up one side of the valley. The way becomes more difficult than down along the stream. We are going to make another day-long personal inspection of the entire border—a challenging task due to the rapid growth of some of the vegetation.

"So, how did he figure out the A/V comms links?"

"He didn't but one of Lester's men, Alain, is a hot shot in that area and re-configured them."

"Goodwin. I saw him just recently. We had a little talk. Interesting."

"Alain's ok, but his view of all this, and I mean the whole mission, is narrow. I think he's overwhelmed by it all. He's a perfect match for Wesley because he doesn't question anything. He doesn't interact with me much either or anyone else for that matter as far as I can tell." Dylan pauses and waits for me to stop and turn to face him. "Speaking of the overall mission…"

"Yes?"

"I'd like to stay," he says in a matter-of-fact way. "Here. I'd like to stay here when this is over. I know you can't make it happen, but I've been thinking: I like it here. I think I could make a go and have a good life."

"Short life, you mean," and I instantly regret my hasty comment. Dylan does not show offense or hurt, but then again he is a cool customer and even-tempered.

"Maybe short by our standards, but a good one."

"Dylan, hold on." I see he is serious and begin to rattle off the obvious objections. "Where do I begin? First, not gonna happen. Nobody is left behind alive. Second, no doc, no medical at all. Third, much shorter life span *assuming* you die of natural causes, which is not at all likely. And, and, and… the list goes on."

"Yes, it goes on. I know. But Jason, it's a real life and something I want to do. And don't say it's a waste. There's a lot I could teach during my time. I'd like that."

"Teach…? Dyl, let's say you mean it but listen, you're making a mistake. You are not of this planet. Yes, the chemicals and code of life are the same, you can digest the food, and there is no basic incompatibility but…"

"But what?"

"But look, the native populations, and I mean all the populations on the planet—animal, plant, microscopic, all—have lived and evolved right here, together, for eons. They are used to each other, for lack of a better term. And they are in a more-or-less stable equilibrium. We are not from here. Sure, we are protected by the med treatments and preventatives, the skin spray coating…"

"Not me. I quit using it."

This stops me in my tracks. "Are you kidding me? When?"

"Don't worry. It's been a while. You do know that lab has been testing and culturing as much of the native biota as they can. I've talked to Jacob about it…"

"Jacob? Doc? You mean, he's said it's ok?" I ask in surprise.

"No, he didn't know at first. In fact he didn't know until my last checkup. He agrees with you, that it's a bad idea not to use the spray. But I still don't think so. Anyway, there it is."

"But back to the main point. It remains a strong possibility that something out there is going to get you. I can't believe you haven't caught something already. You are simply not fine-tuned for this environment." It's then I realize I don't know anything about his background. "Family?"

"None to speak of. There'll be no one left when we get back. If I go back I mean." After a brief silence, Dylan adds, "Jason. Ok. I hear you. I will think about it. At least you know now, and you are the only one who knows."

I am fairly beat by the time we complete our circuit, ending up once again near the natural entry for this small valley. To my great surprise, we hear a loud voice, an amplified voice, booming out as we approach our starting point.

"What the… Is that…?"

"Yep, that is the voice of your pal Lester," answers Dylan.

205

"What is he up to now?" I wonder, still surprised. "I didn't catch what he was saying." We approach the main pathway and just catch a glimpse of several natives. They have seen us first and begin to move quickly but quietly away. I notice that one recognizes Dylan and gives a quick look and wave to him before disappearing. The bright visual warning lights come on and we step into the clearing close to where the natives were congregated.

"Shipley, you reek!" says the booming voice.

That Dylan's a good kid. I mentioned to him that the administrator passwords for the Resource team's private channels had been changed, hoping he could help me get back in. But he kept anything he might have known about access to himself.

I ran into David not long ago, when I was thinking about Dylan's report of monitoring and further treatments for the A&B line. I was in a mood and just asked him straight out if it's true. No fireworks—he just said 'yes' and that was it.

The more I think about it, the more I don't like the way the work Craig and Aileen did with A&B was being undermined. Dylan couldn't say exactly what they were being told, of course, but he was confident it was not helpful. And it was being done not so much as part of a grand plan, but more for amusement. According to my well-tested theory of personality constancy, I have to wonder what other mischief is afoot.

Local Attraction

"So Dylan. What do you think? I mean about his idea to stay."

"If you must know," says Carol, looking at me carefully, "I've thought about the same thing. Hasn't it occurred to you?"

"Carol, what are you talking about? We can't stay here. Wait, you are talking about us both?" She gives me a look. "Yes, of course. And there is nothing more I'd like to do than spend my life with you, but here?"

"Really?"

"Really what?"

"Spend our lives together?"

"Well, yes, of course. I thought you knew."

"I left my mind-reading helmet up on the Hobbe, so no, I didn't know. You may want to make a note to speak out loud when you have a thought like that," she says with a decidedly unamused look on her face.

I am a little embarrassed by my lack of skill in dealing with relationship issues and am thankful she is trying to help me out. "But here? As I told him, it's not gonna happen."

"You've traveled around this planet more than I have and you've seen how beautiful it is. Can't you just imagine? Stop being practical just a moment."

"Ok sure, I like the idea of us spending our lives in an exotic location, back to nature; our rugged defiance of adversity, reliance on ourselves and all that. But at some point, a very early point I might add, you bump up against reality: infection; broken limb; childbirth..." I take a quick look at Carol and see no response. "All these things become life threatening instead of routine. It's asking a lot to sacrifice the advantages we have."

"Way to ruin it."

"I'm just sayin' I wouldn't mind ordering out for food sometime and having it delivered instead of trapping and killing wild animals. I mean, when is the last time anyone's done that? Who's had unprocessed food in our lifetimes?" She's not responding so I add, "You're gonna get tired of pounding grain and sewing our clothes together out of skins and sinew." At last, I detect her little smile. "On the other hand, if we could someday afford a nice place back in the civilized world, I say let's do it. It's going to be a while though."

"Ok, let's."

"Back home, you mean?" She nods. "Think about some places, and we'll do the math and see how to make it

208

happen. We could opt out of any more missions and out of the Academy work altogether. I imagine we'll each have opportunities in civilian positions if we want. Just a thought."

"Alright, let's take the practical approach after all," Carol says and now she is not gently chiding me but instead seems content with our discussion. "Let's do make a point while we are here to get away again every now and then for a few days. We'll never have a whole planet practically to ourselves again."

"It's a deal. If you can make me some shoes out of tree bark, I promise to kill something and figure out how to cook it on a fire."

"No, you don't have to. It is an intriguing idea though, you have to admit. Cave man and cave woman against the world." Carol is silent for a moment and then speaks again saying, "But I do know someone who could give you pointers on cooking raw meat."

"Raw meat? Really?"

"Yes, you asked who has ever done that recently and, well, you might want to talk to Wesley about it."

"You must be joking. Has he gone native? I can't imagine for one second him getting his hands dirty. Why do you think this?"

"Look, I haven't seen it myself and shouldn't be talking out of turn. But I do talk to one or two of his people sometimes and the word is that Wes is not only doing it but that he's hooked on it. You talked about raw meat on a fire—well he's done it, or having it done."

This reminds me of the scene that Dylan and I stumbled on during my last visit to the old bio area. The natives had run off from the gate area, but they left behind some intriguing things; including meat—charred. "I wonder…" Carol knows some of what happened that time and I fill her in on the rest. "You don't think he's badgering the natives to do it for him? Is he using them for something like that?"

"It could be; he's a snake. I told you I don't trust him. Way back when we were still at the Academy, he would deliberately pester me…"

"Pester? What exactly? Pester how?" My hackles are raised; here is yet another reason to dislike this man.

"It's not important now, but I let him have it verbally and threatened to go straight to Dean Carson or higher if he kept it up. That straightened him out and since then when we meet he pretends innocence and ignorance."

"Look, if he's…"

"Settle down, tiger, I told you it's not a problem now. I am doing some work for him but only through his delegates."

"Go on. What work? If I may ask," I ask, still upset.

"It's all legit. He is asking me to work the Hobbe's imaging systems to search landmasses globally for surface outcroppings of specific materials. Or, for outcroppings where we may deduce the materials may be embedded if we don't find them directly. It's all standard stuff."

"Standard stuff? I don't like it. If anything comes up where he tries to get you alone…"

"Hey, I'm a big girl, ok? I can handle him."

I take some breaths to cool down. I'll trust her to handle Brachus.

There's been a lot to absorb lately: Dylan running around without basic protection on his bare skin; now Brachus eating unprocessed meat, if the story I true. What other safety measures is that group ignoring? The actual idea of using animals from here, roasted or whatever, turns my stomach a little. It's possible Carol has it wrong. Her contacts may be feeding her a line. He seems to have a pretty loyal core group, whatever else they might be, and I wouldn't be surprised if he, and maybe they as a group, were to enjoy an ego boost by spreading a rumor like this.

———

"Look, it's the best system ever developed," says Mark in one of his expansive moods in his work area at base camp. "It's really the best there is and nothing beats it."

"But what about the latest version we saw back at training?"

"What, that? Don't be silly. I played with it. It's beta.

Loaded with bugs. Here, take this. Here's to ya."

Mark takes an exploratory sip of his latest batch followed by another and a grin. "That's what I'm talkin' about."

"I have to give it to you, it's just a bad as the real thing back home," says I after my own sip. I am not a fan of his favorite after-hours brew. "What possesses you to drink this stuff?"

"I deserve it," he says. "After all the crap I put up with... You talk to Porter? Well, he's got the right idea. His priority system is the best. Just give me one job at a time if you are going to micromanage me. Or better yet, get the hell out of my way and I'll take care of my end of things just fine."

"So you are not actually brewing or distilling this stuff are you? How is it actually done?"

"Yes, I'm brewing it. What do you think?" Mark answers hastily. He gives his thinning red hair a sweep. "Well, brewing... I am inputting the ingredients in the form of organic compounds, the output formula I modify by hand; the impurities, the aging flavors, are a little tricky. Try something like that on your beta unit."

"But brewing, or fermenting, in the original sense..."

"It's the impurities that make the difference between good, better, and best. What you have here, son, is gold, pure gold," he says, ignoring my original question. He follows this with another sip. "This unit will spit out, no pun intended, just about anything you want. The trick is having the right formula. All the standards are built in for food and drink. Non-standards require someone who knows what they are doing."

"Can it make me a cup o' 'burnin' fire'?" I suggest, tongue-in-cheek.

"Nope. Can't do that yet. Too complex. Need to completely break it down and analyze. Not gonna do it here, at least not unless time frees up. And not even then. Not interested. Something's happening during the processing of those beans anyway; the drying, crushing, and heating makes for a very complex liquid by the time you drink it. You drink it?"

"I have. Not a major fan."

"Are you a major fan of anything? Besides Carol, I mean," Mark adds with his own brand of chortling.

"Inorganics. What about them? Same unit?"

"No. Yes, same idea. Different handling. Ores have to go through preprocessing. They are all different. You have to change setups quite often, believe me I know," he answers and I catch a little grimace on his face.

"What is keeping you so busy? Is everything going all right? Your crew behaving?"

"Crew? Naw, we're basically all runners now, I don't have a crew. We all work for Big Brachus and just don't know it. No, my operation is smooth. It's the damn government jobs that'll kill ya. But never mind that. Take a look at this," he says conspiratorially. Mark pulls a little sphere out of his pocket and drops it into my free hand. I set my drink down and look at the object.

"Is this...?" It's heavy for its size, like a ball bearing, which it clearly is not.

"Yes, it is. It certainly is."

I knew it right away. I look at Mark, look at the glittering object in my hand, and then hold it up in front of my eye. You think you can look through it but you cannot. If you hold it up to a light source it gets brighter but it's not translucent in the normal sense; you can see nothing through it. It is a work of art—an immensely detailed and beautiful object. It's as if ordinary light goes in, bounces around a while and then exits as every color of the rainbow. The surface is an ever-changing assemblage of soft points of every color. I say 'surface' but I can't really focus on the surface at all. You can feel it—it's hard—but the sphere looks more like a cloud, with depth.

"You made this," I say at last, not as a question. I see that Mark is studying me, enjoying my reaction no doubt.

"I figured out the secret. Something I've been playing with on the side. I've got to have some fun in all this too, you know. It's a solution, technically, not a solid—the sphere. A structure built up of just three building blocks, one after the other, atom by atom. It doesn't happen naturally." He looks at me, his eyes gleaming. "I should say molecule-by-molecule." Oh, he's in his element now, as it were. Mark continues, "You've heard about this stuff—ever held one before?"

"Piramon? Never saw it in person before, but…"

"Yeah, yeah—keep it down, will ya? Not many people run into the two main components of this material. One's a metal, the other is not, both are pretty rare. What do you think is the third component? Do you know?"

I shake my head, still looking at the colors. The way the points of color change, it looks like the sphere is moving, pulsing, but it's not. If you hold it without looking, it feels like ordinary metal or maybe glass. Funny, it seems to get cooler the longer I hold it.

"Water. Plain old water. This unit over here can take the extracted raw materials and build one of these in about two of these years here, with my help, spare time only. It's as close to a perfect sphere as can be made. Gravity distorts it a little. Tidal effect…"

"But…"

"Don't ask." Mark takes the sphere back. "You never saw it."

"Is this the government job you mentioned?"

"This? No way. It's my baby only. Wanted to see if I could do it."

I make a show of taking another sip of Mark's liquid 'gold' while I digest what he's just shown me. I hope that Mark will open up some more and ask, "Speaking of making stuff out of thin air, can you make it spit out more components for one A/V cam and transceiver? The mount is ok."

"No can do, old chum. Can't do anything unofficial, supposedly." And at this Mark laughs heartily in his special way that ends in what sounds like hiccups. "Put in a request. I'll get to it when it makes its way to the top of the pile. Which ain't gonna be soon." More hiccups.

"Forget it. I think there's some around I can cannibalize. You are swamped." Another sip for me.

Mark's demeanor returns to a more serious level. "Look, I've got all systems running basically around the clock now, and it going to be like that for a long time. If you really need…"

"No, forget it. I can make do. If it doesn't work out I'll put in a request. What else are you working on? Officially, I mean…"

"Ah, knocking out the list for the Hobbe, slowly but surely. Then there's some special extraction that's eating up time, machine time and my time, that's all. It's not a lot of work really, but it takes some set up time and some hands-on."

"Is that for…?"

"Who else?"

"You mean in addition to the…?" I ask, nodding towards his pocket.

"No. This is done," patting his pocket. "Just a challenge I set for myself. The other things… Well, I don't want to get into it. In fact, I don't know what you are talking about."

"Ok, all right, if you say so. But, answer me this: organic or inorganic?" I presume Brachus may have a favorite beverage as well.

"Too many questions. Can't talk about it. Maybe some other time," says Mark. He finishes his drink. "Inorganic," I hear as he turns away.

> *As Mark said, Brachus is running the show now and David seems fine with the situation. He concern is 'his' line and how it's doing. He receives samples and reports from the field, but no more 'modifications', genetically speaking, are being performed.*

> *Sad to report but Alpha and Beta have passed. They both had a long life span, about ten times the norm for the natives. I am surprised they made it that long what with all the dangers and lack of medical care. Bee went first; and Dylan kept in touch with Al right up to the end. He saw that Al had become a respected leader and that his children and his children's children were many. He*

told us that Al had a nickname for Bee. He translated it as "Mother of Nations."

A chosen few of Al's descendants are being given telomere treatments. This way, in David's view, the best of the best are given ample opportunity to procreate and expand the line; he's said this before. The treatment work is being done at bio camp central by Aileen and Tracy, trained by Vanessa.

There have been reports of aggressive and brutal behavior amongst the natives, but the accepted conclusion is that this is a natural phenomenon and has nothing to do with us. Struggle for survival and so forth. We do know that in any environment with limited resources, conflicts will and must occur in and between species and subgroups competing for those resources to procreate. Any species, including humans. This is a given. But to what extent we are affecting the level of violence I, for one, am not sure.

There is influence, obviously. In a way, that's the entire reason we are here. What I mean is: I wonder how we are affecting the native populations on an intellectual level? Clearly some have seen our comings and goings as we search out and retrieve resources; some have even had direct contact—think of Dylan out in the field, or those select individuals undergoing the life extension treatments. What the natives are able to make out of all this is another thing. Dylan assures me there will be a lasting impact in their history, their legends, their lore. He's in touch with the descendants of A & B, and other populations as well, and tells me that they have long been passing oral traditions from generation to generation; we are part of that tradition. Likewise, written records are also now being kept in at least one case, which are carefully preserved by copying from one generation to the next.

Interestingly, A & B's descendants have developed a subgroup who concern themselves almost exclusively with matters dealing with their limited understanding of us. They preserve and perpetuate the lore, both written and oral. This is to be, I think, expected, as follows: If some see one or two of their own who are treated differently, by communicating or otherwise interacting with mysterious and powerful outsiders (that is, us), those one or two will be seen in a special light by the remainder. Rumors will spread; conclusions will be drawn, right or wrong. And if the chosen seem to live a long time, and be on good terms with us, then those chosen ones will be assumed to be very special indeed, inspiring awe and respect, if not reverence. I am struggling with whether this is, in the long run, good, bad, or neither.

I do believe the Weasel is doing a little prospecting for himself on the Academy's dime. It fits right in with his MO—looking out for number one. The clues are several. He is having Carol search for some specific, and I would assume rare, materials in crustal outcroppings, thus inorganic; he is having Mark do some special extracting as a 'government' job. But what exactly? It can't be too bulky or heavy either. That would get noticed during launch prep. So very small or light, or both, and valuable— that narrows it down. I think Mark wants to talk about it. We'll see.

This business about eating meat from native animals has me both interested and repulsed. Aside from the danger of consuming potentially harmful or deadly chemicals and organisms, the actual consumption of meat is not a problem. It is very unusual nowadays but certainly was the norm and is the norm for developing populations. Check your teeth, the imprint of evolution cannot be denied. Not to mention the fact that the gastrointestinal machinery of the body is perfectly capable of dealing with and digesting this source of energy and nutrients. But, we have moved on from that stage to something better, have we not? Now, some of the fruits and vegetables have been thoroughly tested and have a big green light from Doc. But not so with meat, any meat, as far as I know. I need to corner him next time I go in and see what he says about it.

Defector

I am sort of kidding when I ask about access, trying to make the dreaded 'small talk.' She makes me nervous.

Tracy answers, "Oh sure, I've got 'em. No problem. What'll you give me for them?" she asks as she looks me over with a suggestive expression. "I mean, this has to be a two-way street, so…"

Now I'm really uncomfortable. My mind races to find a suitable answer and judging from her reaction I guess my face betrays me.

"Relax dude, just kidding. Ha ha, that look's almost as good as the one in the picture Les snapped of you on the cam a while back." She returns to my question saying, "Sure, I'll send them right along. Two things though: you don't know where you got them and, don't be too surprised at what you find." She winks, puts a piece of something in her mouth and walks away chewing toward Dylan and Craig.

She's a good looking young woman with her brown hair always pulled back in a ponytail. She makes me uncomfortable for a couple reasons. First and foremost, she has been too buddy-buddy with Brachus for me to trust her. After all, she's the human firewall he set up to insulate himself. Second, she's got a mischievous look about her, in a racy way, which makes me wonder what she's thinking. And I get the impression she enjoys saying things that can be taken two ways. Not flirty like Vanessa, but downright suggestive. Not my style.

And she offered to give the passwords right away. I am too stunned to think properly at first. I guess the first step is to see if I actually get the access information like she promised. Then, see if it works. I gather my bits and bobs for the return trip from bio camp back to base. Dylan and Craig walk in my direction, talking. I'm sorry but Craig just looks way too young to be part of the team. I do know his background and qualifications, on paper, but he's that type of man who looks like a kid, and probably always will. I think he cultivates that look by letting his mop top grow long, among other quirks.

"Heading back I see. Got everything you need?" asks Dylan. I nod. "Porter is ready to go. He'll take you. Thanks for the help today."

"No problem," I reply. "Anytime you need help, or anything really, let me know. Hey, one quick thing. What is she chewing over there?"

"Oh, Trace?" He looks over at Tracy, smiles, turns back to me and says, "That, Jason, is dried meat." Dylan pauses to examine my reaction I guess. "You should try it. It won't hurt you. And it's delicious."

I shake my head, decline to comment and take my leave

from bio camp.

———

"Not you too?" I say to Porter as we head back to base.

"What?" he says, turning away from the controls to look at me.

"Your little snack there. It's odiferous."

"Odiferous? Seriously? Odiferous? Here, have one." And he tosses me a little irregular shred of something of a dark brownish red color. It is greasy, *is* odiferous, and I decline to put it in my mouth; I don't even like handling it.

"You really should get that stuff checked out by Doc before chewing. Or eating. Are you swallowing it? Good grief man, I'm not kidding." I shake my head and wonder what is wrong with these people? I change the subject to one of more interest. "Say, what's up with Tracy?"

"What do you mean?"

"Don't play dumb with me, you know what I mean. I don't think she's spoken two words to me the whole time and now she's totally nice and friendly? That's what I mean."

"Haw! So you've noticed." He says, looking at me to see, I suspect, if he should say more. "You might say they've had a little falling out." He turns back to face the controls. "Or a big falling out."

"'They' being Tracy and…"

"That's right, Tracy and…" he looks at me again and we both know. "You might say she told him off and then told him where to *get* off."

"But, why? What happened?"

"Rumors my friend, rumors. You know you really should try some." He nods toward the dried meat I am holding while he adjusts his glasses with one hand.

"We'll see what Doc says and then, maybe." When we exit the runabout at base camp, I toss the greasy tidbit aside when Porter's not looking. "Where are you off to next? Some secret mission for Brachus?"

"Of course. Top secret. Actually, I'm heading to a super spot—76 East and 14 South—just fantastic. My favorite. Hopefully I can stay a while."

"Loading up ore or…?"

"No, not there, nothing like that there. I won a bet with Wes and he says I can have some time off. Besides, he needs the runabout for a bit. I'm taking it out there to him and, like I say, I hope he keeps it a while. Wouldn't mind being stranded for a few days."

"Is it near those bluffs? They are awesome."

Porter responds only with a quizzical look.

"No, no, of course not. They're west not east. Never mind," I say to correct my error. "I'd like to get back to them sometime. Never got my fill."

"What? Bluffs? No bluffs. Hey, gotta run. Wish me luck!" Porter runs off leaving me alone for a moment in the landing area.

This is a stark and sterile area. The rugged surrounds are quite striking with the sun at this low angle. Bright reds and golds in direct light with sharply contrasting dark browns and blacks in shadow. All against the clear blue of the sky. You can almost see the shadows moving higher. Maybe it's my imagination but I think I *can* see them moving if I concentrate.

———

The alert from my genie wakes me suddenly. What day is it anyway? It's early, but plenty light out; the day is well underway. I'm still groggy, but take a quick look around the base camp. Porter is back. He only got a day or two at his special location apparently. But now I see he's running out again in a big hurry straight to the transport unit. Something is up.

I check my incoming comms and am surprised that there is, in fact, a message from Tracy. It says 'Something just for you. Let me know if there is anything else I can do ;) Codes attached.' I'd better save this for in my quarters when I have access to a decent screen and console.

Now I see not one but *two* alarms! Is this thing working

right? How did I sleep through that? One is a general alert and the other, earlier one, is from Craig to everyone.

What to log first? Most important and most disturbing is what happened to Dylan a short time after I left bio camp last time. The good news—he will live. By a fluke they were near one of the cams so we got to see some of what happened. A big animal, what we would call a cat, was inside the outer perimeter. This has happened before of course; I've seen the tracks myself. You just can't seal out the world completely without building real walls or putting up a dome, which David definitely didn't want. But it never came to anything like this. Anyway, this large cat, easily as massive as a man—probably more—and longer than Dylan is tall, attacked while he and Craig were out and, as I say, near a cam. The video just shows the beginning blur of the attack and the rest happens outside the field of view.

Craig was not touched and used his weapon to dispatch the animal but not before Dylan suffered a lot of damage. It's a wonder that either of them had a weapon the way they have lately been ignoring basic common sense. Lucky. Another lucky stroke is that Lester and Tracy both received the alert from Craig right away and between them they got Dylan to a clearing where Porter could land. We heard it was a real mess and they had to use some pretty serious emergency procedures.

There were barely any vital signs by the time Doc got him. He says the timing was good however, with a little to spare, but not much. He says without the field treatment, Dylan would be a goner. The emergency field procedures were literally a lifesaver. Some of the meds, he says, are the same as we all get for the long parts of the voyage out here and back. He also says not to worry; it's all easy from this point on. Patchin' and sewin', in his words. I don't like to joke about it. Seems like with all his medical miracles, he could fix his cowlick. Maybe nobody's ever had the nerve to tell him he has one.

The access info from Tracy works. I can access the Resource Group's cams for sure. I can also see their locally stored reports and other data. Just for laughs I pulled up a recent official progress report from Wes and tried to compare it to what I find through this new access. Well, first of all, there is no copy of it at all in any of their folders. There were plenty of docs of the same date and roughly the same time but nothing I could see matched what he sent in officially. Is he making this stuff up? Honestly though, his reports don't hold any interest for me anymore.

Carol heard through the 'girl grapevine' that Tracy caught Wes in a lie and some sort of compromising position but no details. What exactly is going on with this guy? I'm telling you here and now that it's difficult to keep a positive attitude while suspecting the 'leaders' of misdeeds and lies. I should say

227

'leader' since it's clear now that David has lately assumed a passive role and Wes is taking advantage. Also, while I think David may be misguided in his quest to hit a home run with his work here, I don't think he's up to anything really deceitful.

Accusation

"It was like slow motion. We both suspected something and stopped and looked at each other, then slowly and carefully looked around. You know how it is when you can sense that someone is watching you even though you can't see them? That was the feeling. And you could for sure hear the rustle of the underbrush when the cat attacked. I froze and thought it was going for me, but it wasn't. For the first few seconds I couldn't seem to process what was happening, then snapped out of it and blasted the cat. I was really worried that my stupid delay would cost Dylan his life," explains Craig. I'll bet this encounter will add one or two experience lines to his boyish countenance.

I glance around. The listeners look at Craig, or on the ground, but not so much at each other. Mark asks, "What were you guys doing out there? Isn't someone watching those cams for just this sort of problem?"

"The cams are set up for motion and sound detection and can respond automatically. But they don't cover the whole area and they couldn't see everything even if they did cover the whole area. I told you, *we* couldn't even see it when it was stalking us at close range. We were out for some work on one of the new cams downstream past the rapids outside the entrance to the bio area. We never made it past the gate on this trip, for obvious reasons."

"Cams outside the bio area? This is news to me," I say. "Is that how the animal tracked you guys in? From outside?"

"I…I don't think so. We didn't make it to the outside this time, but maybe the previous times…" Craig continues, "Jason, you know that right at the entrance to the bio area it's narrow and we've got that under control. You've been there yourself enough to know that I'm right. I think the cat came in from higher ground at the sides. He just was missed." It is clear that Craig is still shaken up.

"These things happen, Craig. Nobody said there wouldn't be danger here, and I think we all are thankful that you responded the way you did."

"Hear, hear," says Brachus, who has made one of his rare appearances at base camp. He is sitting sideways on a chair with one elbow on the back of it. His legs are crossed and the one on top is swinging back and forth.

I add, "What about those cams outside, though?"

"We were asked to set up a series out past the gate, way down where the land opens up. Wesley needs them to keep an eye on things for David…"

Brachus pipes in with, "This is no time to discuss camera placement."

"Anyway," Craig continues, "you should have seen this thing. I mean, it would freeze you right in your tracks. The muscles rippling, the fur glistening with color from a dark orange to black and back. I could just feel the power. But

230

silent, powerful and silent. And just before I got it, it turned and looked right at me. I'll tell you, you *know* it's looking and thinking…"

Someone asks Craig another question but I am not listening.

Carol gives me a nudge and we walk out leaving Craig with the rest gathered to hear about the attack. I take her to the natural rock ledge seat where we sometimes come to talk. Cloud cover has muted the effect of the sun on the mountains. They remain darkly imposing and seem to be poised like me, waiting to hear what Carol has to say.

"You've got to do something," she begins. "And I'm quite serious. If what I hear from Tracy is true, you've *got* to do something."

"Me? Why me? What does she say?"

"Let's start with the easy one first. Wes is playing with the native men like they are animals. He is setting them up for fighting and then he and his goons are placing bets on who wins."

"She said that? Tracy?"

Carol nods.

"I'm not sure I believe it. That's pretty low even for him. My guess would be that she is mad and trying to get back at him."

231

Carol remains silent, looking at me steadily.

"You and I both know that at their stage of development, this society is still very physical. There will be fights for dominance and survival. It happens, and it's not pretty. Now, maybe Wes is watching and passively betting on his favorites, but setting them up? I don't know…" I suddenly remember Porter's comment about winning some days off from Wes on a bet.

"But, she says he is doing just that. Inciting them, and then making sure that a confrontation happens. By the way, the usual result is that only one survives. If we leave them alone and they fight, I can deal with it, even understand it, but set it up for fun and profit? No way." She pauses and waits for my response. I don't have a response and just shake my head.

"You've only heard part of it. Brace yourself. Tracy says that she has nothing more to do with Wes because she caught him doing more than just betting on fights."

I guess I am a little slow because this is not making any sense. "You mean he's actively involved with these fights? But how…"

"Oh you poor thing. When we get you back home, we'll have to get you out in society more. He's 'actively involved' all right but not with the men." Pause.

"Get out!" I say as it dawns on me what she means. "Do you actually believe she's serious?"

Carol doesn't respond directly. "You have access to their data now, right?" I nod. "I said earlier 'if what she said is true'. Poke around there. What I hear is that you will see for yourself what's happening and verify some, if not all, of it. Let me know what you find." This sinks in as she pauses and then adds, "The rest of his people have to know what's going on too, if only they would talk."

As we walk back through the open area at base camp there is a small group talking and laughing. I don't see Craig anywhere but Lester is there. He makes eye contact with me as we move toward their general direction. Carol splits away. I give Lester a "Hey" and decide to try something.

Mustering up an accusatory tone I ask, "What the heck are you guys up to?" after I am close enough so that it is clear I am talking to Lester.

"What, us?" and he indicates the small group, looking confused for a moment. "What does it look like we're doing?" and he turns back.

"No. Come on. You know what I mean," I say as I stop and maintain a serious expression and the same tone.

"No, I don't know what you mean," he says as he turns to me, taking a small step away from the rest. "And now you have my full attention."

"I don't mean to break up your little confab, but we hear rumors about what's going on out there, in the field, where you spend all your time. What the heck are you doing out there?"

233

I see a brief but clear look of worry cross Lester's face. He is silent for some several seconds, then smiles, rakes his hair back, and says calmly, "I don't know who 'we' is and I don't know about any rumors. What I do know is that if you needed to know what we are 'up to', as you put it, you would already know."

"I don't 'need' to know anything. Just curious, that's all. There are some pretty wild stories spreading."

This time, all I get are raised eyebrows and silence. I realize that Lester is probably not going to fall for it but I try one last tack by saying, "Oh, come on, you can tell me. I heard something from Porter about your exploits. I would think you'd like to share something as juicy as that," I conclude with a wink.

This time there is a definite reaction but not what I was hoping for. "Porter? Where is he? I'll find out one way or the other what stories he's spreading..." And he makes as if to go.

"Wait. Hold on. Take it easy." Time to defuse the situation, I think. "You're a little touchy, aren't you? Just tell me what's been going on out there. I hear you've done some exploring," I say with less of a serious expression, losing the accusatory tone also.

"Exploring?"

"Haven't you? I heard something about deep ocean..."

"Oh, that. Yeah."

Did I just see a big sigh of relief?

"Yeah, me and a couple others have taken the two-man down. Deep. Freaky. I mean, there are some real wild creatures down there. If you turn on the floods…"

Lester stops, blinks, and looks at me as if he just realizes something important. He continues, but in a more typical, for him, fashion by saying, "There are pics and vids; they'll be in the archives. See ya 'round." And he steps off. He doesn't turn around but I can still hear him say as he leaves, "I wouldn't pay much attention to rumors if I were you," followed by a low chuckle.

She's right. I've got to do something. Holy shit. How incredibly stupid must he be to keep a record of this? Pictures, videos, records of the fights. Unbelievable. The story about the fights? Not only is it true, it's documented!

Something else that's apparently true: The strain of big natives, the ones who Dylan mentioned long ago are significantly larger than the usual, well, they are in the pictures too. They're real. These are big hulkers and they figure pretty prominently. I didn't look at every picture but the situation is clear. We've got time and location stamps and pictures of lethal fights interspersed with shots of an alternately rapt and exuberant Brachus, along with a couple of his crew.

But, sorry to say, that's not all. Tracy's right too, about Brachus' questionable doings with native females. That's how it looks. There is, thankfully, no visual evidence that I have found of him in intimate contact; otherwise I would have to put my eyes out. But there is plenty of evidence of him misusing them. I have not been to any of his field camps, except of course the bio camp, but I am here to tell you that he's set himself up quite nicely in at least a couple of exotic spots around the globe. And he's using what appear to be female slaves (my term—innocent until proven guilty and all that) in each of them, except bio.

I found the deep sea shots Lester mentioned. Now that's interesting! Really fantastic—the variety and shapes and colors of the creatures down there. There are seafloor and seamount shots too but the really good shots are of the products of evolution. Now, I have to admit that these could be shots from deep sea back home. When you are looking at life in an alien environment like deep under an ocean, you are bound to find incredible things no matter what planet you are on.

Back to a more unpleasant subject: It occurs to me that Brachus (and possibly others in his cadre) may be responsible for hybrid offspring—I'm sure my meaning here is clear. If the children are fertile, then the gene pool here has been really been stirred up, so to speak. And not just Brachus, but you've got the giants and the other so-called rejects out there; others that Dylan told me are breeding for sure. That's going to dilute and distort the gene pool even more.

I'm going to use this aspect in my approach to David. If he can understand that things have gotten out of hand, and that his desire for "our" line to flourish is jeopardized, it may jolt him out of the doldrums to take action.

Whistle Blower

"Mark, I've got to go to David and I'm not looking forward to it. I hope he's in a good mood. Have you seen him?"

"You have no chance." Mark says this using a humorous voice; he is sometimes self-amused, I think.

"Really? You've talked to him?"

"No, not lately but I don't have to talk to him to see he's in a black mood."

"That bad? You never know though; he changes from minute to minute, or used to."

"Not any more. What name does Bevan call him now? Sad Sack or something? He's right, although I hate to ever admit that he's right," says Mark as he putters at his worktable. More seriously now, he says, "You're going to talk to our Commander? I've got a couple things I should tell him too."

"You can't come with me; it'd be too much at once."

"It can wait. He's wrapped up in his own thoughts lately. Mine can wait; I can handle it. I just have to keep pushing

239

straight ahead and I'll be alright. One thing at a time."

"Let me guess…"

"Nope, don't to it. Don't say it. I'll handle it," he says again, looking at me with an 'I mean business' look.

"Ok, ok. Let me know if I can help you. If I survive this meeting."

I *would* like some moral support to meet with David but it's just not right. I don't want to drag Mark or anyone else into it.

I was hoping to meet Carol out on the rock ledge but now she can't make it. I think of sitting alone to plan a strategy but realize that approach doesn't work for me. I have to go into the meeting cold and let the facts speak. There is always the danger of over-thinking the problem. I have found that things rarely go as expected in any discussion after the first sentence is uttered, so detailed planning of a conversation is a waste of time. You can never plan for all possibilities.

———

"What are you getting at?" David says after I start showing what I found.

"What am I…? I am getting at the fact these pictures show improper behavior. Probable betting and instigating of fights for amusement; using of slaves for who knows what."

He looks at a select few of the found images. "These don't show anything. Natives fight, have fought, will fight. We have cams, they caught the action. I don't want to look at it, but some people do. Slaves? What slaves?"

I am struggling to quickly think: have I made a terrible mistake? Is this all a misunderstanding? But no, it can't be. "David, there are reports…"

"From who? Please be clear. If you're making an accusation, make it!"

Instead, as an alternative to speaking, I present the next photos. Photos of Brachus being attended by native women.

"Wait, hold it. Back up. What's this? Where did you get these?"

"Not the point; you can see…"

"Jason. Hold it. Back up. Tell me. Where did you find these?"

"They are part of the Resource team's locally archived data," I say rather abruptly, annoyed that he's asking the wrong questions. I know that I have to keep cool. It is David's habit to sometimes shoot the messenger and I know it. "I stumbled on these in various folders while performing routine maintenance," I lie. I don't want to bring Tracy or anyone else into the picture right now unless I have to. Let the evidence speak.

241

David looks at several of the pictures again. I can see he is paying attention to the time and location stamps. His mouth habit working, I can see him thinking now, really thinking. He is soundlessly mouthing the coordinates of one of the pictures. "Where was this taken?" I give him the common name of the site. "Shit, I've been there. I didn't see anything like this." For some time, David says nothing, and I decline to break his concentration. "Well," he says, looking away from the pictures and back at me at last, "what did you come here for? What do you expect me to do?"

————

"So, what did you say?" Carol asks, later in the day, when we are alone.

"I didn't really answer that question. I couldn't. I told him that I didn't come to him to give direction, only information. And what happens from there is up to him. Things like that."

"Good. And? Go on."

"And then I dropped the idea that the gene pool may be irreversibly tainted. I don't think he fully believes that the so-called 'sterile' natives are mixing back in; I advised him that Dylan's certain of it. And then about the potential, shall we say, contamination from Brachus."

"According to our source, it's not potential, it's actual. What she doesn't know is how long it's been going on…"

"But here's the good news. He gets it. He's sees the

242

potential fallout. David got the business about the pool getting cloudy. He knows that anybody checking into the native genome later, say on the next visit, assuming there will be a next visit, will see something fishy. He believes they will be able to detect one or both key things: that someone, namely him, was fooling around outside the guidelines trying to do something to bolster his own reputation and also that at least one of his crew, namely you know who, has been fooling around sexually with the natives for his own pleasure. Neither one will look good on David's record, and that's important to him."

"Do you think he really believes those things are happening? And that it'll be noticed?"

"I don't know. I have to say that, as commander, he cannot believe it just yet. He has to take it slowly, deliberately. But he knows Brachus; he must at some level believe that this is at least possible. And he trusts Dylan; so he won't easily dismiss that either. He'll look at the files; it's there. He'll come around."

"I see. So you think he will take action now on his own."

"I think he will. I do. In fact, I went to Mark right after talking to David and guess what? He'd already called and commandeered the first available flyer."

"That's something. At least he's moving again." Carol adds, "Jason?"

"Yes dear?"

"I'm proud of you."

———

"I don't know what you are doing but cut it out," says Gleshert the next day during a routine visit. He is finished checking me over and I am trying to figure out why his data upload to the Hobbe is not working.

"What…?"

"I've got enough to do," he says.

"Doc, I'm sure I don't know what you're talking about."

"Can it. David tells me this is all part of a pet project of yours. And I'm paying the price for it."

"No. Nope. I don't have any projects, pet or otherwise. What's the problem?" I get the stare and glare, but it melts back to normal quickly. "What does he have you doing?"

"The only part I can tell you is that samples are coming in fast and furious from the latest generation of natives. And there are lots; it's like rabbits out there. He's having the results sorted a whole number of ways from Sunday and…" He sees that I am listening intently and halts in mid-sentence. "And that's it for today. Finish up what you need to do and scram. Do not tell me about what you find with the equipment unless it's something I actually need to know and even then…"

"Say Doc, one thing. That cup over there with what looks like 'burnin' fire'—is that yours?"

244

"Beat it."

I pass Vanessa on the way out.

"You're not a fast learner," she says, "are you?" And she's not asking a question, but making a statement. "Do you deliberately try to trigger him?"

"Van, what do you mean? I…"

"Nevermind. Scoot," she says

> David's on a mission all right. I try to stay out of his way. But at least he's moving, as Carol said. It's refreshing.
>
> Brachus was in camp again—base camp. It was a sight to see at first. He had been talked to by David, you could tell that right away. His whole demeanor has changed to sheepish. He greets me like he's a normal person, just one of the guys. Pretty disgusting, now that I know that he would never think of greeting me at all if he was left on his own. He pretends to be interested in protocol along with other details he never showed much interest in before. I say disgusting, Carol says amusing. Mark says scary.
>
> I am able to get into the Resource team's data storage and can now access any of their sensors. Interestingly, none of the cams show a hint of anything untoward. All cleaned up. I made a copy earlier of the key graphics and data and put it in

my private storage. I have a feeling those are going to disappear from the original location.

The stream of field DNA samples continues as far as I can tell—but I can't get Doc or Vanessa to open up about it. All quiet. I think it's because nobody wants to get chewed on by David if they say the wrong thing at the wrong moment.

I don't hear much talk around the camp about misconduct. You would think it would spread like juicy gossip normally does. I've only talked about it with Carol, privately, and David officially. I hinted at it to Mark and he seemed to hint back that he knows—hard to say with him. I thought Tracy might be a talker, but apparently not.

Correction

"She did what? Military?"

"Exactly what we are doing now," I reply.

"Really. I've heard her name of course. Lillian. Lily. I like it. And I know about her later exploits but didn't realize she had something like this under her belt. I say I know... Really I just know from the 'incident' at central government."

"That's what gets played up, but she had a whole career before that. I finally took the time to research her. I read a little about her way back, when they announced our ship. Lillian Hobbe, explorer, pioneer, and so on. I think I told you. Right?"

From her look, I sense that there is more on her mind than history and so I hold back any more comments.

"So..." begins Carol, waiting until she has my full attention and eye contact, "About the shenanigans—David is really pissed at Wes? You didn't mention it when we talked about it before." I think I see a slight smile on her face.

"Looks that way. But what makes you think that?"

"People talk; you hear things."

"He didn't get outwardly upset when we talked. I think he was shaken, but hid it well.. But seems he's over it already to me. And I am guessing he's made some conclusion about the effect it all has had on the mission. That's what the meeting is going to be about. Damage control."

"I'm not invited."

"I am and I hope not to get an assignment out of it."

A small group shuffles past our corner table in the mess hall as we take a couple of bites. We talk of it sometimes as 'our' table. I don't know why really. The tables are all the same. It has to be location and familiarity. It's a corner, it's more or less private, usually, and we don't have to check out the surroundings; they are always the same. That's where the feeling comes from. It's 'ours.'

"Mark says he is on schedule for his work; we are about half way through now, assuming no surprises. I'm going to miss this place when we leave. When are we going back to the bluffs?"

"Half way or not, it's a long time yet before you will have to miss it. The bluffs? I don't know when," I say. "You ready? I'm in. Let's do it."

————

The meeting is a small one: just myself, David and Brachus, and that's why I'm uncomfortable. Here we sit, each knowing what has happened but no one

248

acknowledging any of it directly. David has yet to come out with any public statement. I do know one thing: I'd never run things like this.

"There is a problem that needs to be handled right away," is David's opening remark. That's encouraging—sounds like a leader. "The course of the last few, well, more than a few, generations of the natives we've been monitoring have shown a significant drift away from the ideal genetic configuration." He pauses and looks us over; Brachus is not making eye contact with me and has not done so since we first sat down.

David continues, "Let me restate that in a different way. We have a directive, part of our mission, to assess the situation on this planet. To see if things, specifically the human… yes, the human natives are progressing along the path expected and desired. To test that progress, we have a template function based on time and other variables that allows us to make a quantitative determination of their current state relative to the expected and desired one. Beyond that, we have the ability to predict the likely future evolution of the correspondence of empirical data to theoretical. You both have heard this before. Any questions you have, answer them on your own time. It's all documented."

After another pause, during which we are all three silent, he adds, "The reason for the prediction algorithm is to prevent, if possible, a costly delay in the development of this environment. If the prediction positively indicates a problem of this nature … that is, the likely development of a non-ideal or worse, population … if it indicates the environment is moving down an unacceptable path…" David clears his throat before resuming, "we are charged with not only reporting that situation but also with the responsibility to correct it.

"We are going to correct it, and you both are going to help make it happen. Wes, you stay. Shipley, leave us now; I will call you back in in a few minutes."

Ok, it's not exactly what I was expecting but it's something. I had the feeling he was going to try to 'correct' the gene pool problem and that's what he says he is going to do. But no mention of any wrongdoing or censure of Wes. That still might be coming, but so far nothing, not even a hint. He talked about our responsibility to correct it. I would have added 'especially if we caused it' to that statement.

I get David's message and rejoin the meeting.

"I have charged Wesley with overseeing and executing the necessary steps to ensure our mission is successful." He nods to Brachus, who gets up and leaves after a cool courtesy nod to me. "Jason, sit down. We are off the record now.

"There have no doubt been a couple screw-ups, as you well know. And I do thank you for bringing them to my attention." He pauses, and then says, "I take full responsibility. It's my fault, and it's my problem."

"But you…"

"Let me finish. I am not going to let my mistakes up to this point taint the mission. I know what you are thinking and believe me Wesley knows exactly how I feel about… all of this. That's precisely the reason I am having him clean it up.

"Now, your part. I need you to help clean up too," David says, and I can feel a different mood overtake him in that his face has softened and the tone of his voice has mellowed. He works his lip a couple times before speaking. "Did any part of the Resource team's data—their private channel—yet make it to the main system archives? I mean is any of it…"

"I know what you mean. I will have to check but I don't think so. It seems to me that the reason for their insistence on private communication and data storage was for situations just like this and so…"

"There are other reasons for privacy, so don't go there. Back to the point. Please take a look. Verify that nothing makes it through except for bone fide mission documents. If any of it did make it through… well, let me know what you find and…" and David trails off looking as if for me to finish his thought.

It's my turn to pause, look David in the eye, and say, "I understand. I'll take care of it." No need to mention right now that I have made my own copy and have it safely tucked away.

———

"I did get an assignment after all, but my part is easy. Important to David and our mission legacy, and easy in the execution," I say to Carol out at the bluffs. It is late evening and the warm breeze has died. The clear sky holds an impressive canopy of stars and we are on our backs looking up. The hiss of the surf endlessly cycles through its frequency shift: low, slowly rising, rising, and then effortlessly and quickly falling low once again to start over. The waves are coming in at an angle to the shore and so the sound has the additional feature of pleasantly gliding from right to left, north to south. I check my genie but am careful to keep the illumination low so as not to degrade my night vision.

"What are you doing? Do you keep looking at the time?"

"Nothing. No reason. Just checking the proximity alarm."

"But there's nothing out here to be afraid of. You've told me this more than once."

"Have I? That's right, don't worry, there's…" At last a bright speck catches my eye, moving against the background of stars. "There. See? There it is. Right on time."

"What? Oh, there it is. I see it. What is… oh, that's the old girl herself isn't it. That's the ship!"

"Right you are." We are both watching silently for several heartbeats. "Grigor's up there at the moment."

"Yes, awesome. Grigor? Wait, I think… Yes, I see him.

Odd… he seems to be complaining about something," Carol says and laughs.

She's the best. We watch the speck of the ship glide past. I am happy and relieved that I said something to David. It was the right thing to do. I am also happy to be with Carol. I roll over toward her and embrace her. We kiss.

"Don't start something you can't finish," she whispers in her teasing way.

"Don't worry."

The times away with Carol are magical and refreshing. We have already talked about when we can do it again. Where to go? We both like our spot on the bluffs. Sometimes the wind is too much, and nearly constant, but the scenery along the coast, the isolation—can we beat that? Porter said something about his favorite spot, east was it?

The problem with going inland is the loss of the isolation factor. And not just from people, but animals too. It's wild out there. If there were a small island… Carol has done extensive mapping; it's time to check it out.

My part in David's 'correction plan' is done. Brachus has disappeared from the base camp area lately, as has Lester. I met with Craig and Porter together at the mess hall and they are pretty shook up about something. They clammed up when I joined them. You could see from their faces that something's wrong—pale, unsmiling. They are not expert at hiding their emotions. They wouldn't hold eye contact and were slow in responding, even to casual conversation.

Mark seems normal. He's not as swamped as he was, apparently, and has some new little pet project he's doing on the side. Wouldn't show me.

Dylan's not normal. I mean, he's recovered from the cat attack, but he's got something serious on his mind. I know because he stalked right into David's base camp quarters when Carol and I were out once again at the rock ledge seat. We could see his determination as he went in. They were in there a long time and when he came out his expression was grim. Not his usual demeanor at all.

Drastic Measures

"I can't believe it. I really can't." His eyes are misty and he keeps moving them from one person to the next, and then back to the images he is holding in his hands.

We are in the mess hall with a small number of the crew minus Wes and Les, minus David and Doc. Carol left already.

"Can I see again?" Tracy asks. Dylan flips the pictures toward her across the small dining table. They slide and separate and end up near enough for her to grasp.

"You can't hide something like this. It's massive destruction of several adjoining populations in the lowlands." Dylan is livid. "I went to David. I went... I went too late."

"What are we looking at here exactly?"

Dylan peers across at the page she has on top. "Let me see it." She tilts it. "That's the 'before'. Look at it next to the other. The pictures are of nearly the same area. The clouds are hiding some... You can spot the landmarks. Look."

I get closer and look too. The edge of 'our' mountains is just inside the image and I can make out the coastline nearest to us. Those look the same. But other features are different. The one large lake—the one into which the little bio camp stream empties—is different. Its shoreline has changed, expanded dramatically.

"Ok fellas, that's it," says Grigor when he looks up from the images and around the table at all of us. "You see what's happening? You do see... right? What have I told you? These are the people we are takin' orders from? This is what we're here for? Good luck to us all." And he walks away muttering, roughly brushing past Mark, Aileen and Alain.

Although no one says anything, I can see their glances. I can see their looks.

"Mark—wait. Don't go. I need to get down there again. What've you got?"

"Yeah, sure Dyl sure. Jimmy, fix 'im up."

————

"What exactly happened?" Carol asks after we get back. I went out with Dylan to see too. Carol thought he shouldn't go alone. She was correct.

"A few things happened, all more or less at the same time." "The guys are talking. Not Brachus or Lester, but the others are."

"Yes, yes. Go on."

I glance around and behind me; we are at our table in the

256

corner of the mess hall. "I think David got scared. Maybe he scared Wes too. The idea that any 'fingerprints' remain must've done it. It looks like the traces of meddling were eliminated…"

"Is that what Dylan was showing us?"

"That's the main part. The lowlands where a large portion of the people were living was flooded."

"Flooded. But how? I saw… I know about the big lake. Was it deliberately…?"

"Looks like it," I reply and as I look up I see Carol looking over my head.

"That's bull, man. It's the rainy season down there. They were gettin' washed away by the minute." It's Lester. He must've heard some of our conversation.

"Uh-huh. So you guys didn't do anything to…

"It was full, overflowing. It would have gone any second anyway."

"So you did. You 'helped' it along…"

"Look, we saved the people we were told. We saved 'em. We're the good guys here." He rakes his shiny hair straight back and has an expectant look. Expectant and vulnerable.

"You're the… You're somethin' all right." I avert my eyes from him trying to make it clear that we had a private conversation going. "Where were we, Carol?"

Lester leaves without saying a word more. I was expecting a snide closing remark—but nothing.

"What in the world does he mean, the good guys?"

"Carol, look, without picking a right or wrong, I can see both sides. Assume David's worried. He is. He's got to be. Ok, we still have a chance to fix this—I'm thinking as he would now—and get back on track. That's what he's saying. What with the so-called giants, the interbreeding, whatever other supposedly sterile rejects from the old bio camp were mixing in—the genome is messed up. And the evidence is out there. Was out there." I look at Carol to see any reaction before continuing. Nothing so far, she's just listening. "That's what he means—they cleaned it up. From that perspective, it's a good thing."

"Is there no other way…" Carol starts but she trails off.

"Of course," I say, and again look around to see we are not overheard. "The right way is to not let it ever come to this. That's where it went wrong. But it did, and they did, and here we are."

Carol says, "For sure my opinion of David has dropped several steps; my opinion of Wesley remains the same; it cannot drop further. Do you actually think David okayed this? This method?"

"My personal opinion? No. I think he left it up to Brachus. The details anyway. The guys were saying too that there

258

were some relocations. Not many. And also some chemical sterilization, not just the flooding. I'll bet you any money though that Brachus either didn't think the area affected would be so large or else never thought it would get the attention that it has. One of the two.'"

"Dylan was pretty upset."

"Yes he is and I'll tell you something else. He normally keeps cool and calm but he told me that he went to David and said 'Never again'."

The concept of massive annihilation is troubling, and not to just a few of us. It takes a real effort of will to look towards the long term benefits.

David made a general and official announcement about the current status. He emphasized that his work, our work, has led to the happy discovery of one small subset of the population, a family really, that has, in fact, far surpassed our mission target and will, given enough time, surely spread to cover the globe. He has charged Brachus with monitoring them and taking the necessary steps to see that they flourish. That was it.

It amazes me that leaders such as David, but not only him if history tells us anything, seem to have a capacity for self-delusion. That is, in this case, even though inept manipulation and unethical interference by David and at least some of his crew have resulted in the wholesale slaughter of thousands, the right person can spin the situation

259

such that it seems like a good thing. It's as if the fact that we ourselves caused the problem can be forgotten.

Carol and I both feel that, given his level of emotional maturity, leaving Brachus to see to it that the select group 'flourishes' is a mistake. It's just asking for more trouble. Why is it that David doesn't get it?

Part IV

Field Reports

I don't get it. Sure it's a wonder, it's a marvel, but let's go back already.

"Isn't that something?" asks Porter, his glasses more askew than usual.

"Yeah, something," I respond without really looking anymore.

"No, look. Look over there—where the glacier meets the ocean. A sharp line. Looks like it's been cut with a knife," exclaims Mark.

"Mark, you're getting awful excited about this. You haven't been getting out much, have you?" I counter, still not looking. I am not impressed with our flyover of the northern polar region. Ok, maybe the first few minutes. But when you've seen one incredibly vast blindingly white nearly featureless expanse…

"That's all water ice and snow?" Porter asks, looking first at me, then Mark.

"Absolutely, temp and pressure tells it all. It has to be. Maybe some pockets… No, I don't think so; it's all H2O," answers Mark.

"Shall we go down and see?"

"No," I say immediately.

"Right over there. See? Right there—looks like a safe spot. What kind of ground signal?"

"Says we are good. If we sink in, I'll get us right out. Hold tight just in case."

"Am I not here? Can you not hear me? I said 'no'. Am I out voted—is that it?" I ask of no one in particular and their response is to ignore me once more. We settle without incident and these two tourists are already preparing to exit. The blast of arctic air only reinforces my desire to not get out. "Guys. Seriously. Are we not adults? You act like you've never…"

"Come on. Sure, we've all seen ice and snow. It's like a vacation. Come on, we're getting out."

"You have to get out."

"No, I don't have to get out."

Out they go. These supposed adults are making sounds like children out there. It does seem like we are on solid ground. Or ice. I see we are at 90 West and 62 North.

I remember one time we went on vacation to a snowy area—Mom, Dad, Tom and I. I was real young, just in the first grade or maybe second. It was the usual stuff, playing in the snow, sledding. I don't remember what all, but I do remember what happened on one of the mornings. There was a new snowfall, fresh and deep. I don't know where Tom was; when you're young, an age difference, even a couple years, is huge and we didn't hang out like we did in later years. I was all bundled up and out by myself in the bright sunshine in the snow. On me it was deep enough to make walking difficult, but walk I did, enjoying being the first to explore the pristine landscape—alone against the wilderness, sort of. I wandered off and up the side of a small hill, but the wind had blown the snow such that the contour of the ground was hard to judge visually. I lost my footing, turned and fell backwards off the side of the hill into a deep drift. I was OK but at first disoriented by what had happened and by the handful of snow melting wet on my face and eyes. As I lay on my back looking up at the clear deep blue sky through a perfect outline of my body, I realized I was indeed alone. In all likelihood, no one knew where I was and certainly no one could see me. With my bulky snow outfit I wasn't cold in the least, but was restricted in movement. It felt like I couldn't move my arms or legs, surrounded as they were. It's then that it dawned on me that I might have fallen into a serious situation. A moment of panic, and then I realized I had no choice. It's up to me to get out. No one else is coming; no one else knows I'm even here! With some thrashing and twisting I eventually righted myself and plowed my way out of the nearly neck-high drift. The panic was real; the thrill and relief of survival was too.

Well, I'd better go out and see what they're up to after all—just in case they break a leg or something. I don't hear any more laughing and shouting. Worst case, I will have to drag their frozen carcasses back inside. Whoa, it's cold—really cold if I face the wind! Right after I exit the runabout and look for them I catch a snowball on the left side of my face and neck, just below the ear. Perfect. Some snow gets in one eye and I have to wipe and blink it clear. I see Mark grinning like an idiot and preparing more ammunition. I quickly scoop up some snow of my own and retaliate. I miss Mark by a wide margin but to my delight Porter is a better aim and hits him square in the chest. With this distraction I am able to fire off a couple more at Mark and quickly retreat to the safety and warmth of the interior. That's plenty for me.

"Lousy packing anyway," complains Mark as they both finally climb back in, red-faced and panting. "Too cold."

"If you boys are done playing, can we head back now? Please shut the hatch, my hands have almost thawed." Porter has to clean his glasses—they are wet and have fogged over after coming in from the cold.

———

It's not long after the polar sightseeing trip that I have a chance to sit and talk with Porter again. More about his discoveries as he has been shuttling people and materials all over the planet.

"Volcanoes, you say? And active at that?"

"Active and spewing! From complete and permanent ice cover to spewing molten rock. And everything in between. Anytime you wanna see any of it, let me know."

"You're going to kill yourself out there."

"Might be. The volcanic ash is a killer all right. It gets in everywhere and is abrasive as all get out."

"'As all get out'? Ha. That's a good one. Where did that come from I wonder? I mean originally."

"Huh? It's abrasive, that's all. Really abrasive. And it gets in everywhere. I know 'cause I went right thru an ash cloud."

"Oh, I get you alright. I was just thinking of the origin of the phrase 'all get out.' Ever think about that sort of thing?"

"Um, no, can't say that I do," replies Porter with a look of puzzlement. "But, like I say…"

"No, that's ok. Don't worry about it. Thanks for the sightseeing offer, and I'll take you up on it sometime. I bet Carol would like to see some of that."

"Anytime, pal, anytime."

"Anytime? Anytime what? You guys want another go at the frozen north?" says Mark as he approaches and sits with us.

"Yeah, sure, I still have one good eye," I quip. "How goes it, Mark?"

"Oh it goes, and it goes." Mark gives me a look that I

interpret as meaning 'I've got plenty to say but I'm not going to do it now.'

"Hey Mark," says Porter in greeting. "Let's all go again! We're expecting Dylan, Craig, Trace, and Aileen in any minute. Aileen won't come but…"

"Nope, their flyer is mine as soon as they land. And I'm busy with it for the rest of this week. Maybe after that." Again with the look. It's easy to tell something is going on, with Mark, but it's no use trying to guess.

Small talk ensues, which I block out effectively and wonder what Carol would think of a visit to the arctic. I hear the arrival of one of the flyers and sure enough Dylan and Craig and the girls debark and head off to another part of base camp. It crosses my mind that these men and women are the future the dean spoke of. And Porter too. They are eager, competent, confident and, I believe, trustworthy. I can see them fulfilling the vision statement from what seems to me now so long ago. Where do I fit into that vision? They nod as they pass, see Mark's questioning look, and Craig gives him a thumbs up. As I turn back, Mark and Porter are both looking at me.

"Well?" says Mark.

"Well what?" I reply. "Sorry, I've been daydreaming. What's the question?"

"I said, do you have time to give me a hand? I've got to upfit that transport and could use some help. Porter here has told me to go pound sand," he repeats with a wink to

Porter.

"Sure, as long as you don't ambush me with a snowball in the eye."

"You'll like meeting his new girlfriend. Hubba hubba," says Porter.

"Just be careful with your hubba hubba, Jimmy. You might get a nasty shock if you go poking around where you shouldn't," Mark says, laughing himself to hiccups again.

————

I meet Mark later. He is already at work, and doesn't stop when I come in. "What can I do to help?"

"First, don't touch anything. And then, push that cart over here…"

"Without touching will be tricky. Say, what's that there? I see what Porter meant." I ask when I spot something interesting beside his test bench. It's always something interesting with Mark.

He sees what I am looking at, says again, "Don't touch it. Her. You like that? She's my golden girl."

"Classy!" It's clearly a robotic 'girl' all shiny and new. "Is this for real? I mean does she work?"

"Oh, she works. Mostly. I've been printing out parts for some time; my new little hobby. The design has been around for a long time and has been proven out, but to build her you need a shitload of tiny components with tight tolerances. You have to make special tiny tools just to assemble the darn thing."

"She's a beauty, Mark. You do good work. Um... nice job on the exterior form. Where did you say you want this cart?"

"Yep, right under here. This way. More. Perfect, right there. Thanks." And he begins to lift and fit equipment onto the flyers. "Did you get a chance to talk to Dylan?"

"Not really, just hi and bye. Only briefly. He says he will be around a while."

"He's at it again."

"He is? What do you mean?"

"Our favorite leader. He's at it again." Mark keeps working, after looking to see if I get it, but I don't get it. "Can you hold this here while I attach it? Here, it's heavy. And the holes have to line up."

We get the hardware in position and I hold it. "You mean David?" but I see by the 'you must be a moron' look that I'm wrong. "Oh, I see. Weasel. *Now* what's he up to?"

"Only what I hear from the field. I can let you know more tomorrow after I personally deliver this flyer to him." He stops speaking and continues with the assembly. "You know he's still running the show out there. And this is after what you and I both know he's done."

270

"First of all, nothing he does would surprise me. Second, who *wouldn't* predict more shenanigans from this guy? But what do you hear? Do *not* tell me he's got his hands on the native girls again!"

"Yes. No. Not exactly. He's morphed a bit, according to Dylan. Back to his old self after being so sweet and friendly around camp, which nobody could miss. He knows that he's being watched but he also knows that David's given him a fair amount of control. Correct?"

I don't answer but instead look questioningly at Mark.

"Well? You were in the meeting weren't you? I wasn't."

"Oh, from the meeting a while back." I can't think of any reason to hold back so I say, "Blank check."

"Eh?"

"Free hand. David gave him free reign to monitor and shepherd the subjects," I confess. "But they also talked in private; I don't know what was said then."

"I see. That explains why I've heard the 'I can do anything I want' routine from Lester. Didn't you say he pulled that on you once?"

Mark wipes his hands a moment, brushes the hair off his forehead, then starts back again at his work while motioning me out of the way. "At least his new interest has taken some of the focus off the other business that

271

he's gotten me into."

When Mark doesn't follow up, I ask, "What else is he up to?"

"Oh, it's not a big deal, relatively. Nothing to do with his other messes. I'll tell you later maybe, over a cocktail, but not now. Thanks for the help."

As the native generations pass, our target population is steadily growing more or less arithmetically. Field reports show their increase and also comprise a log of the interaction with various mission members. Dylan is playing an active part, even more than before. He is still smarting over the 're-start,' as it's being called. When we talk, he is grimmer than he has been. Still the same, quiet and thoughtful, but with an added sense of resolve.

I've been thinking lately about words. Words as symbols. Words and how they work. For example, nothing changes when an object is named and yet it cannot be denied that there is a palpable feeling of power and control accompanying the act. But how does the simple act of naming—creating a symbol representing a complex object—enhance creative thought and communication? If anything, it's just an act of substitution; long string replaced by short symbol. A long string such as: 'a surface sufficiently elevated and stable, whose normal vector lies essentially anti parallel to local gravity, with enough area to facilitate the handy placement of other, usually smaller, objects. All that replaced by a short symbol such as, in this case, 'table.'

It must be that the sheer number of references in a complex sentence is sufficient to stimulate the mind to higher levels. I think about a sentence like 'The wooden dining table is sometimes used as a work desk but primarily functions as a support for our daily meals and as such becomes a symbol of unity for us as a family.' To write out the basic references for each word and to describe the sentence syntax and qualifiers (such as 'sometimes' and 'primarily' and 'as such') could, for this one sentence, take up an entire volume. That's a lot of power in a small package.

A dream with my hands came again, triggered no doubt by our polar adventure not too long ago. They were my hands, in thick yellow gloves. I was standing next to a snow bank digging and chopping my way into it with no tools, just the gloved hands. I had no sensation of cold. The visual scene was dominated by brilliant white. Progress into the bank didn't seem important but the act of chopping at the snow was the main point. It was fun. There was an enjoyable feeling of power.

Confirmation

Everyone who was outside at base camp heard it. The explosion, I mean. I heard it. It was distant, muffled, but we knew right away it was an explosion. Not huge, no global effects certainly, and we could see nothing from our location. But that's not surprising the way we are nestled in the mountains. Grigor, back on solid ground now, says he felt it and Carol says she did too. I haven't spoken in person to Dylan but he contacted me via genie to say that a whole settlement has been wiped out. Brachus' decision, he said.

"Brachus said it had to be done," Dylan explained. "No other clarification has been offered, nor do I expect one. Here we go again."

"Did you see it?"

As we speak, we are up in the mountains in the next little rocky valley over from base camp. Not a valley to speak of but a notch in between peaks. Mark is supervising some serious work higher up and a few of us have gathered to watch the activity.

A shake of the head is the response, no eye contact from Dylan. He's looking up at the progress of the work, but not looking at any one of us at the moment.

Two of the Power and Energy guys are down from the ship and are working alongside Mark. They are all business and have Porter tied up lifting and positioning equipment.

"This is crazy, what with the wind and all." The sun is just clearing the mountains and the warmth of its rays is welcome.

"Did you know it was coming?" Aileen asks. She and Tracy are standing and leaning back against the stone, full in the sun. I am sitting on the edge of the central formation we've nicknamed Table Rock with Alain, Rick and Chris.

This time Dylan looks around as if trying to see who asked the question and nods and says, "Yes, I knew. I got some of the people that I knew should be spared out of harm's way, but that doesn't amount to much."

"Do you know why he did it?"

"No, not exactly. He's on his own out there and answers to no one. I wanted to be actively involved with the descendants and that he *has* given me. In fact, I think Wesley is glad to not have to deal with them so much on a personal level. His focus, if you ask me, is on a larger scale now. Groups, not individuals."

"I think you're all gettin' worked up over nothin'," says Rick. "These ones had to go; they were outlaws from the old bunch."

He looks first at Dylan, who doesn't meet his gaze, and
276

then at me.

"They're not part of the program. Had to go," Rick repeats, looking, it seems, for a response.

Mark walks briskly through the area, around Table Rock and around us, followed closely by one of the P&E men.

"Mark…"

"Not now. Rick, come with us." Rick joins them as they pass by and out of this area, higher up the notch.

"What does he mean?" I ask, speaking of Rick's comments.

Chris says, "What he means is, the little settlement that was blasted was a pocket of leftovers from the outcasts—the ones that are not part of the select group. They should have been dealt with before, during the re-start, but were missed."

"Little bit of overkill, eh? The way he did it? Don't ya think?" asks Tracy, face pointed up towards the sun, eyes closed.

"Could be, but he said these were retrogressive and dangerous. More animal, less human. He must've seen something that disgusted him because he didn't hesitate long."

"And now he's run to David," adds Dylan.

"Maybe he doesn't want to get stabbed in the back," says Lester, appearing from around the bend of the trail leading into the small Table Rock clearing. He's looking right at me.

I don't respond to his comment, and no one else speaks either.

"Chris. Go find Mark, he needs more help. Where's Rick?"

"Mark took him."

"Alain, girls, come with me. We're heading out. Not you Waters, you wait to hear from Wes. He'll get hold of you real soon I'm sure." Lester and his small troop head back toward base camp.

"So you think he went to David to head off any complaints?" I ask Dylan when we are alone.

"Of course he did. He's a loose cannon, but he learns. I've been out in the field a lot. I see what he's been doing. I've said it before—he has no respect for the people here."

"What do you mean, he's playing around again? Girls? Fighting?"

"Not so much that, although you can hardly talk to him anymore he's so full of himself. No, he's playing war games now."

"War games? You mean like the fights he was promoting before?"

"Yes, but now it's groups."

"Really, how so?"

"You know that there are other populations scattered around the globe, yes? And there have been since the beginning. And they have seen us, accidentally or incidentally you might say, but they are not our primary focus, these others. There is only one population that we are looking at now, the descendants from the re-start, to make sure that they have a fighting chance to multiply and prosper. Right? This is what we are doing. Mark is continuing to replenish and refit for our eventual departure but, in the meantime, that's what we are doing."

"Ok, I'm with you."

"As you can imagine, 'our' population is more or less surrounded by 'outsiders'—various separate groups, not one large one—and there are naturally border disputes. You have an almost constant display of aggression for land, food, women or anything else of value. Some groups have learned agriculture, some metallurgy, others not so much. Threats and force are one way for groups to get what they need or want. So…"

"Yes, so…?"

"So, the cultures have learned that their planet is a rich source of metals such as iron and they are now using and developing that resource. They know how to make both offensive and defensive armaments, as well as non-military tools. These are all manual weapons and tools mind you—

279

they have so far no kind of engine other than animal power. What it means is that they can whip up some ferociously bloody battles that go on all day, decimating whole populations, sometimes one person at a time. Sometimes, these battles threaten 'our' people. I will try to communicate, in various ways, when I see trouble brewing, to see that bloodshed is avoided or minimized. But Wesley, he likes to play military strategist." Dylan offers me a piece of the snack he has been nibbling on while talking. It looks like more of the dried meat. I decline and he doesn't force the issue. "He likes to play war games with these groups."

"You don't mean…" I say as I start to form an image of Brachus, the soldier. "You surely don't mean he is out amid the people, fighting."

For the first time ever, to my memory, I see Dylan almost laugh. "No. Not even. He might do it if he was in no danger whatsoever. Come to think, maybe he has gone out and pretended he's a great warrior. I can tell you this: He would never go out with their primitive armor and weapons. Not on your life. What he does do is assess a battle's combatants, as a whole, decide who's got the advantage, and, if it's not our people, arrange things so that we do have the advantage in some way."

"Dylan, I can see you are not kidding. You are serious."

"No, I'm not kidding. But you may have missed the best part. I said he's manipulating things so that our people win or at the very least, minimizes their damage. You see? He's doing what David asked him to do. He's playing war games, with real people, and he can always point to the results and say, 'See, this is what I was told to accomplish.' Our guys are prospering, multiplying and expanding their territory."

"Are you one hundred percent sure about this?"

"I am one hundred percent sure."

"What is wrong with this guy?" No answer and I don't expect one. "Let me guess, Lester buys into the whole scheme."

"Certainly he does. They assess and plan and execute together. Can I say it? I think they are having a ball out there."

It's clear that he's uncomfortable with the image of these two cronies using people like game pieces. He decides to continue, after finishing his snack, and says, "Do you want to help? I'm tracking the main families, but there are quite a few now and they are dispersing, sometimes of their own will, sometimes not. We are keeping a special eye on those lineages with the highest correlation to ideal. I figure that will give us the best shot at David's vision. I could use you out in the field."

This is something to think about. My contact with the people lately has been essentially nil.

"Don't worry; we can make you look like one of them. Worst case, they will treat you as a stranger, not as an enemy," Dylan says, no doubt noting my hesitation. "You may not even have to mingle at all, just observe from a distance, or remotely, and report. I'll keep you out of trouble, if I can. What do you say?"

———————

"What do you say?" I ask Carol when we are alone a few days after hearing Dylan's proposal. "He says as a couple, we will be more accepted should it happen that we find ourselves in direct contact. And we will."

I am used to her silence as she thinks things over. I like this part. She is deliberate and logical.

"Let's do it," she says at last. "I don't know what will happen, but I would like to think we can make a difference. If he needs help, let's help him. When can he give us the language and customs basics?"

———————

"What, are you nuts? At this late notice?" exclaims Mark when I tell him of our resolve just before we head out. We are going to a remote site that Dylan is using for the time being as his moveable field 'headquarters.' It is there that we will get outfitted to pass as natives.

"But, you already knew about this didn't you? This is why we need you, or someone, to shuttle us out. That's why I reserved the runabout."

"Oh, so that's what it's about," Mark says in an unconvincing tone. "I think I heard a word about it." He continues to putter about pretending, it seems, to be concerned with other matters. "You know, maybe I will pilot you out myself. There might be something interesting I can show …" Mark finishes his thought in a low tone that I can't catch.

"Hmm? What's that? You're mumbling again."

"Nothing. I'm old. I talk to myself." And then, "Right. It's settled. I'll take you. One thing: I may come and get you on short notice. There just possibly will be something you would like to see."

"Something, eh? I have no idea where we'll be. Could be anywhere."

"I'll find you. Just be ready and watch for my message. I'll give you as much notice as I can."

———

Carol and I only spend a few days at Dylan's makeshift camp being trained, before he decides to relocate. His contacts in the field are widely scattered over a large area and he's found a few well-hidden spots to use as temporary bases for his forays into native communities. He continues instructing us at the new location and stresses 'quiet confidence' as our best tool. 'If you look like you belong, and act like you belong, you belong,' he says.

For our first outing, Dylan guides us to a common area in a settlement, a marketplace where food, clothing, and other goods are exchanged. It's early in the day and people are milling about, setting up their goods, mostly on the ground. The few structures are simple and crude. We separate from Dylan, but keep close in case of the unexpected, which of course happens immediately. We are accosted by a merchant who is not deterred by our persistent 'no' and refusal gestures. He seems to insist that Carol look at his wares and soon decides to take me by the arm to stop us from moving away. It is not clear to me if we are dealing strictly with a rude salesman or if there is something wrong with my accent or words. While I resist the pull of the man, I decline to react more strongly so as not to escalate the situation.

Fortunately, Dylan has noticed the problem and comes quickly to our rescue. He doesn't hesitate to firmly remove the merchant's hand from me while I see him smile politely, and hear him saying 'no, not these two' and something about us being 'outlanders.'

The merchant responds meekly, to my surprise, bows slightly, and turns to harass other potential customers physically and verbally.

"What's the secret?" I ask when we are out of earshot of anyone else.

"No secret. Only what I told you. Quiet, confident, and firm. Remember, you are not from around here. You only know a few words of the language. You know how to say that at least. Say it."

With Dylan, we go to a dwelling of some of 'our' people. There must be a large family living in this rude abode judging by the number of children and the level of activity.

"Remember, they will invite you to eat. You *must* politely refuse; if you do not, you will have to eat their food and sit while you do. You're not ready for that. Even if you would eat, it wouldn't work. They would have plenty of time to ask you questions you would not be able to answer." We see that some of the adults look at us and some recognize Dylan. He returns the nod of a couple of the men.

Still a little shaken by our close encounter with the merchant and after a quick glance at Carol, I say, "You are right. Please make our excuses for us. We will meet you back near where we came in to town. You know the spot where we turn off the road."

There are no further surprises in town. Carol and I wait alone together outside the village. We are close to a well-worn path. Close enough to see the few passersby, but not close enough to be targets for casual conversation with them. Our garments are loose fitting and as such allow us to carry essentials not visible to others. We snack on some of our processed food while waiting. I sit leaning against a tree determined to enjoy the wait. Carol is leaning against the tree too, right next to me.

"I'd like to know more," she says quietly. "More about their daily life here. Like, was this a normal day in the village? Or was this 'market day' or something. Seemed like a lot of men were around. Shouldn't they be out hunting and gathering?"

"Good question, but part wrong. The females would be gathering, males hunting."

An old man appears on the path, sees us, makes eye contact, nods as he passes going in towards the settlement. But then he turns around making a gesture as if to ask if he may join us where we sit. As he approaches, we both nod and say, "Please." He doesn't start or make any other sign that our accent or pronunciation is suspect. Nice! We three now sit in silence for a few moments when, unthinkably, my genie makes a loud and clear beep. Our new companion doesn't react. Carol inconspicuously jabs me with her elbow. It beeps again, but the old man still doesn't react. Is he deaf?

I fumble hurriedly and as discreetly as I can, trying to disable audio on the communicator without bringing it out in the open, when the old man turns to us and says, "Shall we go?"

I am too dumbfounded to respond. Carol begins to laugh. I look at her, then back to our visitor.

"It's me you idiot," says Mark. "Carol recognized me right away. She's good." He adds, "You should really use vibrate mode out here."

"What are you doing here?" I ask, still coming to grips with the revelation.

"I heard from Dylan; he's tied up. And there's something going on not too far away that I want you to see. I think you will be interested in what may happen this evening and we have to get going." Mark pauses for a moment, looking me over. "Why so surprised? I told you I might be coming." I shake my head no, but he counters by saying, "Yes, I did tell you and I said that I would give you as much notice as I could. This is it."

After he startled us—no—startled me near the settlement, we hiked to Dylan's field dome camp where Mark got out of his getup. Carol and I didn't change. The runabout was hidden nearby and we were soon on our way. Mark is in high demand, however, and we had an unexpected detour to base camp.

On the way in we three talked about the juxtaposition of primitive development and current technology. For us, it's a simple matter of stepwise accommodation when technology advances at home. Some new technology is introduced and, sooner or later, it is no longer novel, no longer new. Another technology comes along—the same thing. It's similar to watching a child grow. You see him or her every day, you don't notice the changes, but changes there are, and they accumulate. If you don't see that child for a few years, then the changes can be startling.

But here, on this world, the steps from their current state to ours are almost beyond counting. There is no 'accommodation time' long enough, in my opinion. Imagine one of these locals having a look at Amara from orbit, or seeing any number of our myriad technologies—it just wouldn't compute.

Carol agrees, but Mark says no. He says you hand one of them a genie, show what it does and how to us it, they would be all over it. I say impossible; he's just saying that to be contrary.

At base, we separate with instructions from Mark to stay close and ready to go. I have a few moments alone in the mess hall to log these latest developments.

Witness

Unexpectedly, I am joined at a mess hall table by David.

"Jason, how are you?"

"Fine. I'm fine. Are you holding up?"

David nods but does not smile. "Tell me about yourself. I know some of your background; tell me about your family."

I give him the briefest rundown and he perks up when I mention my brother.

"He left, just like that?"

"Just like that. Took some sort of testing job. I don't know the details. Couldn't take being cooped up in a cube. We left just after I found out."

"Well, good for him. Sometimes you have to have a change."

"He's always had some odd ideas. Like his limits and borders ideas."

"Yes, limits and borders. What about them? Go on."

"He's always had a thing about limits. It's a kind of universal principle with him. He thinks limits are everything. I mean, they cause everything." I pause, but David doesn't respond. He's thinking and working his habit. "I'm not saying it right. He can explain it to where it starts to make sense. Limits define everything, that's what he says. You know, the blank sheet of paper concept."

"No. Explain."

"Ok. Students go into a class. The teacher says 'write a one page paper.' What happens?"

"Ok, a one page paper. On what topic?"

"Exactly."

"Exactly?"

"If the teacher said 'write a page on your family' the students could begin immediately. But you see without the limit, without the topic, you get a blank stare from most, me included, because neither they nor I have any idea what to write. And he says the topic is irrelevant – could be anything at all. It's the…"

"It's the limit that makes it go. I see. He has a point, your brother. Very interesting."

"If Tom were here, he could tell you more. Like life itself. Without the limit of the cell wall, inside from outside, none of us," indicating we two, "would exist. Limits. You see?"

"I do see. Again. He is right. I will think about this some more for sure. Did he have any words of wisdom on how to use this principle? How do you put it to work?"

"I wish he were here. I can't tell you how to use it. Sorry!"

"Jason, thanks. Good talking to you. I needed a break."

————

Mark pilots the three of us out of base camp and back in the general direction from which we lately came. He's being all secretive except to say that there is something we should see. For a change, I'm not watching our course or coordinates closely and instead enjoy the view of the landscape passing below us in the afternoon sun. I seem to see a worried expression on Mark's face as he looks back at us. No, he's looking at Carol. This makes me worry now too. Where is he taking us?

We land and exit the vehicle. From our vantage point we overlook a wide and flat valley. Mark uses field binoculars and then hands them to me.

"Take a look."

I see there is activity on the valley floor.

"What's going on?"

"The natives are restless as they say."

"Restless? They're more than restless. They're fighting. They're attacking one another," I say as I continue to scan the action. "So this is one of the battles... I presume one side is ours? Can you tell which is which?"

"I can't. But if you can hang around, we'll find out." Mark looks first at me, then at Carol. "Do you want to have a look? I don't recommend it."

Carol shakes her head and asks, "How did you know about this?"

"Got a tip."

"What do you mean 'we'll find out'?"

"Just wait 'til dark and then we might see. Can I see those again?" he asks. I hand over the binos and Mark scans the area some more. "There. Western side of the valley. You can see him."

"What? Let me see..." The valley runs generally north and south and the sun is setting over the low hills on the western side. I can just make out the unmistakable shape of one of our flyers. "So that's Brachus? What's he up to?"

"Can I see?" asks Carol. She takes a few moments and then says, "No kidding. There he is and Lester too."

The view through binoculars shows clear enough that the bloody battle has been in full swing since well before we arrived. The casualties, dead and wounded, are strewn grotesquely on the ground as small groups of men now rush forward, now are beaten back; other groups rush forward, get beaten back and the whole scene reeks of

292

chaos and disorder. Dusk spreads, the conflict before us continues. From our distance, we are spared the full horror of the slaughter. Still, we can hear the din, albeit muffled and indistinct.

"It's getting dark. I'm ready to go," says Carol, clearly not enjoying the spectacle.

"Hold on, just a bit more," answers Mark. He's looking again towards that western side of the valley.

"There. There it is. Look. You don't need the binos."

Sure enough Carol and I both look and see lights have come on from the spot where we saw Brachus. I'm shocked and look to see that Carol is too. Mark is watching our reactions. The lights create a wide but intense beam and illuminate the field of battle such that the momentarily bewildered combatants could continue their struggle. And continue they *do*.

"That's what I wanted you to see" says Mark. He explains that he was charged with providing the light array on the flyer. "It's not clear if they are stooping to the level of instigating these clashes, but they have no qualms about interfering with them. If it seems like the 'good guys' need assistance in the form of intelligence of the enemy's whereabouts, strength, or tactics, or if they need a couple more hours of daylight to complete their victory, Wesley is happy to provide it." We turn to go. "What do you think?"

"I'm not sure if this is what David imagines when he says to ensure our people prosper and multiply," I answer.

293

We have gotten pretty good at blending in and fending for ourselves. Dylan's still our guide and protector if we get in a jam. We help gather information about the number of families, their offspring and their settlements and in doing so help keep an eye on their spread and multiplication. It's interesting that the people themselves—'our' people—are helping by keeping strict records, orally and, more and more, in writing, of their lineage.

Their elders are charged with maintaining lineage records and communicating amongst their extended families. These same elders also perform rites and rituals for various social functions and important milestones in their society. I'm not comfortable with all of their actions; some seem based on bad assumptions and superstition. But I have come to agree with Carol that this behavior is normal. After all, some of the interactions we are having with them, intentional or otherwise, are so outside of their experience as to be baffling and at least a little frightening to them. They have to make something out of it all, and so they do.

One of the rites Carol and I witnessed that I don't like is this business of ritual sacrifice. The use of oils and grains and other foodstuffs is one thing, but animals are another. It's taken on a life of its own so to speak and seems to be widespread. What a waste and for what purpose? It's an odd thing for a society to latch onto and perpetuate.

Dylan recounted to us of a time, many of their generations ago, when Wes coerced natives to bring him some of their food. This was back after David first effectively ceded control of field operations to Brachus. Anyway, the natives brought in some fire-cooked meat and that was it. Brachus loved it. Dylan believes the current ritual, believe it or not, stems from that first incident. Doubtful. But it had to start somehow and there's no reason to believe that if he asked for it back then and liked it, that he wouldn't keep on demanding it if he could get away with it. What I see, though, is a great waste of otherwise perfectly good food.

Brachus is right about one thing: The aroma of meat cooking over open flame is absolutely intoxicating! I have yet to eat any but I can't say I'm not tempted. It makes the prospect of eating our standard processed fare unappealing and monotonous to say the least.

Demonstration

"Everyone, we have reached an important milestone in our mission."

David stands just in front of his base camp quarters on an improvised riser. It is a beautiful, clear, calm day. The sky is the featureless deep blue that reminds one that the infinite blackness of space is just beyond. When the sun rises above the mountains it will be a different story, but now cool morning prevails. David is at his most charismatic in appearance, gesture, and tone. Carol catches my eye discreetly and indicates with a movement of her head and her eyes that she too notices that David seems better.

"We have been on this planet for almost exactly 2,500 years as they are measured here and we should all feel proud to be part of the success we've achieved as a team. Most important, although we have lived through many generations of the local inhabitants, we have not lost one single member of our crew. Dylan?—ah, there you are— Dylan gave us a scare a while back when he tried to serve himself as lunch down at bio camp. He is living proof you can't keep a good man down." Some reserved laughter is heard. "Seriously though, thanks to all for taking care of yourselves and each other, and a special thank you to Doctor Jacob and Nurse Vanessa for all that they do to keep us healthy."

David visually locates Doc in the group and Gleshert looks around as if uncomfortable with being singled out. Vanessa, up front with the women, turns around with a big smile and bows. Before continuing, I see David search out Mark Arwyn in the crowd and Mark gives him a nod.

"So, today. It's a special day. We have placed the entire official record of our mission up to this point—that is, ship log, ground log, R&R progress…"

Someone says "huh?" and David hears it.

"That's 'repair, refit and replenish' the Hobbe, our ride home, in long hand. We've placed mission records in a capsule to be sent back to home base. We've included all of the data and graphics gleaned so far from our survey of the planet—space- and ground-based—all of it. All of the genetic information gathered, not just from the people here, but from much of the biota as well, is in the capsule. In a few moments… Yes, a question?"

"So, aren't we going to make it back? Why are we sending this now instead of taking it all when we go?" asks Craig with a grin, but with concern in his voice.

"Good question, Craig. Look, we are going to be heading back, and sooner rather than later. The reports I'm getting suggest it's nearly 'all systems go' for the return trip. And yes, we will have all of the data I just mentioned and more with us when we do go. But in the early days genetic expansion missions like ours were not as routine as they are now. There is still danger, don't misinterpret, but we have learned many lessons over time on how to make these voyages safer and safer. It was a decision long ago that, rather than lose the data from an otherwise successful mission, an archive should be sent separately via a method that is nearly 100% assured of making it home. By the way, it was our ship's namesake who returned the first GE mission archive capsule, Commander Hobbe.

"Besides, it offers us an important opportunity to test the auxiliary acceleration system we will use ourselves when the time comes. Mr. Arwyn tells me that we are ready to witness the deployment of said capsule and the test of the double L. Is that right Mark?"

"You are correct, sir," says Mark and he then talks quietly into his communicator.

"Before I get any questions, Mark, why is it called the double L system? I seemed to have missed that somewhere along the line."

"What's that? The double L? You know, if I could think quick enough I'd make something up, but I can't. I think it's the inventors' initials or maybe the manufacturer's designation."

"Ok, never mind, it's a homework assignment. In any case, Mark is going to take over now. Those who want to go with him, can. We will all meet back here at meal time."

"This way," says Mark so that all can hear. He speaks from his position near the back of the group and begins walking away toward one of the several narrow passages out of the base camp common area into the surrounding mountains. "Follow me, those who want to see first the test, then the deployment."

Mark stops near Table Rock, waits for those who have followed, and then, when he has everyone's attention, points to a structure high up on a nearby peak.

"There are three of those," he says. "They are on precision gimbals. Now, take a look at Porter up there." He points and we see Porter high up in the sky in the solo flyer. He appears motionless. "I'm going to enable the three units and have each of them lock onto Porter. His flyer has been equipped not for acceleration, but for detecting and returning a beam normally used by each of the ground units for adaptive optics correction. Don't worry about what that is; it's just a way to cancel out atmospheric turbulence or non-uniformity so we get a steady and true beam. In our case, for this demo, the adaptive signal will be redirected to the exact middle of the three gimbaled units, which, by the way, is where we are standing right now."

Mark fiddles with a comms unit which I recognize as not one of our standard-issue genie models.

"Listen up. Do not, repeat, do *not* look up at Porter again until I tell you it's OK to do so. Alain, what did I say?"

Alain stops talking to Tracy and pays attention to Mark.

"The return beam won't kill you but you will need

300

someone to lead you around after if you look directly at it. Now, everyone watch the sender near the top of that peak."

I look but for a few seconds nothing happens. Then the unit moves. And it moves quickly, pivoting gracefully, and then remains motionless.

"If you can all see these…" and Mark holds up two flat white sheets, blank. "Here Carol, push that button when I tell you."

Mark hands the comms unit over and moves to a spot next to Table Rock whereon he puts one of the sheets.

"OK, now, Carol." We watch the sheet and there appears a bluish-white nearly circular patch of light no bigger than the palm of a man's hand, sparkling with a large number of tiny speckles. It reminds me of effects I have seen with lasers.

"This beam is coming from Porter up there, see?" And Mark passes the other sheet back and forth between Porter's flyer and the first sheet a few times so we can see the spot disappear and reappear. "Carol, press that button again."

She does but nothing happens to the image on the sheet.

"Now, we know the beam is over here," Mark says, indicating the sheet on the rock, "so it's safe to look up. First look at that sender on the peak."

We do.

"Now look at Porter, and then back at the image down here."

We see the unit near the mountain peak is moving—not as quickly as before, but it's moving. Porter is moving too, executing rather large moves in three dimensions. Yet the image on the sheet is completely stable except for slight changes in its outline and the ever-present sparkling scintillation.

"It's tracking him. Nearly perfectly. OK, third time for the button please, and then I will take that, Carol. Thanks." He fiddles some more with the comms unit. "Watch up at the peak again." We do and see the sender swivel again, this time pointing almost straight up.

"Demo over. The capsule David mentioned is in geosynchronous orbit right now and all three double L sender units are locked on it. When I give the go signal it will trigger its launch phase back towards home. These accel units will act in concert to give it a boost beyond what its own engine provides, the same as they will for us when it's our turn. Questions?"

"The light's gone—the beam we were watching."

"Yes, right. That was for demo only. A test of tracking and stability. Think of that same beam, but now split into three, one sent to each of the ground units up on the mountains. And instead of coming from Porter in the solo flyer, it's from the return capsule. In actual fact, there is

302

nothing else for us to see here now. It's happening, and it's automatic, and we may as well head back. The senders are moving, tracking the capsule, but their movement is so slight that we can't see it. Anything else?"

"Wait, so the capsule is on its way? You said it was in orbit, but now it's heading straight home?" asks one of the assembled team.

"Straight home."

"Hold on, chief," interjects Grigor, "that's not right. Not straight."

"Alright, alright. Grigor is correct. Straight, as in 'no stops before it's picked up at the receiving end.' The capsule started off in orbit before it received the initial thrust to get it headed on its way. The entire return path is a complex curve if you want to nitpick and as the capsule picks up speed it does become closer to a straight line."

"But the gimbals here have a limit to how far they can rotate, so how…"

"Good one. Good question," Mark interrupts. "You are correct, the three units will follow the target, but eventually the rotation of the planet puts them out of line-of-sight to it. They then wait until the line-of-sight is restored, re-lock, and continue to boost the ship, or capsule in this case. Most amazing to me, the impulses they provide do not decrease in power with distance; the beams they send remain compact and collimated to a fantastic degree.

That's the beauty of the system really."

Carol asks, "Are we really going to leave these complex units here when we leave? Isn't that a violation of mission policy?"

"As far as exact policy, you need to get with David. But I do know our safe and speedy return trumps almost anything else. As far as equipment, well, look around. I picked this area for our camp for a couple reasons. It's isolated, inaccessible without pretty advanced technology and determination, and uninhabitable to a large degree. The units on the peaks up there have a life span of, say, a thousand of these years and when that's over, they will tumble down in pieces. Now yes maybe someone will find pieces at the bottom of a ravine someday, but they won't know what to make of it."

I keep hearing talk of home, of going home. So far, homesickness has not infected me. At the capsule launch lunch meeting, David cautioned that we are here for quite some time yet and all need to stay safe and focused. He did, however, make one or two changes in responsibility, from ground-based tasks to departure-related tasks. More activity specifically related to departure will help placate those itching to go.

Carol remarked on David's mood. She thinks it's a good sign and we are both relieved to see the change. After seeing and hearing of Brachus' and Lester's latest hands-on manipulation, it would be a good thing if he got more involved.

Carol thinks I should say something to David—again—and that now may be the right time. Master Brachus has little to no regard for the native population, the human population, here and it's time to do something about it, she says. I say not again; give me a break. I don't want to be the Whistle Blower of Amara. She wonders if I could get Mark or Dylan to join me to form a broader front. I say no, no, no. First, I think David would balk at something like that. It would seem like we are ganging up on him, and that would be a correct interpretation. Second, if anything is said to David, I think it should be done only after he has seen some of the goings-on personally. He may not need me or anyone to prompt him after that. It would take me out of having to say anything.

Our visits to the field are fascinating. These are real people, primitive culturally, having little or no technology, but real people none-the-less. Their primitive condition suffers from nothing that time won't solve. Some of the things we have seen are heartbreaking: the sicknesses for which there is not even a glimmer of a cure; the crippling injuries with no hope of restoration; the high mortality rate, short life spans, senseless slaughter—all of the trials and tribulations that primitive societies must endure. We see tragedies such as these, knowing that even if we have solutions for them, which we do—most of them anyway—it is not feasible to apply these solutions on a societal or global scale.

There is simply no infrastructure to support it. None.

On the other hand, the various populations with which we have mingled are very interesting. What captures my imagination most is how they are dealing with their ability to think and explore and discover. The results of the recent, relatively speaking, expansion of their memory and cognitive abilities are visible everywhere: Language, written and oral, is ubiquitous and increasingly complex; tool making is exploding, including the making of jewelry and other adornment; the use and expansion of agriculture supports an ever more rapidly increasing population.

Social, governmental, and moral aspects of their development are weak however and I don't know why. Reading of the history of similar missions, I find that this scenario has been discovered before in populations similar to ours here. I can only guess that the raw nature of their existence up until now has instilled a sense of survival that is brutal first, and incorporates other niceties second. If there was some way to jump start them onto a more civilized path—now that would be a feather in our cap, like David said he wanted early on. Maybe this idea could be used when approaching him...

In the Forest

"No. Absolutely not."

"But, we need you. Where do you want this?" I ask, holding up some scrap wiring I think Mark can use.

"In the bin there. No, and that's it. I would be as guilty as Wes in David's eyes. Not gonna do it. Forget it. Besides, you've got enough without me adding anything. Here, toss this too," Mark answers, handing me a dirty cloth.

"Toss it? In the same…?"

"Yeah, in the bin, in the bin."

"I don't think we do have enough. It's all verbal. Unless… Look, can you arrange to have David see some of the things that we've seen? Get him out into the field? If he could witness some of the carnage…"

"No. And just so you know, I've solved my problem with that government job I may have mentioned earlier.

"How…?"

"Easy." Mark grabs out a clean rag and putters while continuing to talk; mostly to himself, it seems. "Unless he knows how to work it without me, it's over. And he doesn't. Should be enough to set him up and payoff whoever got him this gig."

"What? What did you say? You're mumbling again."

"Nothing. Never mind. I say too much. I'm old; I babble. Besides, I'm guessing at things." Mark rubs his eyes, looks to his left at the patient golden girl assistant that he's assembled. "What do you think, young lady?" he asks it, or her.

She brightens and flashes her 'eyes' but does not respond otherwise.

"One of her best features—she doesn't talk," he says to me with a grin. "Look, you don't need me. Get David to go out with you to the field. Take him around. There's plenty you could show him. If you explain it the right way, make it all touchy-feely, he will suggest going out himself. 'See the results of his hard work' and all that bull. You know how to do it."

"Mark, listen. Think about it. If you know of something happening out there that would open his eyes, like you did for Carol and me, let me know."

As I pass out of Mark's work area, Porter is coming in holding a small box of what looks to me like used metal brackets and pieces of plastic.

"In the bin," I say. "It all goes in the bin."

―――――

We camp out in a remote area with Dylan. It's a pleasant area, wooded but not densely so. The overhead canopy inhibits growth at the ground level. Evening has fallen and we have made a fire. In between conversation, the sound of the fire is all I can hear.

"I've got to say, I haven't done this in forever," I say, staring into the flickering flames. Their constant motion, changing shape and colors is mesmerizing. We three don't say much for a long while. My focus is now on the surfaces of the logs at the base of the fire. These surfaces are checked with red lines against black and gray. Gray ash, I can understand, but it changes to black and back again to gray quickly in what must be waves of heat. The red lines glow brighter, with occasional sparks, as the fire crackles and sputters. In some areas the glowing orange-red of hot burning wood dominates, in others the glow is a deep, deep crimson. Dylan tends the fire and drops another log in, and a huge burst of sparks, yellow, orange, red, fly up in twisting patterns. "You've got the proximity alarm on, right?"

"No. Do you really need it?" Dylan asks, looking at me. He looks back to the fire. "Ok, I'll set it, but I'm telling you we are in no danger here."

"This planet is wide open isn't it? I mean the human population density is incredibly low compared to the available area isn't it?" Carol asks, looking at the fire.

"And the animals—they don't know what to think about fire. Curious, but more afraid. They won't approach."

The wood in the fire settles, crackling and sparking itself into a new configuration of temporary stability. I like how the fire is self-feeding up to a point. Unburnt pieces fall through gravity closer to the heart of the fire. It's a skill for the fire-builder: how to place the logs to maximize this effect?

"I don't mean to break the spell, but what can you tell us about the latest happenings? Are you able to keep up with the tracking?" I ask, looking not at the fire, but at Dylan.

"Yes, for the most part, with the help from you guys. And thanks for that. I also get a ton of info from Wesley's group, believe it or not. From Rick Groth, Lester, and the others too. I think Wes wants to be visible doing something that he thinks David will have to approve of—the end result I mean."

"You mean, he is tracking the line—oh, yes, of course he is. But what about details—do you get that too?" Carol asks.

"I took a page out of Jason's book and started keeping a log. But the gist is this: Wesley is tracking the prime descendants, as it were, and takes care to see that they survive even if he has to intervene blatantly. Do I have to mention that he is ruthless with any natives that get in the way of his plans?"

The light evening wind is in our favor; smoke from the fire rises above us before drifting away. Dylan pauses to rearrange and stoke the fire. He seems at home as he moves around from light to shadow and back. He hands Carol and I something after which we see him take a bite and start chewing.

Without thinking, I start to take a bite. "What...what is this?"

"Good, huh?" Dylan asks with a smile. "That, sir, is real meat. Salted, smoked, shredded, dried, and compressed. What do you think?"

Too late to turn back now, I think, and cautiously bite off a small piece and chew.

"Well?"

I look and see that Carol has already had some and is looking at me smiling while chewing, with eyebrows raised.

"It's... delicious. The taste is strong, but good. Are you sure...?"

"Don't worry, it's safe. Carol?"

"Yum. Tasty! You made this yourself?"

"In the village. With help. If this is your first, we'll stop with that piece. Your system is used to our rations and may find this a shock."

We chew in silence, watching the fire burn down, until our samples are gone. It really is good. I could get used to it. Dylan carefully places another log. The shock initiates the necessary swirl of sparks.

"But, as I was saying… He follows them. He rescues them, he talks to them, and he scares them."

"Scares?"

"You know, like at the entrance to bio camp valley? Lights and speakers on the ground, or with drones. Flames even. He will startle them; give them messages or instructions to help them out of a jam or to find sustenance—whatever. It's a game to him."

"We saw a bloody large scale version of that with Mark. Major influence during a big battle. It went on for half a day. Gruesome, but he knew 'our guys' would win in the end."

"If you call that winning," says Carol.

"I worry about the frequent and obvious interaction. The people know they're dealing with something way beyond their ken. Wesley's developing some sort of a hero worship or cult mentality out there. Jason, Carol, it scares me. Ok, they are multiplying, yes, but they are also becoming dependent on outside help, on being given tips, instructions, advice."

"I see what you mean."

"Yes, I know you do, but there's another side. Wesley likes it too much, in my opinion. Even when he's not playing army with them, he's enjoying the rest of it. The

312

controlling, the threatening, the fear. Once Chris, that is, Chris Seaborn, talking to me and Lester, let something drop, accidentally I think. He said that Wesley had sent a large group to the mountains, our mountains mind you," and he looks at both of us before continuing saying, "and they became lost, desperate and dying. Well, he stepped in with water and food. Our food."

"Really?"

"That's what he said. Apparently this was the prime line of descendants, or one of the prime, I don't know, and couldn't afford to be lost. They said Wesley took their leader aside, personally, up in our mountains to try to act as a mentor or something. They were laughing about the show he set up with fireworks and whatnot."

"Our mountains? Not at base camp?"

"No, no, but in our mountains near base camp for sure. I don't have the coordinates or anything."

The flickering flames lend an eerie and intimate cast to our small gathering on this distant planet, one that has become a home away from home. Deep red dominates the fire now, with small blue and yellow flames licking first at one spot and then another. I see the occasional green colored flame appear and disappear. Must be a trace of copper in there somewhere.

Dylan makes ready a place near the fire, sits and lays back, and doesn't say more. Carol and I both look up and see stars in the black sky through and beyond the dense forest canopy. The breeze must be stronger up higher as the treetops sway majestically against the starry background.

Carol still says David must be confronted and I am beginning to agree. Why does it always have to be me? I think Mark will help if we really need him, no matter what he says now. Dylan has already helped by sharing what he has seen and heard. I knew from the start that he is not convinced that our collective actions are for the best anyway, even without a loose cannon like Brachus around. I think he can be counted upon should we need him for support.

The questions are two: how to convince David that he needs to step up and retake control of the mission, specifically the field operations of the Resources group. I doubt he can be convinced verbally. I believe at some point David will have to see for himself what is going on; Carol disagrees. Second, it is my firm opinion that we have to be ready with an answer when he asks, 'What do we do?'

I am finally forcing myself to take the time to read more of the mission histories in the database. It's a lot to plow through, but there are good ideas in there. Something may apply to our situation.

I am still elated from our camping out in the forest primeval with Dylan. When we were out at the bluffs, we at first retreated to our little dome to sleep. Not so in the forest. It was just magical and

Carol told me she feels the same way. Dylan says the prox alarm was on but I wonder; he seems to take a lot of chances. In the morning, the fire was still smoldering, the air was cool and crisp and there were any number of birds and small furry creatures flitting and scurrying about. I remember thinking in amazement at the time that here I am waking on a strange but hospitable world surrounded by unfamiliar plants and animals, vulnerable in many ways, and yet with the strong feeling that, yes, this could be a fine home to me, to Carol, and the others, just as it is to the native people.

Surprise

David eyes me suspiciously. He pushes his lower lip out, draws it back. He looks away and rubs his right temple with a slow circular motion. "Again? Really?" He turns his head back to me, elbows on the table in his base camp quarters, and puts his fingertips together. "Is it personal? Is there something you've got against him?"

I don't think this is the time to confess my visceral dislike for Master Brachus. It would only serve to cloud the facts. "No, it's not personal David. Not last time, and not this time. You saw the evidence from last time yourself. That was not personal. It was factual," I answer calmly. "And it was a situation that only you could address." I pause so as to leave room if he needs to comment. "And you did."

David drops one hand to the table and his eyes flash, but just as fast as Mr. Means shows up, he departs again. "Ok. Alright," David says with resignation in his voice. "Tell me."

After laying out what I see to be the main issue with the current situation, I summarize the key point that I worked out earlier with Carol and say, "Look David, if you agree that genetically these people are on the right track, then it remains to us to try and leave them heading in the right direction as a society, if possible. Our current tack is based on punishment and the enforcement of arbitrary rules. It's harsh and, I believe, a dead end; a failure after we leave. But if we could change that direction, if we could change the emphasis from punishment to reward then we would have something; something self-sustaining. Something that the people themselves could understand and promote now and into the future. David, it's something you could take back home with you as a legacy."

———

"Whatever you told him worked, apparently," says Mark a few days later.

"What do you mean, worked?"

"He commandeered one of the flyers again and has been covering lots of ground out there. Back and forth. He's out as we speak. I peeked at the on-board memory and he's not sight-seeing; his movements are to the field locations of Wes' team plus a few stops in between. What did you tell him exactly?"

"Has he said much to you? What's his mood?"

"Mood? He hasn't said anything to me. All business. He's in that focused state where he doesn't really see you. Some people get like that. They're there, but then again they're not. Whatever you did, you've got him thinking, that's for sure."

Mark brushes his hair off his forehead although it doesn't need it. He looks on his worktable for something, but then turns and walks towards the back wall of his shop. He looks older now for some reason. His limp is more noticeable than I remember. But when he turns back, his grin is in place and he looks right at me and says, "Wes, on the other hand, is going to be pissed as hell." I deliberately don't react. "He's going to know it's you, you know. You're a real troublemaker, you know."

"Come on, it's not me. Not just me. You know it and you agree, too, but you don't say it. Besides," I protest, "if it's anyone, it's him. It's his attitude. He and his pals are out of control. Or should I say, in control. That's the whole problem."

Mark's right though. No matter how it turns out, there is a high likelihood that Brachus will assume it's me who's the 'complainer.' And, he's never said anything, but he must assume that I'm the one who blew the whistle when I showed David the hidden Resource team media. Lester let on as much. Lester has been loyal to him right through; his other crew not so much. But they haven't ratted him out to David to my knowledge.

I know that, politically, David has to tread lightly. After all, we are all going to come through this adventure and out the other side together. Brachus is still going to be here, and the whole team will have to deal with it and work together, uncomfortable or not.

———

"Let's get started. Sit down."

David remains standing. He looks at every one of us as if

he's taking attendance. If my memory is correct, this is the only time, on the planet's surface, that the entire mission team has been assembled. No, wait, at the archive capsule sendoff we were all there too. We are in the mess hall and the seating has been arranged like a small classroom in neat lines all facing David. Brachus is sort of loitering in the front of the assembly off to the side of David. I watch closely as David nods to him and indicates with a head movement that he, too, should be seated. Brachus grins and totters over on his spindly legs to a front row seat, making a show of politely asking the nearest person for permission to sit.

David looks like his old self again; the David we met back at the Academy, charismatic David. He remains in a casual posture, not speaking, still looking the gang over, not engaging any one particular person. Comments or greetings he answers only with a smile or nod; a question thrown to him by Grigor he cuts off with his hand by using a 'stop' gesture and shaking his head and turning his attention elsewhere.

After everyone is seated, the gathering becomes quiet. I feel the tension slowly increase as David, arms folded, remains silently standing and smiling, but not broadly. Next to me, Carol reaches over and takes hold of my hand. I look at her as she gives it a squeeze. I can tell she is pleased by the way David is commanding attention. I am not as pleased; I would rather he get on with it. I am afraid that I may get called out for blowing the whistle on Wes' activities.

"Chris. Chris, where are you going? Please sit down."

"To get something to drink?"

"Sit. Please. I won't be long. Sit. Thanks."

"Everyone. Please. Yes, it's really me. The rumor that I've been replaced by one of Mark's robots is false. And just to be clear, I have not been locked in my quarters contemplating how to clone myself and populate the entire planet singlehandedly."

I too am starting to like what he's doing. Capture the crowd, disarm them with humor.

"We have come to another milestone. Everyone, the last phase of our mission is about to begin. And the culmination of that phase is our return. Our return home, to civilization." He again slowly scans the group. "This last phase is going to require some changes, and that's what we are going to discuss now." David unfolds his arms and stands erect, shifting his weight evenly to both feet.

"First, I am told that the Resources team has more than fulfilled their task of locating, extracting, and delivering the raw materials we need for R & R…" David pauses in mid-sentence apparently to assess whether there is a question about his meaning. There is none, although there are a few murmurs, and he continues, "… and so their function will change for the remainder of our stay. They will now be tasked with the work of prepping the Hobbe for our return and will be split into two task forces, one supporting Mark and technically directed by him on this end, the other task force at the other end, up top, under Grigor's technical direction.

"The focus of the Processing and Fabrication group—it's more than just Mark alone now—will continue the good work of that department for a time. But that focus too will change as it transitions into re-cycling mode, cannibalizing this base camp, as well as our other outposts, before departure."

"And the flyers," adds Mark.

"And the flyers, one at a time" repeats David, nodding a thank you. He moves slowly as he talks, walking from side to side in front of the group. "As we get closer to departure, each of you will reach that time when you have to say goodbye to this world. One or two at a time, you will be re-assigned to your ship-board duties until at last we can make one final ascent leaving only the double L system behind." David lowers his head, turns, and calmly moves closer to front and center, where he began his address. He leans back, but does not sit, on the stool provided for him and crosses his arms. He remains silent for a moment, looking over the assembled team until the scattered hushed chatter stops.

"A few words about mission objectives. The documentation of the conditions here—animal, mineral, and vegetable—is complete. And I would add, is a complete success, as is the recording of planetological parameters. The verification of evolutionary goals for the native population is also complete and will be well-received back at GE central. And here, I want to add something personal," David says as he scoots back and up onto the stool, bringing both feet up off the floor and onto the lowest rung of the stool.

"About the people. There is a high correlation of the progress of these people, genetically, to the ideal. It was with some trepidation that I investigated, as you all know, the possibility of pushing their numbers even higher. I am now prepared, without hiding my sincere relief, to share with you the news that this goal has been accomplished."

I can see one or two faces showing mild confusion, as if they don't know whether to cheer, clap, or quietly wait for more. A couple others smile and nod at David; Wes gives him a thumbs up, but I swear it looks like he's doing it for our sake, not for David's, as he makes sure his gesture is visible to all. It is refreshing to see David ignore his childish behavior and quietly regard the assembled team before continuing.

"Several on our Resources team—Dylan, you are one of them—have played a large part in seeing that the strongest line, or now I should say lines, of genetically advanced people have got a solid foothold in the environment and have a real chance at not only surviving, but prospering and eventually dominating the planet. And that is a real achievement that will set this mission and all of you apart from the ordinary." There is a general light applause, and any tension among the audience members seems relieved. "But that phase is played out and over. 'Our' people, if I can call them that, will have to make it on their own from now on."

David's glance now rests on me for a moment before he says, "During this close-out phase of our mission we are going to take a stab at giving them a push down the road to cultural maturity. Genetically, we are done. But culturally, there is a long way for these people to go. I believe we can help them. Shipley? Jason, I want you to assume responsibility for this effort."

I am shocked, but try to keep evidence of it off my face. The result is that I make no response physically, nor can I think of anything to say. After a few moments of delay, during which several turn partway around to see my reaction, I look and see Carol looking at me with concern. She raises her eyebrows and I discreetly shake my head 'no' and manage a weak smile. I determine not to say a word but instead to simply return David's gaze.

> *I was blindsided! I know that baboon Brachus set this up. I'm a communications officer, not a social psychologist! Aside from the insult of not being consulted before the announcement, I have a deep sinking feeling as I struggle to think what to do with this responsibility. Carol and I talked this over already and we have a vague idea what needs to be done, but how?*
>
> *Carol rightly mentioned that at no time did David address Wes or mention him by name in his speech. And that's surely a slight to him. And neither was he given an opportunity to sidle up next to David and pretend to more importance than he deserves.*

She's right about that too; David handled the Wes part of it very well.

Since I was given the task, I'm taking it. I met with my new group—hand-picked of course. Carol, Dylan, Craig, Porter. I've asked Mark in as an advisor only; he's fully occupied already. No decisions yet, just identifying those of us whom I will count on. Specifically not Brachus, Lester, Rick, or Chris. They are all tied too closely to exactly what needs to be corrected.

The current situation as extensively documented by Dylan, and witnessed by a number of others, including myself, is quite harsh. It's based on the people recognizing that yes, they do have some sort of guiding force that wants them to prosper and multiply, but that entity ensures compliance via fear and force, sometimes overwhelming and merciless force. And he, meaning Brachus, has set down a number of arbitrary 'rules' for behavior to satisfy his own preferences and tastes; his own ego.

In all this, they as a people have been given some guidance, it's true, but it has been piecemeal and sometimes contradictory. Dylan emphasizes that he sees the people, when they are faced with major decisions, motivated by fear rather than more mature guiding principles.

Leftover Dreams

"We've got to try to break this cycle of endless war, endless killing. And at the same time we've got to leave a strong and lasting sense of societal and individual responsibility."

I found some interesting case histories in the archives. The concept was reported as having good results in different but similar situations on previous missions. I did a lot of thinking about it and bounced it off Carol. It's a good idea. I think it'll work. It has to work; we only get one shot and then we are out of here.

"The first idea is this: we need to send a clear message that the lessons they've learned in the past are not necessarily the best. In fact they need to be updated with a new, simple and clear set of principles. The principles have to be presented in a compelling way, a way that will impress and be remembered—hopefully forever. That's where the second part comes in."

I have ideas on how to do all this, but want to save them until I get buy-in on the general plan.

"It's not going to be easy; I'll need all of your help to make it happen," I say and cross my arms as I try to adopt David-like gravitas and charisma. I can see by Carol's wink that it's not exactly working. But I know this team is on my side, and they all want to help; I've talked to each of them individually.

"Having said that, the second part is going to be trickier to pull off than the first. I've settled on a concept but we will want to kick a few of your ideas around too."

"Jason, Tracy said she would like to help, if you think you could use her."

At the beginning of the mission she was in tight with Brachus, or so it seemed. No, not 'seemed,' she was. She was the human firewall between him and the rest of us.

"Carol, since she talked to you, will you please tell her thanks, we'll let her know."

Porter says, "What about that second part you mentioned? What do you mean 'trickier than the first part'? What are we up against?"

"I don't know how much you've seen of the constant warring, the bloodshed of the so-called 'our' people and the surrounding groups. Well, some of that was encouraged by Brachus and Lester. They would make a kind of a game out of it. What it has done is instill an attitude of 'might makes right' and an attitude in 'our' people that they have a 'destiny' to prevail. These are attitudes that will not serve them or any population well going forward.

"I know David has a special interest in the lineage he has

been following but as most of you must know, there are other scattered small populations over much of the globe. Some message of cooperation and coexistence must be sent, in my opinion, so future generations may peaceably cohabit this planet."

"But how? What is your plan? Jason, I think I can say we are all on board, but let's get this going. Where do we start?"

It's now or never to get this plan on the table and fill in any holes we can detect; I push on.

"The first part, instilling a new set of principles has to be done in such a way that it's the talk of the land. It can't be a quick 'here, read this' kind of thing. It's got to be implemented in a powerful manner that cannot be ignored, to make sure it will be the stuff of legends and lore for generations to follow. We have to replace the paradigm of fear and punishment with one of hope and reward. These are principles that we've all learned. Common sense, you might think, but it's not so to a new society. And they need these ideas if peace and prosperity are to thrive.

"The second part has to have the same enduring quality but with added danger—danger to one of us. We have to teach a lesson that will replace the endless cycle of deaths and Wes-worship with a symbolic or ritual sacrifice that will serve as the proxy for all others." I look over the group one at a time and repeat, "All others—now and into the future."

"Wait—who are you? Symbolic proxy? Where did you come up with this stuff?" ask Porter. We all look at him to see his half-smiling quizzical expression.

This breaks the tension a bit, I can see, and Carol follows with, "Yes, Jason, tell us. Where *did* you come up with this?"

"All right, I did a lot of research. There is a ton of history out there and some good ideas from previous missions." I stop for a few seconds to make sure they are all listening and say, "But look guys, this is serious. Forget about our official directives; forget about David for a moment. What about these people? I think if we can help them we should."

"I'll second that," agrees Dylan and there are nods all around.

"There has certainly been no lack of native interaction already, for better or worse, and my plan does not alter that, but the players have changed—to us." I pause to let this sink in.

"Let's assume the prediction made by David is correct and the genetic tracking and shepherding is over. The people are *the* people, genetics aside. Let's try to make a positive difference in their development."

We are meeting in my quarters. It's a bit cramped and I suggest moving out to the mess hall. Mark is there, happily, and I begin to lead the way to join him. He is chewing and nods when I point to the empty spaces at his

330

table. Before I sit, I see Brachus just outside the hall entry, motioning for me to come. I'm not going to avoid him, so I excuse myself for the moment.

"Yes?" I say upon approach.

"Quite a little team you've got there Shipley. Quite a team."

"Yes, they are. How can I help you?"

"You're not going to make any difference out there you know. They're animals."

"Really? We will see."

"They understand force, that's about it. And they understand me; they listen to me."

At this, I make no response. I look into his eyes. They dart from me towards Mark's table, and back.

"I know what you've done," he says, voice lower than before, "and I won't forget it. I'll be watching. One mistake and…" and he trails off.

"And…?" I prompt, but he declines to continue. "Look, you did your job; David said so. What's the problem? I'm going to do my job now."

"No problem. None at all," he says, with his big-toothed grin.

I can't resist adding, "You've got them jumping through all kinds of hoops, don't you? You've bullied them into treating you like a king or something. You think that makes you a leader? Someone to respect? Is that what you're getting from this?"

"At least I don't go around behind people's backs slandering them to their superiors."

"It's not slander if it's true, Brachus."

"You don't know what's true and what's not, you're…"

"Ah, but the videos! Your own pictures and videos. I wonder if any copies of those still exist?" The grin disappears. "I wonder who would like to take a look at those back home? Tell you what, let's both hope those don't have to turn up again, ok?" No response, but the eyes don't dart anymore. They are looking at me steadily. "Now, if you don't mind, I've got a meeting to attend."

Silence for a heartbeat, then the grin reappears and Master Brachus says, "Most certainly, do attend to your meeting." And he turns and walks away from the mess hall entrance.

"I hate to bring this up again, but you said something about danger to us, or one of us," says Porter when I rejoin the group. "What danger? And which one of us?"

"Well, James, one of us has to die," I say solemnly. After a pause I add, "Someone has to die, James, and it's going to be me."

Mark stops chewing and looks at me and says, "Whoa, hey now! I'm just trying to have a quiet bite to eat here and people are dying already." He resumes chewing.

I should have warned Carol about that last part, but I have to say she can keep her composure phenomenally well. She, too, looks at me, but only until I return her gaze. Yep, I should have brought that out more gently but talking to Brachus put me in a mood.

"I think we'll need to hear more details, Jason," is all she says to the now quiet gathering.

> I had to go over everything again with Carol; she was not thrilled, let me tell you. Oh, she's on board all right with us trying to do some good, but she was not at all convinced about the bomb I dropped at the mess hall.
>
> We had a follow-up discussion where I explained more about the historical examples. We came up with a plan that, while not perfect, is workable and something we all at least agree upon. A couple details were worked out, this time as a group. To be convincing, it's got to be one of us; to be impressive and memorable, we have to work as a team; to work as a lasting symbol, there must be mortal danger. They will understand that.
>
> There haven't been any more run-ins with Brachus. I did get the evil eye from Lester, but that's it. I believe both Chris Seaborn and Rick Groth have seen the light; I will bet you that David had a talk

with each of them. Groth has asked me to let him know if there is anything he can do to help.

We decided that the best venue in which to execute our plan is right in the heart of the region with the highest density of 'our' people. And we agree that the entire plan must be completed within the span of a single generation. There has been enough interaction over the past generations that the people know we are here; at least they suspect we are around and have an interest in them. Because our technology is millennia ahead of theirs, we can guess they think of us as magicians, sorcerers or gods. We know Brachus did not discourage the latter idea, but that's ok, it'll work in our favor to engender respect and attention.

If we can turn blind obedience into self-improvement and introspection, all the better. If we can replace fear of reprisal from a false god with love and respect for a teacher, we will have success.

Step Up

Dylan is invaluable to us. Without his knowledge of the people, customs, and languages, it would be tough sledding out there. Our plan becomes more firm and fleshed out every day. Although the principles we will try to instill are simple and basic to us, they may not be as easily accepted as we would hope. Our biggest challenge is to make sure the message is propagated down through the generations.

The foundations for the plan are already being laid. We do not believe dictating or otherwise writing and delivering a code of ethics will work; it's got to be something the people can feel and experience and relate to emotionally. Besides, the vast majority of the people are illiterate.

"I'm happy with the bird's eye view; do not trouble me with minutia," says David, or should I say, Mr. Means, right after he hears and okays our plan. I am disappointed by the curt treatment. He nods and leaves us rather abruptly with, "Carry on."

I wish he hadn't cut us off, but so be it. I remember that this is how he treated Brachus too; he gave him authority and let him go without interference. He did agree to assist with a last small bit of genetics, and I am thankful for that as it will, I'm sure, make a big impression.

Dylan has agreed to assist me in my language skills, and, trust me, this will be my hardest part. We talk over the danger again: the necessity for mortal danger; the likelihood of imprisonment, at the very least; the real chance that rescue will not come in time to save me without, or even with, all the medical miracles that Gleshert can perform.

———

Dylan seems unusually quiet. We are in my cramped quarters again. It's getting more and more Spartan around base camp as departure prep continues.

"You guys are missing the show out here," Mark says as he sticks his head into the meeting.

"Glad you could make it after all."

"Not my fault, I was tied up with Seaborn until David just sprung me. Greed is going to undo that boy," Mark says shaking his head.

"Huh? Who?"

"Anyway, never mind. Have you come up with anything for me yet?"

"Mark, just keep the runabout and the solo flyer intact as long as you can, and keep them available for us. Once we start rolling, it's going to happen fast. What show are you talking about?"

"Hah? Oh, I'll tell you later. For the flyers: I do what I can, as always. Porter, you still certified to fly? It's been a while," Mark grins. "In the meantime, I've got to go do one last odious errand. Later," he says and disappears.

I have a thought and get up and look out the door, thinking to call Mark back. Across the common area, Chris Seaborn is nodding to David, who is clearly not happy. Chris sees me looking and moves enough to put his back to me while still facing David. I guess so I cannot read his lips or hear what he is saying. David, in this same moment, sees Mark and calls him over. I'll have to catch Mark later.

"Jason."

"Jason."

I close the door and turn back to my group. "Yes?"

"We need to talk," says Dylan, looking at the table in front of him. He raises his eyes and looks right at me, then Carol, and finally back at me. "Look, we've got something wrong. I knew it from the beginning but I had to think about it a while before I could say anything." I see by his mood that this is something serious and sit back down in the seat I left moments before. "Jason, no offense, but you can't pull it off. Not by memorizing your lines, not with remote prompting, no how, no way. You can't do it."

He looks quickly at Carol again.

"But what are you saying? We all think the plan is as good as it's going to get…"

"No, it's not that." He looks down at his hands. "I'll do it. I have to do it."

"Dyl, what are you…"

"Jason, hold on," says Carol. "Are you saying you want to be the teacher, Dylan?"

"I will do it. I feel they are my people. I know them; I have had friends among them over the years. I'm telling you like I told Wesley and even told David, although I don't think either believed me, these people are more advanced than you think. They are not as far from what we would consider basic civilized society… I know, you don't see much of that out there… but I'm telling you I'm right.

"Besides, that's not the point. I can pass for one of them. I've done it; I know how to do it, easily. Jason, you just can't say the same. No one on the mission team can." He stops speaking and I don't know what to say. "You know I'm right. To pull this off, it has to be one hundred percent believable. No, I take it back; it has to be absolutely real. Anything less will fail and we will waste our time."

"Dyl… I appreciate what you say, but I have a responsibility…"

"To do it right. Yes, you do have that responsibility," says Dylan as he interrupts and finishes my statement.

I look from Dylan to Porter to Carol. Carol does not betray her thoughts or feelings although I can imagine she would welcome this change to the plan.

"Dyl... let's think this over. If you want to talk privately..."

"I'm doing it. Let's get over it and on with the program. I know we haven't completed any non-reversible actions, so let's move forward."

———

"I can't deny it would be a relief to me, but, that aside, he is correct."

"How so?" I ask Carol when we are alone later.

"Come on, you've never been at ease with the people, 'our' people. You know it and so do I. And he's right that we have one shot and it's got to be real; they will see through anything else."

"But... if he doesn't make it..."

"We all love Dylan, but it's his decision. I don't want to see anything happen to him any more than you do. We can do our best to protect him, but he wants to do this. You've seen him from the beginning: He has a special feel for these people. Sympathy, rapport—whatever you call it. Just think how much it would mean to him to have a chance to do something really significant and positive for them. He *will* make it, but even if he doesn't, remember that he said he wanted to stay here..." Carol stops speaking abruptly and turns away.

We finally came up with a plan for propagating the ideas that we will be promoting. It's a simple train-

the-trainer approach. Dylan is comfortable with it but doesn't think one generation is enough to do the job of training let alone the rest of the plan. After much debate, we all do finally and at last agree that one generation it is. We are counting on the impact of the experience to be strong enough to push the ideas forward in time.

And the issue of Dylan being the focus is settled as well. He is correct and I, and the entire team, consent to the risk that he is assuming.

The mother has been selected. David assisted us in fertilizing her using genetic material supplied by Dylan. Dylan visited with her and she was told, of course in non-technical terms, what was done and to be expecting a special child. Time is really short now and a lot has to be done. We are making sure to give advance notice to as many of 'our' people as possible and in a way that they will long remember.

Prep for departure is progressing apace. The archive capsule signal confirms the double L system is performing well. Recycling is having a dramatic effect on our base camp; it's disappearing. We understand field sites have all been cleaned up and cleared out. David is spending most of his time up top; Grigor too.

I have lately been reflecting on the meaning of all this—the mission. More than the mission: the whole program of missions. Even more: the concept that we, as a people, should make it our business to interfere with planets the way we do. Maybe interfere is not the right word. Modify is better perhaps. Make no mistake, I understand if you have an undeveloped tract, it only makes sense to clear it, use the materials it provides, and make the land productive, whether it is an unused field of arable land in your back yard or a planet in another solar system. My doubts arise from the question of whose field is it anyway? First come, first served? Sure, we are paving the way via seeding but I see no record of how many of the seeded planets had preexisting life, primitive or otherwise. How many had viable life, different from ours fundamentally, perhaps incompatible with ours, but life nonetheless? Did we destroy it, and so what if we did? Tough questions all.

Moving Forward

"They're certainly buzzing about it. The word got out all right," reports Dylan.

"I used the solo flyer and floodlight for the big night," adds Porter. "Just to make sure the location stood out."

"Does everyone know what to do?" Nods all around answer me. "Mark?" I ask into the open comms unit.

"Yes, but I'm clear as to the next couple steps only. After that I'll be needing some help. I'm old, I forget things," Mark says via the small comms speaker.

"Yeah, sure you do. Me too. Okay then, keep an eye on your messages. All of you. We've got to pull together in case of the unexpected. The primary thing—well, there are two things right now. Keeping track of young Mr. Dylan," I say with a smile, but noting Dylan's negative facial reaction I realize too late that that appellation is too flippant, too soon, or both, "or I should say, his stand-in, and, second, making the several preparations in advance of Dylan's, *our* Dylan's, appearance on the scene." Nods again, and an 'over and out' from Mark.

"You've all heard this already… The quick life cycle of the natives means that it won't be long until the real show begins. It is a critical part of the plan that Dylan's child be raised among the natives as any other. He must be fully accepted into and known by the locals. It turns out that we have been very fortunate that the boy does indeed bear a striking resemblance to his father—a trait that will help immensely, and one that we are counting on.

"There are a number of events that we all agree will create a lasting impression, and they require a fairly complicated setup. Doc is helping us with a few of his powerful tools and drugs and we have his commitment to assist should we need it in the case of an emergency."

————————

"Do you have any idea at all what you're doing?" asks Gleshert when I come to him for supplies and instructions on how to use them.

"Only in theory. Something similar has been done before. We have the advantage of more advanced techniques, but one thing we do know is that the unexpected can and probably will occur."

"Just give me all the notice you can," he says, with a different tone—his more human, less grouchy tone.

"Will do," I say as I turn to leave the tiny supply room at base camp. The med facility has not been affected yet by the slow but steady teardown and preparation for departure.

"One more thing…"

I stop and look back at Doc, my arms full.

"Watch out for him; keep someone with him."

I put down the case that contains the heavier part of the supplies he has given me and turn around to face him.

"Doc, I know how you feel, and we all feel the same. You probably know what I'm going to say… He has to carry through the final act on his own. I personally will monitor him—he won't have any of his regular gear, weapon, or communicator with him—and will let you know if he needs you."

———

"Tell Tracy she can help," I say to Carol when I get back to my place, which has morphed into the headquarters for this operation. "She's been out with the natives, yes? Mingling and whatnot? Knows the local language in the area?"

Carol nods, "I think so."

"If she can do it, I want her to go to the village where Dyl … the stand-in I mean, lives and talk up the ideas that we agreed upon. And specifically to the women; I think we are doing all we can with the men. And then if she could fan out and visit neighboring communities … just keep the rumors going, play up the birth, you know, and the rest."

"Alright." And Carol adds, "Do you want me to go too?"

"No. Listen; tell her also to be careful. Be discreet, take

precautionary measures, no chances—you girls know what I mean. You, stay here. I want you to keep tabs on the team, their locations. What's the latest?"

"The latest is that our boy is the spitting image of his dad; and Dad says he's ready to go anytime. I am here to tell you Dylan is very impressive. He is going to make a real impression down there; heck, he's made a real impression on me. He's got a strong presence—you've seen it. He's quiet, confident, and most of all firm. I don't see him getting flustered at all."

"I do know what you mean. And that's where I would fall down, I'm sure. He's got, like you said, presence." I stop to think and then add, "Let's see how Tracy feels and if it's a go, give her some time to do her thing. Then we make the swap."

"Hey."

"Hey," Carol answers as she thoughtfully looks at Dylan when he enters. She's hit the nail on the head; he's got a new presence. New? Or am I just noticing it now? Dylan greets me as well and sits. I begin to say something more but get waved into silence.

"I will cause conflict out there. I don't mean wars. But I will say my piece in public, first to attract crowds, with your help," looking at me and Carol and gesturing so that we know he means the team inclusive, "and then to confront their native leaders, those who have a stake in the status quo.

346

"I will try to do it so that the object of their wrath is me, and me alone, as we planned," he explains. "But there's also got to be that carrot, a reward. If the messages that I leave are to spread, there has got to be the promise of a reward. And that promise has to outweigh the pressure from the rest of society."

"Yes, that's…"

"Wait. Yes, I know what you are going to say. That's the plan. You've got to help me find those among the people who are willing to carry on after I'm gone, after we've gone from this planet. They are going to have to be able to articulate the message and able and willing to spread it. I've got a couple ideas; there are a few fellows who are about the right age, whose families I know from the field. But let's work now to line up others; we don't have much time."

I talked to Porter; he had no contact with the people as part of his job shuttling ores and other resources back and forth for David, Brachus, and Mark. And he has no desire now to get up close and personal, especially in a crowded village. Nevertheless, he's agreed to pitch in when and where he can.

Mark's advice is short and sweet: 'Use the contacts that Dylan has identified, and then use their like-minded friends to build a small network to help carry on. Done. No sweat, no strain.' And that's what we'll do. They are identified, but Dylan will have to contact them himself and confer upon them their charge.

More and more non-essential items are being recycled, or returned to the ship. We are to give a list to Mark and his helpers of what he can reprocess, discard, or pack to keep. Mark sent his own message right after saying that there is a strict weight limit; if we go over, he will choose what to eliminate, so be careful, he says. Don't be the last in line, he says.

The swap needs to be made; should have been done by now. The concept was to physically remove the stand-in from the area. He'd have been fine; set up in a good location, with strangers— friendly strangers who know Dylan from his field work—who would take care of him until he becomes part of their society. He is young and strong, with skills. He would have had a long and happy life. But Dylan blocked it.

Showtime

"Jason, I'm addressing you and you alone. It's not right and I can't allow it. I will not allow it. That's why I stopped the transfer."

"But…"

"No buts. You surely aren't going to ask me why?" Dylan says, looking steadily and only at me, not at the rest of the team. "Are you?"

"No, of course not," Carol answers for me, for all of us.

I sit down. Only Dylan remains standing and continues saying, "The plan goes forward. I have talked to the boy. He now knows about me and wants to help. There are some small things he can do; he will be a 'cousin' and help by working in outlying areas to spread the word. No one will be the wiser."

"Can we be sure this is a better solution?"

"Better? It's the right solution. And the only one. He deserves to have a voice in all this and to be among his people. Now, where were we?"

———

"Isn't this a bit deceptive? I mean, the costumes, the makeup. Look at me!"

"Rick, we need you. I don't suppose you could talk to Chris…?" Rick doesn't speak, but I can see that the answer is no. No mind, we are what we are and will make do.

"But, what I was saying…"

"Yes, I know. But it's a sure way of getting their attention. Like I told you all, we need to get maximum exposure and this is one sure way to do it. The girls are pitching in along with Craig, Alain—even Porter is out there right now," I explain.

"I don't know. I don't like it. I mean, it could get dicey. You see?"

"No, we are going out among the masses—the poor people. These are the ones who are looking at basic survival from day to day. They are not your enemy. You'll blend. Besides, we are using a team concept; you'll be working with at least one other, always."

I can see two things: He's not totally convinced that he will be safe and, second, that he's resigning himself to do it anyway.

"Thanks. We do appreciate it. The whole program will be over in two of their years. We are about half way through

350

right now. Talk to the team, they will tell you how it is."

"Who's the new guy? Hubba hubba!" says Tracy, just coming into the remote temporary camp some are calling 'the green room.' Hey, Rick, you should show off those muscles more often."

"What's the news?" I ask.

"It's a madhouse…"

"See? What was I saying? Hey?" interjects Rick.

"The crowds are buzzin'. And they're getting bigger by the day. Are you his speech writer?"

I shake my head. "No, not me."

"Whoever, then. He can really wrap them around his little finger, man. I'm tellin' ya!"

"Who's up?"

"You. Carol's next. She's in position and Dylan's supposed to see her tomorrow. Should be a good show, but… Yes? What?"

"No, nothing. Sorry. Go ahead, what else?"

"I was just sayin', Jimmy or one of 'em has found a family that are all sick with something. Pretty bad fever or what. Should be a snap to fix with one of Doc's potions. Easy for us—probable death sentence for them without it. But

351

it should wow them some more for sure. It might be that Carol will have to wait a day or week for her show."

Tracy is looking Rick over again and says, "There is a problem."

"Rick, you're done in here. Tracy will take you out and brief you, get you oriented." Turning to Tracy I ask, "Problem?"

"Yeah. He's in demand. *High* demand. The people are seeing things they've never seen, cures that are unheard of. They obviously think it's him—can't imagine technology or real medicine. They all want a piece of him."

"No, that's good. As long as he's safe for a while longer, we want the buzz as big as we can get it. Sounds like it's going according to plan to me."

"If you say so… Say dude, you're up!"

She's right. I have to go out and do my part again as well. We have planned several incidents for various locations and each one takes more or less setup. Craig and the others been out for almost a year now for just that reason. They've got to be believable as 'one of them' so that when Dylan comes along, the plan goes off without a hitch. Total believability; it's top priority.

———

"Where does he get this stuff?"

I'm tired and trying to rest from a long stint among the

352

people and crowds. I don't open my eyes. "Stuff?"

"You know, the speeches or stories he's telling."

"Yeah, I've heard him too. What about it, Jason?"

I open my eyes, but do not turn to make eye contact with anyone. "Come on, you've heard it all before; standard ideas, right? There's nothing surprising in what he's saying to them."

"Ok, but the way he's doing it—I mean, sure, it's seems like the basics all over again. Things we know by heart, or should know anyway."

"That's it, it's the basics we learned…"

"But, the stories…"

"Look," I say with some irritation due to the rest time I am losing, "I told you guys—there is history from other missions. But the delivery—that's all Dylan. I've heard him too. He's awesome." What I think, but don't say, is that there is no way I could have managed as well. Not a chance. He's a natural. "What's that?" I ask.

"We were just saying about the stories—they are… interesting."

I close my eyes again, knowing that I've only got a short time before heading back out. "Has to be. Literacy near zero. Lots of oral tradition though. Got to have stories with a message that can be passed along."

353

"It's all common sense though, really, from what I've heard."

"Common sense to you and me maybe. Look, there are some things people know are right, right?. Maybe they can't say it, but they know it. We all know some things without being told. But many times it takes a person to articulate it, to say it out loud, for it to crystalize into a concrete precept that a people can rally around or at least agree upon. And if it's said by a person of authority, a persuasive speaker…"

There is some additional low talking, but I do not pay attention.

I open my eyes again and slowly realize that I did get some rest after all. I am alone. I check my appearance and my task details and head out. As usual, I can feel my tension rise as I get closer to populated areas. Lately though, it's getting easier.

I say as little as possible even though I do have a certain level of comfort now with the people. I am a familiar sight in and around the small community on my current assignment. I've made sure of that. There have got to be questions about my situation but so far there have not been any incidents. I can laugh off or otherwise deflect questions about my past, family, livelihood, and so on without difficulty. It's important though that I'm visible and visibly hurting. One of Dylan's supporters has been kind enough to put me up when I do stay in the community overnight. It's crunch time now and tomorrow's my day.

———

I hope it's enough. There is a following for sure, but is it enough? My interaction with Dylan went off without a hitch and the locals are suitably impressed by any measure. For my part, I am still playing the role of the thankful recipient of Dylan's attention and have joined the growing group that makes up his following. My part is over for now and I am glad to be able soon to slip away and head back to the green room.

Rapid fire events now consume most of the team's time. One after the other we are all contributing to good effect. There's a ways to go but a large part of the plan has been carried out successfully.

The stories from the team are incredible. Each situation has its unique quirks and surprises. Nothing goes just as expected but I guess that's to be expected!

Carol drew some stares when she said her piece. I didn't notice anything; it must be that she speaks the local language with a peculiar accent or something. It didn't matter; Dylan's response to her was simple, instructive, and well received.

Danger

"It's working. They are amazed."

"We suspected as much. When technology and medicine are in their infancy, essentially unknown, they just can't fathom that one of their own could do what he has done."

"What he is still doing!"

"You should hear him speak! I was in the crowd at several of the venues. They can't get enough."

"I will say the magistrates or whatever they are called are not happy. They are calling him a liar and pretender to the throne and other things. He's getting the attention we expected, from all sides."

"Porter, I am surprised to see you enjoy mingling in the crowds."

"Not 'enjoy.' Wrong-o. I don't talk, I keep my head down. Besides, I am a blind man out there without my glasses. Most of their gibberish I don't pick up. Have to report on the sly. Tracy, you need help out there? I'd rather be with him than in the city."

"Ha, you're doing great. Keep it up. We need you there

bud."

"Porter, you won't have to go to him. We are directing him to you."

"Oh, yeah…" Porter says as he apparently remembers.

"James, you are the one that has to turn him in."

Porter's expression changes subtly. He swallows before nodding and looking around our small group. "Mark, I'll take one of those cocktails of yours now."

This was another hard part of the plan to agree upon. In order to build up the recognition, the notoriety, in order to get the message out and have the largest impact, we need to have the biggest possible confrontation. There are no mass media, there is no electronic communication; hardly—even printing is a long way off for these people.

———

"I met with him outside the city," Carol says. "He's a changed man from mission kickoff. It's something to see. He acts as if he were made for this role."

"When does he… Hey, Mark, come on in. You don't look happy."

Mark sits without speaking. He has aged again, going by his appearance. His laugh lines are prominent, but he is not laughing now. After making sure his thin reddish hair is in place with a sweeping motion of his hand, he says, "I'm getting badgered. Again." He looks at me and I believe I know what he means. "I've just about had it. I'm officially done with field resource work. *All* field work." He gives himself a shake as if warding off a chill, and says, "Forget about it. Back to where you were when I barged in."

"Right. Are you sure you don't need help with anything? We could give you a hand…"

"Nope. We're wasting valuable happy hour time people, let's go."

"Where were we?" I ask Carol.

"When he goes in…", she reminds me.

"Yes, when is he going in?"

"In?" Mark asks, a confused look on his face.

"Dylan. Into the city."

"Right."

"Craig will let us know the actual time. The day is set; it matches the current plan. It's tomorrow, Jason. There promises to be a lot of people in the city and more coming along with him."

"So, this is it."

———

Carol and I prepare ourselves and enter the city. Now,

359

other than Mark, my whole team is there and able to mix in with Dylan and his followers. It's a relief to me that I have learned the language enough to be comfortable. Creature comforts are another matter and after a day or two I can only wonder how civilization of any kind can survive infection and disease in these primitive conditions without antibiotics and other modern remedies. Not to mention personal hygiene.

"I'm going to do it now," Porter says to us in the native tongue. With his outfit and makeup, it's hard for me to tell if he's nervous or not. He moves off and I lose him in the crowd. There is a bit of commotion moments later. The crowd erupts with shouts and accusations, threats and pleading; the tone smacks first of authority, then defiance and, finally, bitter acceptance. Dylan, I see, in the midst of it all, remains calm, almost radiant.

I hear it first, and then I see part of the crowd turn angry once more. I feel a sharp twinge of panic when I realize that it is poor Porter they have turned against. Damn it— we should have foreseen this! Dylan's loyal followers would of course not view Porter's action favorably. I search faces frantically to see if there are any others of my team around while pushing my way forward towards the knot of people harassing Porter. Nobody! It's clear that it's only a matter of seconds before he will be in real trouble.

I grab for Porter and reach something, not sure if I have him or not. It is him! Pulling him back and then behind me, I give him one final shove away from the mob and release my grip. At the same time I continue to press forward while indicating as urgently as I can a false direction to fool the angry crowd. This ploy is working. I hear shouts of 'There he goes!' echo and support my deception.

I turn and glance behind me in time to see Porter hustle away as discreetly and quickly as he can. That was close!

A hand clamps my shoulder and I look back now to see an unfamiliar face—an unfamiliar face with a familiar grin. It takes only a moment to process the grin and realize it belongs to Craig. He nods, removes his hand and turns to move away without saying anything at all. I am at last able to exhale and relax, knowing now why the misdirection worked so easily.

———

We have done all we can do here for the moment. Carol and I head out of town and decide to stay at least one more night in one of the places that Dylan used in his recent travels. We meet a teammate on the way.

"I thought I might see one of you out here." Porter, shaken but intact, looks tired. "Have a seat," he says.

"You did good. Glad you're all right."

"I'm ok. I still don't know how I got out of there."

"Say 'thanks' to Craig the next time you see him. You're out. Come with us if you'd like. We're going to stay."

"No. No thanks." Porter looks with a blank expression

from me to Carol and back. I wonder how clearly he can see us at this distance. "Nope. Really, I'm fine. Say…"

"Yes?"

"They're really stirred up. I mean, that could have gotten real ugly real fast. Do you think he… I mean, what will they do…?"

"He'll be fine. It's all according to plan; it just feels different when you're in the middle of it as it happens."

Porter doesn't say more and we leave him sitting with his forearms on his knees. He's removed some of his garb so he'll not be recognized even if someone spots him. He's done the last part of his job and can return to base camp.

That leaves Craig and Tracy in town to monitor and report developments. We will give it some time before we head back to base.

———

The message comes in from Craig only a day or two after we left town: "Dylan under interrogation and trial."

Communication is one way for the most part. We can't expect any of the team to monitor their genies when in town.

From Tracy a little later in the week: "J Hope u know what you are doing. Can't believe what I saw. He's taking a beating."

This from Craig within minutes of Tracy's message: "OK alert Mark. It's heating up. Looks bad for the home team." Then: "Mark standby. Looks like tomorrow."

We change our plan and decide to stay put until things play out. No thought of returning to base before then. Time seems to slow down and we pass it in silence.

The next day I hear from Tracy first: "Horrible. Going to be sick. What are they thinking??"

Craig, to me but the whole team is copied: "Mark, prepare to come and extract. Will let you know as soon as it is clear. Doc, it's bad."

The hours pass. We can only imagine what is happening.

We finally hear the report, planned both as a signal to the people themselves and as a signal to us, and brace for the next message.

"It's over. It's the worst case of all we discussed. Mark, get close and come on my signal." Craig sends coordinates in the next message.

The clock starts now regarding Dylan's chances to survive.

"Wasn't pretty. Going to need attention soon. Hurry," is the next message, this from Tracy.

We start on foot toward town.

"Worst case, he said," says Carol.

I nod. We keep moving.

Then a series of messages: "Not looking good. Lots of damage. Time passing. Worried."

We make it to the coordinates Craig sent. Gruesome, barbaric. I am getting sick to my stomach, as Tracy had earlier. Carol is taking it without much expression; she is a rock. I don't understand how she can walk through here.

At the absolute earliest moment, we call for Mark. Doc came too. He's not happy, and this time I don't blame him. He's not talking except for barking a few orders. Between us and using Mark's gear we get Dylan stabilized and out. Really gruesome work and not pleasant at all. On top of it all we had to wait an excruciatingly long time so that he could be taken away in secrecy. That was the worst of it for me—the delay.

> *Doc did what he could on site, but you could tell he was worried. Two things are against us: elapsed time and the extent of the injuries. Even taking into consideration the preventive measures Dylan used earlier in the day in anticipation of the worst, hope is hard to come by.*
>
> *Dylan is back at base camp now and is in the med center. I have been afraid to inquire. We know this is not like the cat attack. Worse. There is a real danger of losing him.*

One thing certain, he will not be able to participate in the next phase. Time is short and I absolutely do not want to abandon the plan. Which means there is no getting around it, someone has to go. What to do?

Tracy is the only one who remains in town. She has sent in a couple reports. We've got her made up to look quite old now, so she is able to get into places almost unnoticed.

Part V

Finishing Touch

"The physical injuries are more than I've had to deal with in a long time. Ever, in fact," says Gleshert to the entire assembled members of the mission. "Be that as it may, his biggest problem is with the brain."

I look at Carol and the rest of the somber faces. I look back at Doc and am jolted because he is staring right at me. Wait, he knew the risk—we all did, especially Dylan.

"The good news, and there's not much good news at this point, is that physically he can be put back together. Before the ordeal, someone, either Dylan himself, or one of you, administered the protective drugs I gave him. Without them, the elapsed time would have been too much. As it is, I still don't know how much cognitive function will remain."

"When will you know?" someone asks tentatively.

"He's undergoing a restorative procedure. This takes time. As a further complication, I'm transferring him upstairs. Like everything else, the base med center is going away soon, and he's going up when it's safe to make that move. That's it. No more questions."

———

"It could've been worse, you know."

I give this some thought. "Yes, you are right. There is some hope," I respond. Carol, Porter, Craig, Mark and I are meeting in my quarters.

"Jason, you've got to go in his place."

"Yes, I suppose I do." I'd already thought of that and I don't relish the idea. "I don't know if I can pull it off though."

"Snap out of it man, you can do it," Mark says suddenly, somewhat out of character.

"There is no time, Jason. You'll look like him enough to pass after we get you in the same outfit and makeup. Didn't we at one time discuss this as a possible back-up plan?" I nod, and at the same time realize that this is something I have to do. They are right, there is no time left. A couple days have passed, it's time to go. "You've listened to his talks?"

"Yes, all of them. More than once. Caught pieces of a couple in person."

"Forget about looks, we'll take care of that. It's your demeanor that will carry the day. Just repeat his message as best you can. They will pick up from there." And I know 'they' are the contacts and supporters handpicked by Dylan.

———

370

Preparations are going quickly and we, including Mark this time, take off in the only flyer still available. It takes two trips. I am dropped off first and make my way into town without incident. I need to find that core group of Dylan's. Unlike Dylan, I am carrying my comms unit and other essentials for this extended stay.

Tracy sent a group message. Mark has made a good show, she says, and the fact that Dylan has 'disappeared' is all the talk. The others are helping to make sure it is already spreading like wildfire. Mark has headed back to base; he's says to give a shout when we need extraction.

When I approach the first of the contacts, I am almost overcome with fear of failure. But I press on knowing that this is nothing compared to what Dylan had to face. I am met first with indifference, funnily enough, then with shock at recognition, then disbelief followed by awed acceptance. It's amazing to see! I meet the others—same set of reactions! I am still nervous as hell but am struggling, successfully I think, to hide it. I speak as little as possible, but when I do, I use my 'Dylan voice' and demeanor such as they are. So far, not a hint of trouble. It's reassuring to see one or two of the team occasionally milling about incognito in the background.

———

I continue to travel about with one or another of this group and instruct them to spread the messages that Dylan taught. What I wouldn't give for a decent pair of shoes! I feel I am handicapped by the crowd; they won't leave me alone. I, as calmly as possible, use their awe as a kind of shield to isolate myself for a few moments alone to think and recharge. "Well done!" "Keep it up!" "I love you!" are the messages on my communicator. That last one is from Carol.

———

I've done all I can do out here. I'm tired. It's time for the last show, as it were. I signal to the team and they coordinate with Mark until we are all clear as to timing and location. I make my few parting remarks and the 'extraction' is made to great effect and wonder. Me, I'm hanging on for dear life while trying my best to appear nonchalant! Once I'm up in the runabout, we head back to base.

It's a great relief to be done with my part among the people. I get positive feedback from the team, but on the inside I'm not so sure. Dylan was the right guy for the job and I am sorry he couldn't complete it. Other than Mark, the rest stayed out in the field and have split up to make sure things get started on the right foot as planned. Porter has the flyer and is making trips back and forth, but I can tell he'd rather be done out there as well.

———

"I know you told me to take care of him, protect him."

"You did all you could," says Doc, but I get the feeling he's not saying all he's thinking.

"He knew the dangers; he wanted to do it."

"It was his decision, he's a big boy."

"Look," I say, "I don't know how we could have done more. It's a terrible thing. Really, the delay was the problem, if I understand you correctly. Without the long delay, the outcome would have been better.

"There was nothing else you could do," he says outwardly calm but now I'm quite sure he's upset with me.

I sit silent for a few minutes. He gives me the medical 'all clear' from my long exposure to the people and various pathogens out in the world.

"Or could you?" he suddenly asks with that frozen stare of his. "Did you have to engineer this last project of yours? Is it really that important? Why not let them be? They have to figure out life on their own, just like we all do. Is there anything we can do, really, that will have any long-lasting effect, other than what we've already done?" He turns his stare away and says, "What a waste."

"Doc, David agreed," I say in defense. "I'm not saying the plan wasn't mine. Ours. And it's my responsibility. David saw the effect of Brachus' interaction. He agreed that we should try to do something to correct it. In my view, we owed it to the people to try to help them back on the right path." No response from Doc other than he quits fiddling with his equipment and returns my gaze.

"There is a precedent," I add, and this time I get a questioning eyebrow raised as a response. "It's in the archives…"

"I'd like to see that," he snaps.

"No problem, I will send you the link. And, yes, I do think we will have a long term effect. Tell you what, look at the report from the mission archive and we'll talk again."

The stare. And then, his expression breaks from the confrontational stare and Doc resumes puttering about the little lab. "I'll read it."

———

"Where's your stuff?" ask Mark as he surveys my quarters.

"Already gone. I travel light."

"Hah, what? Already gone?"

"If you mean my personal items, they are already gone. Carol and I packed together and she said you took it."

"I took it? Where is your stuff again?" asks Mark as if he didn't comprehend at all.

"With Carol's. You have it already. You OK?"

"Oh. I have it. OK, if you say so."

"I marked all the equipment and tools and the rest. You see? Anything not marked, you can dispose of as you please. More trouble from Brachus?"

"Ha. Not for me, but for somebody. He's coming for you next, you know."

"No, I don't know but let him come. What's it all about?"

"No comment. I'm out of it. Gotta run, see ya."

"Mark?"

"What?"

"Somebody once told me 'relax, they can't leave without you, plenty of time', or something to that effect. Remember?"

> *Gleshert gave out some guarded good news. Dylan seems stable and whatever else happens, he will be coming home with us.*
>
> *There have been some final data acquired that are troubling. We have underestimated the total native population. It's not a large error but on the other hand it's statistically significant. I haven't discussed the portent of this with anyone, not even Carol. I should, though, at least talk it over with her. What it means is that 'our' people, the so-called chosen ones, may not be enough. They and their progeny may not be able to dominate the planet after all. It depends on relative reproduction rates. We can only hope now that the train-the-trainer approach we took works and works real well. If it doesn't, there's a good chance that competing philosophies will emerge and delay the hoped-for advancement.*
>
> *The more I think about our reward or 'carrot' idea, the more I like it. It's not a false promise, but I do agree with Carol it might be misleading. After all, they won't have the technology for many hundreds*

or thousands of years to perform any of the medical miracles they have witnessed. But the promise is real. They have seen that it can be done. Further, long ago their ancestors witnessed and recorded the long lifespans that are possible, again with pretty advanced technology, but that are certainly possible. Part of Dylan's message was, if they believe and promote his teachings, that the promise of long life in a more ideal world is a real possibility. It's our hope that, coupled with the senseless tragedy they witnessed in the brutal 'sacrifice' of Dylan, they will begin to renounce the primitive behaviors of insane wars and violent aggression based on greed and lust. It's a shame that during the time Brachus held sway in the field he, in his quest to fulfill David's desire that the prime lineage be protected, encouraged wars and battles. It will make the transition that much more difficult.

Carol and I are both having second thoughts about the inclusion of an aspect that was raised and accepted by the team: that of a threat. The overall message is one thing, but we decided to include a threat that we will return in the future to see how things are going. In other words, 'you'd better behave 'cause we'll be back, either to welcome you into the larger universe of civilized worlds or else...'

No matter now. Nothing else can be done. We are all done. It is what it is. The small steps that we've made on this mission are over, for good or ill. But if we move back and take a larger perspective, it's rosy. What used to be a molten ball of iron is now a nearly ideal habitat for life. The life it has is compatible in a fundamental way with ours. The people on it, while primitive, have the potential to join our larger society, someday, as equals. Like I said, rosy.

Misstep

I don't believe it; here he comes again. This time I offer no greeting, no nod; I just look. I am in the middle of what used to be my base camp quarters dismantling, sorting, and crating.

"Hey, there he is. Just where I left ya'," says Wes sort of to me, sort of to himself. The grin is wearing thin, that's for certain. I choose to continue only to look, waiting for him to continue with whatever his business is. "You sure you won't help me?"

"I don't think so. I've got all this…," gesturing at the remnants of my quarters. "Tell me again, exactly, what do you need help with?"

"Like I said, some help with my gear and other stuff from our visit. I'm overweight, and I don't mean here," he says, rubbing his abdomen and grinning still.

I am real tempted to make a comment but stifle it. "What kind of stuff?"

"Just some… keepsakes. What does it matter what? I just need some help." I don't respond and the grin disappears in a flash. "Forget it. I'll get them myself." He starts to turn to go, but stops himself and says, "I understand you are under your weight limit. I presume you won't…"

"How do you know that? Never mind. Go ahead?"

"You won't mind if I use up some of your allotment, will you, old pal?"

I turn away, and think, not of his question, but of his nerve. "Yeah. Ok. Whatever. Knock yourself out." Anything, to be done with him.

————

It is with some amusement that later I see Brachus lugging two cases, one in each hand, and a smaller bundle under his left arm, across our base camp common area. He came from somewhere over behind what used to be Mark's raw materials storage area and is heading to the uplift staging platform. He has to stop now and then to re-position the bundle by sort of hopping and moving his left elbow in and out. It's a sight. He doesn't see me in the small remnant of the mess hall, the only place left where there is some shade, but I can see him, no grin now, sweating with his effort.

Just as I am leaving my table—*the* table, as the rest have already been recycled—I see Brachus hurry off empty-handed in the same direction from which he had just recently emerged. 'More?' I think. I watch him long enough to see that he's going out beyond Mark's works, out of our base camp area entirely. As he enters and begins to climb one of the narrow craggy fissures that lead up into the surrounding mountains, I lose sight of him.

"You ready?" asks Porter as he and Craig both approach just then.

"You mean to go help him?" and I throw a nod towards Brachus' direction.

"No, can't. I'm prepping to take another load. And you with it. And Wes if he's ready."

"Me neither. I'm heading out for another sweep. The final one," adds Craig.

I'm puzzled and I must look it.

"We've been visiting our remote sites making sure we've collected everything. Not supposed to leave any hardware or anything, you know. Erase the traces, and all that."

"Of course. Are you finding anything out there?"

"Yeah, sure. There's always something." Craig pauses, glances at Porter before continuing. "There have been a few visitors too."

"Oh?"

"I've talked to them, such as I'm able. All that time helping you out there paid off—I can talk to them."

"No kidding. Be careful."

"No worries. The visits don't amount to much. I'm sticking to Dylan's program as best I can…"

381

"Anyway, you're scheduled to go up next, as soon as you are set," interrupts Porter.

"I see. Yes, I'm ready."

———

On my way up to the ship I ride alone with Porter and a full load of cargo. I scrunch in near a bulkhead. There are bundles, crates, various-sized cases, bulk material—all strapped down tight for ascent. There are remnants of Amara here; I see traces of reddish dust and grit on some of the pieces. A souvenir from our travels. I wonder about cross-contamination. I mean, we are careful enough, as I understand it, to decontaminate everything and everyone uplifted to the Hobbe but what about the other direction? Are we sure that we don't bring contaminants with us down to the planet? I've heard all about the protocols in place, but you never know. Too late to worry about that now.

We ascend and I move closer to a small viewport to watch the receding surface of the planet on which we have spent so much time. I think of Carol and how we have become close during this stay, of David and his struggles as a leader, of course of Dylan and his passion for the people down below.

The port allows for only a limited glimpse; it is the last close-up view I will have of this world. I try to embed it in my memory knowing all the while it is a futile effort. The images and videos I and the rest of the team have captured will substitute for our limited and imperfect memories.

———

 "Where is he?"

"Are you asking *me*?"

"Yes, I am asking you. Who do you think I'm asking? I'm looking right at you!"

I've inadvertently triggered the appearance of Mr. Means. "I don't know where he is. Last I saw he was hauling a couple cases of goods to be transported up. They came up with me and he was still down there." I want to add that I'm not in the habit of tracking the moment-by-moment whereabouts of Master Brachus, but think better of it.

David Means eyes me suspiciously and works his lower lip. Out, in, Out, in. "He can't be reached; his communicator is broken or dead."

"David, I checked all genies for proper operation just a couple days ago. Maybe he doesn't want to be reached."

"Doesn't want… What do you mean?"

"Maybe there's a simple explanation. Is everyone else accounted for? Lester? Tracy?"

"Yes, yes, both here. Tracy's been working with me and I've had Grigor and Lester working together on resource stowage and inventory for a few days now.

It takes an extra effort on my part to stifle a smile as I picture Grigor and Lester trying to get along.

"Give me a few minutes. I can check for him from here. Even if he's not responding, there's always the safety beacon. Even I don't know how to disable that." As I walk away I hear David talking on his communicator with Mark.

Just as I suspected, Brachus' beacon is active and strong, although he does not respond to me either. The safety beacons of the others on the surface have a strong signal as well. That's Mark and Craig. Porter's is out there too but weak. He must be in transit.

Carol is not in her shipboard work area, and I decide not to look for her in her quarters in case she is resting. I tentatively fiddle with Carol's optical equipment, but give up for now. I prefer to wait rather than mess something up. I doubt anyway if the view is sufficiently detailed enough to see anything useful at base camp, but David's angst earlier has me thinking about Brachus. A look can't hurt, so as soon as I can I will take a gander.

———

Carol and I maintain separate official quarters, but spend a lot of time together even so. I have just 'today'—our time cycles are going to get way off again, now that we are back aboard ship—set up my small personal space with the few items that I unpacked from her cargo boxes. And I'm helping her unpack her things now. Grigor appears at the hatchway abruptly and says, "Better check your screen mate. Someone's trying to get your attention."

I make my way back to my screen. He's right. Holy smoke, I am picking up emergency signals from the surface! David is trying to raise me on my comms unit too and the persistent emergency alarm has just begun buzzing in the ship. Why oh why did I choose just this one time to leave my genie in my quarters?

"Hey, David, yes I'm here. I'm looking at it right now. They're all three going off down there. No, wait. Just two. Brachus' beacon is strong, but he's not sending an emergency signal. Oh, here you are," I say as David appears in my quarters.

"Hang on," he says. And then to me, "I just dropped Mark. Pick him up now."

I get Mark on the speaker.

"Mark, it's Jason and David. What's going on?"

"It's not good. I got your message about looking for Wes…"

"I've got his beacon, strong."

"Well, you can quit looking for him. I found him. If you can, get my video feed on your screen and get Doc in there with you. It's bad news."

David summons Gleshert as I pull up Mark's video feed. I can't quite figure out what we're looking at as Doc joins us. They are now both looking over my shoulder at the shaky video from Mark down on the surface at base camp.

There is an overlay on an adjacent screen showing the guys' beacons on top of a terrain map. We can see they are not in the camp proper but just outside in the rugged surrounding area.

"What are we looking at Mark? Can you hold her steady?" The image zooms out, steadies, and then we see. "Mark, is that what I think it is? What happened?" The image now resolves into the far away figure of a man. Or what used to be a man.

"Guys, I'm here with Craig…"

"Hold on, we're getting another emergency signal here!" I interrupt.

"That's Porter. We tried to reach him before he left the ship to come back down. He's probably just getting my frantic messages right now."

"Mark, what are we… Is that Wesley we see?"

"I'm afraid so." The image zooms out again and Mark does a pan over to Craig, showing that they are in fact not in camp, but in the mountains. On one side is a steep, nearly featureless rock wall, on the other a precipitous drop-off. He slowly lowers the view and we see that it's a long way down indeed. "He must've fallen."

"Mark, steady the cam and zoom in as tight as you can. I need to see the damage right now. Is the solo flyer still operational?" asks Doc.

David shakes his head no while still looking at the screen.

"No, it's just been dismantled; some parts recycled already. Would take a while to re-build."

"Steady." Doc looks at the screen. He catches David's eye, then mine, shakes his head, and says, "Mark, a little above and to the left. See that dark area?"

"Yes, I do. We saw that earlier. Looks like he had a bad fall and there is no soft spot anywhere on the way down."

"What do we need to do?"

"David, look at it. There's nothing *to* do. We can fix a lot of things, but I can't put that right. Too much damage. Too much time. Getting there; getting him out. Mark, is there any way down there?"

"Absolutely not. Not without equipment and a way to air lift him up. It's sheer."

"Air lift? Rope, winch, cables, a stretcher basket. Come on, man!"

"Hold on David. To what purpose? Risk more lives? For what? I'm telling you, even from just the video feed, there is nothing to be done."

Doc looks at David and holds his gaze while saying, "Mark, save any images you can get. Also get the surroundings and any other clues to what happened. We're going to need them."

David got depressed again, and I don't blame him. He commented that all officers were supposed to be on board by then, but Mark and I both replied at the same time that we couldn't control Brachus; no one could—he did what he wanted to do. And that's when David walked out.

As much as I didn't care for him, it's a shame to lose Brachus; it's a shame to lose anyone. He's the only casualty for the entire mission, aside from what happened to Dylan. Now more than ever we have our fingers crossed for Dylan's survival and recovery.

The last load has been uplifted. All persons are accounted for except the one. The decision was made to use an incendiary device for a makeshift cremation. There was no choice. We couldn't leave him like that; we couldn't get down to him. It had to be done. Carol didn't watch.

Carol hasn't said much about the loss of Master Brachus. We agree it's a shame, but it's safe to say that we both think he brought it on himself. After all, what was he doing out in the mountains instead of up here safe aboard ship? I do have my suspicions, based on the few clues Mark dropped over the years, but have kept them to myself.

Should I have gone to help him when he asked? Maybe. I'll have to live with that, I guess. I notice that no one else was out there helping him with his 'keepsakes' either.

Discovery

"Do we know what happened?"

"I was…" Craig says, "I finished the final sweep and was prepping another load for Porter when I see I got a call from Wesley to come help him. I told him hold on, I'll come, but in a few."

"Yes, go on."

"I knew which way he went. I'd been that way before but never very high. I went up but then I figured maybe I'd missed him. I tried to raise him, but there was no response. I thought of going back—it's not really a path up there, it's a narrow ledge with gravel and…"

"We see the graphics," David says as he shuffles through the images Mark recorded and are now being shown on the screen.

"I kept going and found the bundle that I told you about."

"Is there a picture of that?"

"Maybe, but never mind. Here it is right here," says Mark as he puts the wrapped package on the meeting room table.

"Craig?"

"Well. That's when I saw him. When I leaned down to picked that up," indicating the bundle. "I called Mark, told him, and hit the e-button."

"And?"

"That's it."

"Alright you guys, what was he doing up there?" says Mr. Means.

There is some silence as Mark and Craig look at each other. "Getting that bundle would be my guess," I venture, to break the silence.

"Wait, there's more," says Mark. "David, click through those images. Here, give me that thing." David does, and Mark searches quickly and says, "There. See it? Let me zoom. There."

We see a dented and beat up case, scuffed, broken and dirty, laying way down on top of rubble at some distance from the body. David sees it.

"There's one of our cases," adds Mark. "I made a bunch of them for general use. He must have been up there getting it too. Or maybe he was going to put that in it," indicating the item on the table. David draws the bundle close and unwraps it.

"Yes, I agree. That would make sense. I saw him with

something similar not too long ago. He said there were 'keepsakes' in it," I add. David spreads the wrapper, opens the pouch inside and dumps the contents onto the wrapper.

My hunch all along has been correct. I know right away that we are looking at raw and valuable gems. They are not cut or polished, but that's what they are all right. I see the same look of recognition around the table.

"Mark?" David says more as a statement than a question and turns to look at Mark steadily.

Mark doesn't answer at once, but I can 'see' his mind working. He finally says, "David, Wes would bring in special shipments from the various resource sites, have me process them in between my regular work. He would come by later and pick up the output. I would venture to say that we are now looking at the output."

It's David's silence now that indicates to me it's his turn to process what he's just heard. "I see," he says and stands. "Grigor, wrap this back up and jettison it with the waste."

He leaves the room. We sit for a few minutes, silent. I for one am trying to decide if the meeting's over or not. My thoughts wander and I imagine the gems as they enter the atmosphere and wonder if they will vaporize before impact or if they will survive the fall.

———

"There's going to be an inquest. You know there will. We

should've kept that bundle of gems," Carol says later.

"Maybe he thinks the images will be enough," suggests Mark.

"It's wrong mate, it's plain wrong, one wrong thing after another," adds Grigor. "Markus, what were you thinking? Your cut?"

"My cut? Get lost. My cut. Just make sure you don't take *your* cut before ejecting them."

"All right, all right you guys, cut it out. I don't blame Mark. Remember Brachus was basically running the show down there for a long while."

Both gentlemen hold their tongues until Grigor says, to no one and everyone, "What *is* wrong, though, is tossing out valuables. Those should have been kept and added to our coffers. Wouldn't hurt to show some return on this trip."

———

When we are alone, Carol asks, "Do you think David's trying to cover it up?"

"What? No. There is no covering it up. We are coming home one headcount short. One so far anyway," I check Carol's face to see if she takes my meaning, "and there's no getting around that, period." After a moment, I realize I may have misunderstood. "Oh, you mean by tossing the loot? I don't know what he's thinking there. My first guess would be that it was just a knee-jerk reaction, with no plan at all."

"You're probably right about that. He's that way."

"I do think that Mark is worried, though."

"But he was acting under orders from Wes. He had no choice."

"But not official orders. I will bet you any amount that Brachus left no trail of this business. None. He went to a lot of trouble to hide the stuff too. No doubt he didn't even trust his own people enough to let them in on it."

"I still can't believe he's gone. If he'd asked for help…"

"Carol, he did ask me for help. He asked Mark first but Mark refused; he told me so. He'd had enough I guess. Then Brachus came to me. I know he didn't want to; he never liked me from day one."

"So…"

"So I didn't actually tell him to go jump off a cliff…" I say without thinking of the reality of the situation, but it hits me as soon as I hear my own words. "I mean, I didn't outright refuse. But I held off answering long enough for him to go away. And he asked Craig and Porter too I think, as we all heard at the meeting…"

Carol just looks at me—no change in expression, no comment.

"I guess I should've helped. He just rubbed me the wrong way and I didn't feel like doing him any favors. I didn't think it would end like this."

"Of course not."

> The general mood is changing from somber to homesick as we near departure. At least that's how I judge the crew. My duties now, by comparison to the wide open and exciting environment below, seem dull and routine. The varied and complex links to base camp, and other sites; the connections to remote cams; the surface and atmospheric monitors—almost all gone. The more or less constant accumulation, transfer, and storage of data has now slowed tremendously. The one planetary atmosphere monitor remains active and will for a long, long time, but it's not sending to us, it's sending home.

> I keep busy, but for the most part I am in an unusual state of mental transition. All of us have our physical boundaries well defined now, as well as our duties. Our horizon, instead of including vast vistas of mountains, seas, clouds, and open land, instead of being painted with practically every color of the rainbow in the sky, rocks, and leaves, is now limited to the next partition and, aside from vivid instrumentation lights, to a shrunken palette of muted hues.

> I find myself bugging Carol now and then for a hi-res view of the surface. That view, however, like my memories, is a faded substitute for the real thing,

dimmed and obscured by the intervening atmosphere.

We are all scheduled to see Doc for pre-launch check-ups and the beginning of treatment for the flight home. Dylan is already fully under for the return trip. Gleshert says it is for the best and will give the restorative cure time to work and ensure the highest chance of a positive outcome.

Carol read up on the history of the Hobbe itself and on its namesake, Lillian. She, Lillian that is, created a big stink back home a long time ago on her very first mission as commander. The one document she read says Lillian dealt with a rebellion near the end of a planetary stay. A group of her people, both male and female, defied her orders and prepared to stay behind, essentially forming their own seed population on an otherwise uninhabited world (uninhabited by humans, that is). Unfortunately, during an altercation three members of the rebellion were killed by the commander. The rest of the rebels abandoned their dream and reluctantly joined the returning mission.

The revolt jeopardized the successful completion of the mission since they were now short three critical crew members and the attitudes among the remainder varied from hostile to loyal, from angry to indifferent. Well, they did make it back in one piece. But, as a result of the mission review hearing, an official inquest was scheduled to determine the guilt or innocence of the commander relative to the lost crew members. After the inquest, it seemed certain that further action would be taken against her—action which could easily have ruined her career and reputation. Long story short, Ms. Hobbe defied protocol and went public in her own defense. The overwhelming popular support she received engendered a response from government officials who pulled the appropriate strings to make the whole matter go away. Her popularity due to her image as a strong leader able to make tough decisions remained high for the duration of her career and life.

Out of curiosity, I checked more mission histories, this time not for details but for frequency of visitation. It looks like our promise to return to this planet may take a lot longer than we guessed down below. It will be a minimum of five thousand of this planet's years before a return, and probably much longer.

It's time to wind down and begin to think of home. What will it be like? What has happened?

Carol and I have talked of the future. What's next? Another mission? A different career? It would be a dream to fulfill our fantasy of retiring someday to a property with some space, some natural feature or beauty, maybe a waterfront home. I am afraid we were spoiled by the beautiful areas we were able to visit and enjoy together on the lush, largely uninhabited planet below. It doesn't seem, no *matter how I figure it, that it will ever be possible for that dream to come true.*

Final note before we catch a wave: We have left orbit; the double L system is engaged and working. I've already seen the doc and am groggy. It's time to save my work and check out for the bulk of the journey home.

Getting Up to Speed

I will never get used to that. I will say I was expecting the
weird sensations and this time, while they are
indescribable, I can at least now assume they are normal
for this mode of travel. Be careful, set timer, relax.

I remember talking to my dad when I was very young. It
was a quiet time and we were alone. We weren't doing
anything but sitting; he may have been reading, I'm not
sure. But I was sitting beside him looking at his face the
way young kids do. In an adult, this sort of staring or close
inspection would be considered rude behavior, but as a
child it was just 'looking' with no other motive than to see.

"Dad, you have a black spot. There. On your cheek."

"Yes. I do."

"Where did it come from?"

He looked at me and thought for a minute.

"I got it long ago, when I was just a little older than you,"
he said. "I used to work on a train, you know, like the ones
downtown? But this was an old, old train and it needed fire
to run."

399

"Fire?"

"Yep. Fire to make it go. I used to shovel coal into the fire to make it burn hot."

"Coal?"

"Coal is a black rock that burns. I will show you sometime." He takes a moment to touch the black spot with his finger and says, "Anyway, one day, as I was shoveling coal into the firebox of the engine, a little red spark from the fire flew out and blew back and hit me right in the face. Right here. And since then, there's been a little black spot."

As kids do, I accepted this explanation without question. Near as I can recall that was the end of our talk, although I did think about what he said for quite some time. I still think about it. Since then the image I have of the spark as it flies off of the blazing fire, glowing and swirling through the air, inevitably making its erratic way to my dad's cheek, has remained vivid.

As I matured, historical fact began to clash with the story. Coal-fired engines were a thing of the past—the distant past. How can this be? In the way that happens with children and parents, I both believed the story and doubted it at the same time, trying my best to reconcile the discrepancy.

As an adult, I have convinced myself that Dad was telling a story, an interesting and harmless entertainment for his son, perhaps invented off the cuff. I also choose to carry the image of a brave and strong engineer faithfully stoking a fire in the face of certain danger. And I always will.

It won't be long now before we are back. I find myself thinking of family more and more. Carol and I will have our separate personal things to take care of and then sometime later will get together to discuss the future. I wonder if she's game for another mission, or if this is it. I could go either way.

————

"Remember, we've been gone a long time. Things have changed. It's going to be a shock," David announces at one of our wrap-up meetings. "Many if not most of your family members have opted into the LP but let me tell you that life goes on. I know from personal experience that nothing is perfect."

"LP? You mean LMP, longevity medical, yes?"

David nods. "It means long life but it doesn't mean infinite life. You will see clear signs of aging in those you left behind, assuming…" David looks around, seemingly to make sure everyone is paying attention, then continues, "… assuming the best case scenario."

Resuming, he adds, "I am required to tell you that you… me, all of us, will be attending mandatory debriefing. It's then that you will be brought up to speed on the news of the world such as changes in government, laws, and the like. As stable as we have been over time, as a society, you simply have to believe me that there will be surprises.

Changes at the Academy—I presume you know that the staff there, unless they have a family member on a long term mission, are not part of program—are to be expected. And we may safely assume that there have been one or more disasters, natural or otherwise."

David checks his genie and during this pause there arises a murmur amongst the crew, I guess about the expected changes David mentioned.

"David, what about Dylan?"

Dr. Gleshert doesn't wait to be acknowledged, and answers right away, "I am keeping him under and he will transfer to a proper medical facility as soon as possible. There is no other news. He's stable but I cannot make any other statement at this time."

"Back to homecoming." Quiet prevails again. "There is a second debriefing. This one will be private with your families or descendants, depending on your individual case. It's during this portion you will learn their fate, good or bad. I am required, also, to tell you that things happen. Sometimes people choose to opt out of longevity before you return, for whatever reason—this happens more than you might think. Sometimes accidents happen to the healthiest people, due to bad luck. Look at what happened to Wesley. What I'm saying is, be prepared, as best you can, for this second debriefing. There is bound to be an emotional shock, hopefully pleasant, but possibly not. Jason, are we set?" David says, and looks for me at the table. I nod.

"Ok. We are now close enough to home and in communication range, so why aren't we all overloaded with incoming calls and messages from home? It's blocked. All communication for now is routed through the ship's equipment and any incoming not critical to mission completion is blocked. And will be until debriefing. The reason is obvious, I think. The stack of incoming would literally overload each of our devices. Even if the device could handle it, we would each be overwhelmed catching up with messages from the years we have been gone. And by the way, you will be given suggestions on how to deal with this problem once we are back on the ground. On a personal note I can tell you this from experience: Do not start looking at the oldest messages first. If you think about it for a moment, you will understand why."

———

One nice thing about having access to communications passwords is that I can get my messages if I want to. He is right, there must be literally millions. I'm not going to attempt to go through them all, but for the text and other typed messages I am using filters to sort, and then keywords to bulk delete the ones that I know I don't want.

I have been long curious about my brother Tom and, strangely, filtering produces only a very few about him, and they are old. Real old. One is from that Jeff Sanders guy, copying Tom, and blasting Brachus for misleading him about trying to help with his career. He said that not only did he, Jeff, not hear from the people Brachus said he would set him up with, when Jeff talked to the people themselves, they said Brachus never contacted them at all.

Worse, he said that when he checked the receipts on the several messages he sent to Wes—this was back before we got out of communication range—they all showed they were read within an instant of each other. He knows, he says, at least from the Ming message-handling protocol, that this is a pretty good sign that they were never read: They were instead most likely group-deleted to the trash. At least, that's how their system worked at Ming: It would send a receipt at opening *or* at deletion.

The most recent message from Tom is ominous. It is short and says, 'J Am erasing last line. No limit now! Goodbye T' and nothing else. I don't see any other messages from him. I decline to search anymore and will wait for debriefing.

> *It's hard to believe after all this time and all that's happened, but I am back on home planet ground as I write this! Debrief is over—the first half of the first part at least. There is no way to absorb all this. The world I knew is now chronicled in history archives and while there is, as David said, a great deal of continuity, the names have all changed, even some of the language.*
>
> *For the next part we have been given time to meet and talk together as a group while having access to media. This is and has been an enjoyable session; a time where we can all share the surprises and changes. One more day and we break up the mission crew and meet privately for the second part—the family reunions.*

David said his goodbyes first. He was professional about it. I have to wonder if he will consider this mission his last. I don't think his experimentation results were what he was hoping for, but on the other hand it would be a big commitment for him to take on another mission.

Mark and Grigor are going to get together before the families come. They have asked me to join them. They say that others from the crew will be there but I decline. I need to talk to Carol about what she is going to do in the near future, once we are cleared to leave. Other than that I am in the mood to be alone.

So far we've had no update on Dylan. And I've heard no fallout from his 'accident' or Brachus' sad end.

Home Again

Parents, if any, come in first.

I thought I was prepared for the unavoidable effects of aging, but even so I have to work to avoid displaying my shock at her appearance as she comes in. The lines on her face have multiplied and deepened. Her hair is all gray, almost white. It's my mother all right—if I look at the eyes, there is no doubt—but numerous changes have ganged up as if to try to hide the rest of her from immediate recognition.

"Mom. How are you? Where's Dad?"

"Oh Jay, it's been so long! Look at you!" She looks first, holding me at arm's length, then hugs. When did my mother get so short? Her voice is soft and small, not how I remember it at all! I notice too that her hug is weak, not like the smothering hugs from before. "They warned me you would be different. But how different! You have turned out well, Jay, and so handsome!"

We must've both heard the same warning speech. How you never notice changes in people when you see them often although they are changing little by little all the time. But after a long separation, the cumulative effect of the small changes can be startling. The eyes, the smell, these have remained the same.

"How are you?" she asks, holding me again at arm's length and giving a little shake.

"I'm great. I'm good. It's good to be home. Mom, how's Dad? Where is he?"

"Jay…" she starts. But I can see without hearing any more that he's not coming. "Jason. Your father is no longer with us."

"Mom, why? What happened?"

"It's too much to tell right now. We will wait and talk about it," she says with determination. I see her eyes glisten, but no tears. "It was a long time ago. He did not want to continue the treatments."

"Didn't want…"

"He saw all his friends pass, oh, and not to mention Tom…" She put her hand to her mouth and stopped in mid-sentence as if she had not meant to say anything about Tom.

"Mom! Not Tom too?" I say, not really asking for a response. She hangs her head, but manages to nod.

"I… I just got a strange message from him," I say. Mom looks up, not understanding. "I mean I just picked up an old message that he left a long time ago. I didn't understand it. He said 'goodbye' in it."

"A... a voice message?" she asks, with some difficulty.

"No, no, not voice."

"Oh, Jay, I would have liked to hear his voice again." She wipes her eyes. "But I am forgetting. There is someone else here for you to see." She totters, rather unsteadily to my eyes, with short little steps to the door and signals for someone to enter.

I don't get it at first. This big strapping young man looks familiar, but...

"Come on, don't tell me..." this man says, in a voice and tone I do recognize from somewhere.

"Jared? Oh, you've got to be kidding! But how? How... how are you... I mean how did..."

"How how how... Ha! I am fine, how are you!" He says, laughing at my confusion.

As we shake hands and hug I start again, "How..."

"I can fill you in when we get home. You are staying with us, yes?" He gives me a questioning look but does not wait for my response. "I wish I could say there were more people here to greet you, but instead you are stuck with us." I gather the few personal items that I have and begin to walk to the door with them. "You do remember I tried to join the Academy when you did?"

"Yes, but you were too young or...?"

"Ah, but I made it the next try. Man, I've got more missions under my belt than you! One was short and local, but the long one—Jay, look at me! They put me on the LMP!"

I put my belongings into one small bag for the trip home. We meet with Academy personnel for a final exit interview, get my official release, and head out into the world I left so long ago.

We don't talk at first as we make our way. It is disorienting to see what used to be a familiar metropolis, now studded with so much that I don't recognize. I see the occasional building I know and point, "Look!"

"Yes, but look over there. Look how tall. That one is new to me, too. Say, didn't that used to be where the park was?" asks Jared to no one in particular.

"No, not the park. I think that's still there in between somewhere. I can't see it now, but not the park. Not there…" suggests mom.

"It was close to here all right. But come on. Hurry," and Jared picks up his pace like a schoolboy showing off a new toy, "and look here Jay. Remember this spot?"

I do remember. It seems incredible, but I do. Sometimes Jared and Tom and I would take the train and ride. Ride just for fun, going nowhere in particular. It was cheap enough public transit and we could entertain ourselves riding, looking and laughing at the people and sights. Sometimes we would come to the central terminus, near to where we are right now, and walk through the big city, looking for things to do or see.

It was in this very spot, this street between buildings where we spent many hours playing. At some point the street was closed off so that it became a dead end. No traffic at all. It was a silly game we invented here—'curb ball'—that was it. The street seems to have shrunk during the intervening years to alley status but it is the same place all right. It's a normal street with sidewalks and curbs but largely unused because it is so short and leads nowhere. If you loft a ball up high from one side towards the other, just so, it could hit the opposite curb when it comes down. Not just hit the curb but, if you did it just right, maybe one out of 20 tries, the ball would hit the curb at just the right spot and shoot straight back at you right along the pavement. It would bounce away from the curb staying on the ground with no vertical component at all. Not easy. I guess the frequency of good hits was just right to keep us trying to do it again. Ridiculous waste of time. But we had fun being together.

"Do you remember Tom going on about the rules? 'Limits define everything. Everything.' Remember that?"

I can hardly believe this dirty, dark street is still here. I look to see that Jared is watching my reaction. "This is it all right," he says, apparently reading my mind. "See, here are our initials over here," pointing at the blackened, scuffed wall.

"What? No. Impossible," I respond as I move to look where he is pointing. There is nothing there but dirt and the accumulation of graffiti on top of flaking paint on top of more layers of the same. I look back at Jared; he is smiling and shaking his head.

"It was right there, I swear cuz!"

Mom seems quiet and withdrawn to me, another sign of aging no doubt. She never liked Jared that much when we were young but now she seems to be amused by his wise-cracking manner.

———

"Mom, have you been living here all alone?" I ask. Our old house is long gone but I recognize some of the knickknacks and pictures. My old footlocker, of all things, still exists. It's filled with my stuff from before I left on the mission, undisturbed—a time capsule.

"No. Jared's been in and out since…" she answers. I learn that Uncle Joe has passed, and Nancy too. "I get together with the girls each week." The 'girls' are mission wives and mothers who have opted into the program, same as her. "I really do miss the garden. Remember the garden? The only times I got really mad at you kids were when you would get into the garden. My one little space, and you seemed attracted to it like magnets!"

For now my official address is with Mom and Jared. Jared is waiting for another assignment. He figures one more short mission and he will join private industry in some capacity. What capacity? He doesn't know yet. That's keeping his options open, he says. Oh well, who really knows anyway? I thought the Genetic Expansion program would be best for me. And I thought it would help define my career path too. But now I don't know. It may be post-mission lethargy, but I don't see any clear path for me. For now, I am content to spend time here, catch up on what's happened, if that's even possible, and get together with Carol when we can.

The inquest summons was waiting for me when we first arrived home. Now, that's some quick action on the part of the mission board. It only shows my name; I wonder if we all got one. Carol and I decided to hold off contacting each other for now, figuring that it's best to try to re-accommodate to family and all the changes without complicating life further.

I told Mom and Jared about the planet we visited and the unlimited space there. Wild and untamed, and room for gardens galore. I do have pictures and videos but put off showing them. I don't know why; it seems too soon.

They asked about the mission and I recounted some of the happenings, but not all. They asked about the accident. I gave the briefest summary I could. Jared related some of the excitement he experienced on his adventures too.

In my footlocker I find something new—a plain envelope with my name hand-written on it. Inside is the following note:

Jason,

Don't be sorry or sad for me. I have had a wonderful and fulfilling life. It overflowed with marvels, more than anyone could reasonably ask for or expect. I certainly didn't deserve to have a wife as supportive as your mother; nor could one find better sons than you and Tom. Don't be angry with me for my decision, but it will soon be time for me to go. I have chosen to forego any more treatments and will be happy and satisfied to end this final chapter naturally.

Your loving and proud father.

Questions

There is little chance of seeing Carol here. I don't know if she was summoned. We are, or were, a small crew and they probably summoned the whole lot of us. But I am here alone right now. It's a bare, small room and the door is closed. Two men in civilian suits sit side by side at a small plain table. No insignia. I am sitting in one of two chairs facing them. Why two chairs? Do they question in pairs? There is a recording device in plain view on the table.

"What exactly were your duties?" they ask. I answer.

"And when you say 'shipboard', you mean you had other duties while on the surface of the planet?" I answer by explaining that I assisted David with his genetic documentation work at the bio camp. I think it's best to answer the questions simply without too much detail. Detail will only raise more questions.

The questions and short answers go on. The inquest officials are both professional, courteous, and non-confrontational. They nod and accept everything I say which, of course, is being recorded. Only one of them speaks directly to me; occasionally they talk quietly between themselves.

"Where was Commander Means at the time of Master

Brachus' accident?"

I answer, qualifying my statement with the fact that I don't know when the accident actually occurred.

"Switching gears for a moment—please describe what you know of the circumstances of Ensign Water's injuries." By this they mean Dylan. I describe what occurred as simply as I can and emphasize that we were all deeply distressed not to reach him sooner than we did. I ask what news they can share of his present condition. "None," is their answer, they are sorry to say. "Be aware that there are some open questions about his injuries and the events leading up to them. By your admission, you were a participant in at least some of these events. While these questions and their answers are beyond the scope of our meeting today, they will be addressed in the future."

I nod.

"What was the consensus of the crew regarding Commander Means' style of leadership, his ability to command?" I decline to speculate on the rest of the crew's opinions, but do offer my view of David and his ability. I choose to phrase my comments so as to highlight David's positive attributes.

I am asked a similar question about Brachus. I answer that I had little interaction with him. "He kept mostly to himself and his team; socially we did not engage," I add.

"What do you know of Master Brachus specifically as it relates to his accident? What was he doing at that moment?" I say that, to my knowledge, he was alone at the time of the accident and so I don't know exactly what he was doing at that moment.

"Can you speculate?"

"Yes, I can," I say, and for the first time I see a mild reaction from the officials. "I believe he was retrieving personal items that he wished to bring back home with him."

"What makes you think that?"

"Because he told me as much." Definite reaction this time, and I see they make eye contact with each other for an instant. I notice now for the first time that the two inquisitors could be related. They look alike in a familial way.

"What did he say?"

"I saw him carrying items to the staging area for uplift—we were preparing for imminent departure—and I asked what they were. 'My gear,' he said. 'Keepsakes,' he said."

"Is that all?"

"A little while later I saw him, Master Brachus, heading back in the same direction from which he came when I first saw him with his load. I presumed he had more to retrieve and didn't think any more of it. We all were packing and making ready for departure."

"And what was the nature of the 'keepsakes'?" they ask. I respond that I do not know.

"You do not know?"

"I do not know. I never saw the contents and he did not say. There was a small bundle recovered at the accident site which the Commander opened during a team meeting on board ship sometime after the accident. Inside that bundle were what looked to me like raw ore and crystals."

"Are you sure of that description?"

"I am in that I did not touch them or inspect them up close."

"What became of the bundle and contents?"

"David left it in the care of another crewmember for disposal. I never saw it again."

"Which crew member?" they ask. I hesitate to answer.

"Jason, you realize this is not a trial. We are here to ascertain as many facts and details as we can regarding two things: first, the circumstances surrounding the tragic loss of an experienced and valuable officer and, second, a separate inquiry into the circumstances surrounding the life-threatening injury to Ensign Waters. We conduct these interviews to help make a determination whether or not the facts warrant a further action."

"A further action?" I repeat.

"Yes." Silence fills the room.

"David left the bundle in the hands of crewmember Bevan," I say reluctantly, seeing no other choice. Grigor is not going to be happy. The officials speak together for a moment but I can't hear what they say.

"It seems that an inventory of Master Brachus' belongings removed from the ship did not reveal anything beyond ordinarily expected items." I don't respond even though their expressions indicate they would like me to.

"Well?"

"I'm sorry, was that a question?" I ask. "It's possible they didn't make it up to the ship at all. As I said, I was already on board when the emergency signals were received."

More muffled discussion between the two officials ensued.

"That will be all. Thank you."

"I hope I was able to help. It's a shame that an otherwise successful mission should be marred by events such as these. Dylan is a hero in my mind and Wes—I mean Master Brachus—well, I didn't get to know him in depth, but any death is sad, especially so close to the end of our mission."

We all three stand and shake hands politely before I turn to leave.

"Oh, one quick thing. Sorry," the one asking the questions

says before I get out the door. I stop and turn back to face the two men. "The body—it was unrecoverable?"

"Gentlemen, I believe it was unrecoverable without heroic effort and danger to other crew members. You've no doubt seen the images of the area; you know we had little equipment left on the ground. I don't see how it could've been done."

"Yes, yes, of course," says the one that has been doing all the talking.

———

It's too far to walk all the way home, but I feel the need to do something physical. I decide to skip the nearby central terminus and walk to the next one. Past the new and old buildings, the dirty dead end street, past where the park should have been, and when I had walked off the remains of my inquest mood, I took the transit home.

"Mom, did Dad ever talk about his shoveling coal?"

"Shoveling what?"

"Coal. Did he ever work in a mine or on a train shoveling coal?"

"Shoveling coal? What are you talking about, shoveling coal? Who shovels coal? Where did you hear such a thing? Shoveling coal."

"No. Never mind, just a crazy idea."

"Coal? On a train? Is someone playing a trick on you?"

"No. Nothing. Never mind."

Again with the speedy decision. This can't be good. A summons to trial came for me today, exactly one week since the inquest. Who are they going after? David? And why? Sure David's not a perfect leader, but Brachus caused his own problems. And Dylan, well he, I'm sure, would be the first to blame only himself for his suffering. Maybe they are looking for a fall guy, any fall guy. I like to stay out of political intrigue but I know enough that it sometimes works like that. There's a dead body, someone has to be blamed.

Funny, I get no response from Dr. Gleshert. I wouldn't put it past him to delete my messages upon receipt if he's in the wrong mood. He did tell us that Dylan would be transferred to a proper facility so it's possible that Doc doesn't have an update to pass along. No news is good news and that's the saying that I'm going with here.

There's still been no contact with any of my shipmates since the debriefing. I'm missing some of them already, mostly Carol. Each one must be going through some equivalent of what I am going through. Even so, you would think consideration would have been given to the notion of keeping in contact. We were together a long time. Debriefing should have covered this.

A Question of Innocence

Answers

"We are in session. Commander Means, I am under the impression that we, you and I, have an understanding of the seriousness of this proceeding. Is that a correct assumption?"

"Yes, your honor, it is."

"And is there that exact same understanding between myself and the honorable members of the bar here representing their respective sides of this case?"

"Yes, your honor," they respond practically in unison. "There is."

"I would like to remind all participants in this case—litigants, witnesses, representatives, interested parties, and visitors—that the defendant is on trial for negligence and dereliction of duty as Commander of a deep space vessel resulting in the death of his second in command, Master Wesley Brachus. The penalties for a guilty verdict are by no means insignificant and may indeed result in further civil prosecution. Let us proceed keeping the seriousness of this case in mind and act and speak accordingly. I would issue a warning to all of you: do not make me feel the need to repeat the terms of this understanding."

Judge Compton employs a few moments of silence as his gaze passes slowly over the room and its occupants. It is clear that his words and threat have had their intended effect.

He resumes, "Now, if the bailiff will please find and remove the person or device responsible for that incessant clicking noise… It's coming from over there," the judge says as he points toward the offending sound. I did not notice it until now, and just as I do—it stops. The persons in the area whence the sound emanated do not move or otherwise betray the culprit. The bailiff, halfway to the gallery halts, waits, and then looks back at the judge who, in turn, scowls, waves the bailiff back to his post and says, "Gentlemen? Proceed," indicating with his eyes first the representative for the defense, then for the prosecution.

"Thank you, your honor," begins the prosecutor. "I repeat my question: why would your second in command, who you admit was on the surface on the planet without your knowledge and in noncompliance of protocol, ostensibly wander off into a desolate and dangerous mountain pass?"

This time David maintains composure and answers the question using an appropriate tone. I see Carol looking at me and she makes a silent and subtle gesture of 'Whew.' I agree.

I am still confused as to how we ended up with a trial. Past missions, both deep space and local, have suffered losses before. Forget about space missions, all endeavors whether scientific, military, civil, what have you, involve calculated risk. In our careers, the risks are pointed out multiple times and in detail. Sad to say, we have had the occasional loss of an entire ship and crew, and yet cadets continue to enroll, to enlist, and to volunteer. Who is to blame for these losses, or for this one in particular? Not David, surely.

And who's to blame for Brachus' actions but he himself? Still, one wonders: Why the trial? Who benefits if David is punished for something he did not cause, nor had control over? Or did he have control? Maybe he should have stepped up and reined Brachus in. It's true that he relinquished the bulk of control of field operations to him, and for a significant length of time, but that's a commander's prerogative. And maybe he should have enforced the order for officers to board according to protocol. But how? Brachus was easy to read in one regard: He was out for himself only. How do you control that?

Dean Carson is on the stand now. He's being questioned by the prosecuting attorney about the impact of the loss of Master Brachus on the Academy. He answers, "Wesley, I mean Master Brachus, will be missed terribly. He brought a lot to the program, and had a long and bright future ahead of him. I would add that I considered him a personal friend."

"And what is your opinion of Commander Means?"

"Commander Means has likewise been an asset for many years. He is certainly experienced and we are fortunate to have had the benefit of his service and dedication. But," he continues, "a complex procedure has been established based on the evaluation of losses in the past. A protocol that is specifically designed to enhance the safety of crew members exists. It must be followed. It must be enforced."

"Your honor, would you please instruct the witness to answer the questions without embellishment? He was not asked about procedures or enforcement," objects the defense attorney.

"The witness will restrict his answers to the topic of the question."

"On the topic of protocol, Dean, please do explain what you mean. Why is the protocol as it is?"

"The current protocol, the one in effect at the time of the tragedy, is the end product of years of analysis of empirical results. In other words, as each misstep or, in the worst of cases, loss, is incurred, an analysis is completed to determine what could have prevented the loss. As we have applied this procedure again and again over the years, the protocol has evolved into what we have today. Sometimes the guidelines are misunderstood or may appear cryptic, but each one is there for a reason. And that reason is to increase safety."

I don't buy it. The dean supports the prosecution; ok, I get it, let's move on. I notice the judge is preoccupied with something. The prosecutor stops in mid-sentence, and looks towards the bench. The judge, noticing his look, orders him to continue.

There is a subtle humming, or vibration, pervading the courtroom. It is of low magnitude but it is there and it's continuous. It's the building itself–heating, cooling, filtering. I lose interest in the dean and the monotonous back and forth of question and response. My attention wanders and it is with some effort of will that I maintain what I hope is the appearance of alertness.

"… and Mr. Carson, is it not true that you are in the so-called LMP?" asks David's attorney. At this, I am brought back to full attention. Exactly the question I would have asked!

"The LMP?"

"Yes, Dean. Why certainly you know the acronym for the life-extending medical treatments that you have been receiving for some time. A very long time, in fact. Isn't that true?"

"Your honor. Relevance? This line…" interjects the prosecutor.

"Your honor, I believe there may be a stronger connection between the witness and the deceased than mere friendship. A connection that may cloud that objectivity of the witness and may influence his testimony. It is in the best interest of my client, not to mention in the best interest of fairness, that this relationship, if it exists, be brought to light."

The judge stares at the defense attorney for an instant or two before saying, "You may continue in this line."

"The LMP, Dean? Is it true?"

"Yes, of course it is true, as you well know. And it's not a secret."

"Is that a treatment that is normally reserved for extended-mission crew and their immediate families?"

"Yes, normally, but…"

"Dean, do you qualify under either of those categories?"

"I do not. But it was considered wise, in the name of continuity, to extend…"

"Considered wise, by whom, I wonder? Don't answer that. Instead consider this: There is a long history in our society wherein learned men and women consider term limits to be the wise choice."

The dean doesn't answer, the prosecutor objects, and I am ready to stand and cheer for this breath of fresh air in the proceedings.

"I have no further… Wait, there is one last thing. I understand these treatments are quite expensive. Who is paying for them?"

The dean smiles and relaxes visibly. "I am," he says calmly.

"Oh really? On a dean's income? Thank you. No more questions."

The trial went on at an excruciatingly slow pace punctuated by brief moments of headway eliciting in me primarily boredom interspersed with short bursts of mild interest. I have to say I coasted along quite happily for a while after that cross examination of Dean Carson. Maybe David's lawyer is not so bad after all. Is he bluffing, or does he know something? Either way, he had the dean flustered.

Poor Mark and Craig. They both had to take the stand, being the ones who found the body. Craig was nervous and came across as totally believable. Mark on the other hand did not betray one iota of nerves. He did a workmanlike and professional job answering all that was put to him with short and succinct answers. I'm not sure how a judge and jury would interpret his demeanor, but to my eye it was a great job—vintage Mark, but without any of his corny gags. He said that Brachus had special ores processed, but that he, Mark, did not deal with the output—Brachus picked it up personally. 'Was the output part of the so-called 'gear' or 'keepsakes'?' he was asked. 'I do not know,' said Mark.

My signed statement has previously been accepted into the court record and I do not expect to have to take the witness stand.

So far, it seems to me it's all been about character. Prosecution tries to demean David's and that of his witnesses; defense tries to bolster David's while bringing into question the character of the witnesses for the prosecution. If I had to call it, I would say David is losing. Prosecution hammers on the fact that David did not have Brachus safely on board at the time of the accident and that this was the primary cause of the whole affair. A simple matter of not enforcing the rules.

Defense has been trying to raise the question of why Brachus, ignoring the widely known deadline for boarding, would remain on the surface for 'keepsakes'—whatever those may be. I would be hammering away at the fact that Brachus was amassing gems and probably other valuables for his own personal wealth using mission equipment and personnel. What is so difficult about it? I know Mark knows; am I going to have to say something? I really don't want to have to be the one. Not again.

Judgement

The row of small high windows along one courtroom wall admits beams of early morning light. These beams create a series of bright parallelograms slanting across two of the remaining walls, heavily distorted by the corner, the room trim, and wall décor. I swear I can see them move, creeping slowly across the wall and down as the morning progresses.

I see Mark and Craig have joined the gallery; I presume this means they will not be called as witnesses again. Tracy is here too, as she has been throughout. Boy, could *she* be a witness as to Brachus' character. I have to say that for the first time ever, she looks uncomfortable to me. None of the usual flirting, winks, and what not. No eye contact at all. She's out of her element for sure.

We are experiencing one of those inexplicable delays during which, to the naked eye, absolutely nothing, and I mean nothing, is happening. There is the occasional low murmur of hushed conversation riding on top of the ever-present hum of the building itself.

The defense attorney begins speaking, addressing Judge Compton. My attention is drawn back to the proceedings when I hear something regarding Ensign Waters. Suddenly, an undercurrent of whispers passes through the gallery like a wave. I can see surprised glances pass between not a few of the people. Carol too seems excited and is smiling at me for some reason. When I give her a questioning look she just makes a head movement toward the back of the gallery.

I don't see it. Just then an attendant opens the courtroom doors. A figure enters. One of the strips of sunlight, at that moment, is positioned such that it falls slanting across the person illuminating his head. I hear a muffled gasp from somewhere in the room. The face is familiar and I am confused, looking from the face and the white hair to Carol and back again, not able to work it out. I can see now that the figure is supported at one side by an aide who has one hand on the left elbow of the white-haired person and her other hand on one of the courtroom doors.

The figure turns and says something; his elbow is released and he starts slowly walking unassisted through the gallery toward the bench. He is smiling slightly and, as his pace is slow and deliberate, looks from side to side. When he is about half way down the short aisle, he looks my way and catches my eye. Now it clicks; Dylan. Dylan is here. A rush of emotion clouds my thoughts for a moment. It's a lot to grasp. He's back!

The bailiff holds the gate open for him and Dylan makes his way to the witness box. The progress of his recovery was unknown to me until this moment. I've heard of trauma or medicines causing hair to turn white, which is striking enough, but that's not the only difference. His movements are slow and deliberate—ok, that could be part of his recovery. But the way he scans the room, the way he commands our attention...

"The defense will show that Master Brachus did indeed defy Commander Means' general directive to return shipboard, and further that he did inappropriately use mission equipment and personnel for his own personal enrichment, and the enrichment of others," says David's counselor as he scans the gallery significantly, "at least one of whom is in this room."

Another buzz rises in the crowd; the judge ignores it. Dylan is sworn; he is asked a few general questions to establish his identity, rank, duties and so forth. He is thanked for appearing, in consideration of his condition.

"Not at all. I may move slowly, but I feel fine."

Then he is asked if he knows why Master Brachus may have stayed behind and what he may have been doing when the accident befell him.

"I believe I do."

"First please tell us in your own words what you believe Master Brachus was doing outside of base camp just before his accident."

"I believe he was retrieving a cache of highly valuable minerals and compounds, mostly gems."

"And why do you think this?"

"Because he showed me some of the gems, and mentioned he had a lot more hidden in the mountains near our base camp."

"Can you speculate why he would confide in you?"

"Because he was drunk." When the murmurs arise this time, the judge calls for silence.

"Did he say anything about the gems; who they were for, for example?"

"Yes."

"Yes? Go ahead. Again in your own words. What else did he say?"

"He repeated several times that he, Brachus, is 'set for life' and…"

"Yes, go on."

"He said he was set for life even after 'paying off that bastard Carson'."

"Exact words?"

"Exact words, as best I can recall."

Many eyes are upon the dean and yet he maintains a stoic visage and erect posture—no visible reaction.

"When you heard of Master Brachus' accident, did you

436

make any conclusions?"

"None, other than I was not surprised."

"And now, to what or to whom would you assign blame for the accident?"

"I would blame greed. The greed of Wesley Brachus," said Dylan in the same calm voice he has used from the start of his testimony. The judge again has to call for silence. I turn to see Carol—we are not in the same seats as before—and I give her a silent 'wow' expression. She nods.

The prosecutor is allowed to question the witness. "Mr. Waters, do you remember anything after your injury near the end of your stay during the mission, anything at all?"

"I do not."

"Mr. Waters, are you certain your memory is working correctly now?"

"Yes. It is working fine."

"Well, how could you know that? My understanding is that you suffered pretty severe injuries and that these injuries affected your brain. In fact, you are still recovering from your trauma, isn't that the case?"

"Yes, that is true."

"And yet, we are to accept your statements as true without question. Do you have any proof of any of this? Was someone else with you at the time, or…"

"Yes, there was one other there with us,"

"And who would that be?"

"Lester Glavin."

There is a delay while the prosecutor reads something on the table near his seat. I can see Lester in the gallery. He is fidgeting and his usual smirk is gone.

"We have a sworn statement from Mr. Glavin; he mentions nothing that supports your testimony."

Dylan looks pleasantly at the prosecutor but does not say anything.

"Do you have any proof of you statements?"

"No, I don't have any proof."

The prosecutor smiles at Dylan and turns to display the same smile to the rest of the court.

"But someone here does have proof," adds Dylan, causing the prosecutor's smile to disappear.

The prosecutor turns back to face the witness. "And who would that be?"

"Jason Shipley."

I am shocked, to say the least, and try, but can't think of what he means. I feel the eyes of those in the courtroom upon me. I can see only Dylan's calm face, as if I have tunnel vision somehow, and he is looking back at me from the witness stand.

————

For the life of me I don't know how I got to the witness stand, or how long it took to get here, but here I am! I look out to the gallery and can at first only find Carol. Some kind of blindness has gripped me. Now I see Dylan still in the courtroom and sitting way back, against the far wall, to one side of the double doors. I think that if those doors open inward, he's going to get hit.

The sun has moved higher. There is only a single remaining beam of light passing thru one of the high windows. A bright flash attracts my attention. It's Vanessa. She is in the gallery. I almost didn't recognize her when I first saw her in her street clothes and jewelry as she is now.

The counsel for the defense asks me if I can confirm Dylan's testimony. I stammer out something—I'm sure it's nonsense. My mind wanders and I think about what I must look and sound like to the courtroom. Must focus. Then he asks me if I have any records of the mission unknown to the court.

All of a sudden it's clear! They want my private archive! It contains a backup of Brachus' group's folders.

————

A recess gives me time to access the requested data. And it gives me time to recover my composure. I produce the entire media archive for the court without filtering; there is no choice and no time to do otherwise. Of interest to the court are the images that back up Dylan's statements. The folders containing pictures and video of Brachus and his shenanigans in the field aren't hard to find; there are quite a few. Some elicit rumblings and tittering from the gallery and it takes a while to find the important ones.

Just as Dylan said, there is a video of him and Brachus. You can tell it was taken by Lester because Brachus refers to him by name and you can see his, Lester's, hand and arm sometimes in the frame. On the pinky of the hand is a silver ring with dark red stones. We watch the scene unfold. Brachus is drinking (one of Mark's concoctions?) and rambling on about something. It's not clear at the moment what he is saying. Suddenly he seems to achieve a bit more clarity than was evident up until then, grins at Dylan, winks at Lester behind the cam, and offers to show Dylan 'something.' That something turns out to be a box of stones that Brachus describes as 'rocks of a special nature,' and he follows this comment with his biggest grin. I hear someone on the gallery laugh quietly. During the showing off of his box of loot he does indeed say, just as Dylan testified, that he, Brachus that is, will be 'set for life' after settling up with Carson.

My attention drifts from the media presentation to the various people in attendance. Dean Carson remains emotionless in the gallery but this time his posture is not so erect and his eyes are cast downwards, not forward as before. The video, incidentally, shows two native girls—it's easy to see that they are not crew members—nearly naked, one delivering what looks like fruit to the table at which Brachus sits with the rocks, the other refilling his cup; Dylan's cup remains untouched during the entire sequence. The girls, however, do not remain untouched by Brachus. The video shows him rudely pawing at one as she tries to pull away.

The video is stopped when the cam zooms in and follows the movements of the girls as they exit the crude hut in what looks like a tropical setting. I can't place the location; I'm quite sure I was never there. The judge has to call for order more than once as the gallery erupts into pockets of chatter. The defense attorney talks to David; David looks relieved but also dazed; the prosecutor objects to the use of a video that he had not been privy to; Lester twists his ring to try to remove and pocket it without attracting attention—he fails in that attempt.

The dean continues to sit quietly, staring down. I see people around him whispering and talking, but not to him. In the crowded gallery he looks, for all intents and purposes, alone.

The judge calls both attorneys to the bench, along with the bailiff and an attendant officer. I think they are working out what to do next.

> *Several things seemed to happen all at once after the video. I could not tell you what all took place— it's a blur. David caught my eye at the end. We didn't speak and I never got close enough to talk to*

him. Several of the crew got together after adjournment, Carol and I among them. For once, I enjoyed letting the small talk wash over me and even threw in a couple inane comments of my own for good measure. It was a good feeling. The overarching emotion? Relief.

Mark was Mark. He had exactly two of his favorite drinks and disappeared. Grigor was in a positive mood, told a joke or two, and gave me a 'well-done' toast. Vanessa flashed in and out; Tracy stayed and held her own for the time I was there. She said she wanted to "check out local talent of the male persuasion." There were handshakes all around. It felt at last that we had proper closure for the mission. Doc never showed through any of this; don't know why. GlassHeart indeed.

Funny about Craig. He never said much to me but was clearly part of the group and enjoyed himself. He has changed a little too. I saw it then for the first time. A future commander no doubt. We parted after a warm handshake.

Carol and I said our goodbyes to the group and left together. The transition to peace and quiet was sudden and complete as we stepped outside. The sun was down, the sky was clear, and the temperature just perfect for a still evening. We strolled in silence for a time until we came to a large greenspace in the city. In the relative darkness we found a place to sit and watch the stars wheel slowly and majestically overhead.

Just in Case

The Academy is searching for a new dean, the charges against David have been dropped, and Lester had to do some fast talking to explain his part in the scandal. The Academy as a whole, I understand, has undergone scrutiny to weed out whatever corruption may be left. It's for the best.

The inquest into responsibility for Dylan's injuries has come to nothing, mostly because of Dylan himself. He takes full responsibility for the 'accident' and explains that, look, he feels fine. He is fine. No harm no foul. It's a relief to get all the legal stuff behind.

"Jason, I'm so proud of you and how you handled yourself up there."

"Handled myself? Up in court? You're kidding! I think I blacked out for most of it. I can only imagine what I must've looked like and said."

Carol and I have gotten together at my mom's place. We've both been relaxing after the tension of the trial. We're out on the balcony.

"It's nice out here. It's a little small, but it works; it's nice. Say, isn't it something about Dylan?" she asks. "He's a new person. You know, physically he looks great, all in one piece, but there's something about him. A maturity now, I guess."

"Not to mention the hair. I didn't recognize him at first."

"Yes the hair, but more than that. It's hard to explain; maybe more time is needed for him to return to his old self."

"Actually, I like the new Dylan. Really, it's just more of the same. Remember? He was very impressive at the end of the mission."

"You got a delivery, Jay," Mom calls from inside.

"Ok, thanks, we'll be in later."

"They're putting it in your room. It looks official."

"Ok, thanks. What? My room? No, mom, tell them the storage room for now. I'll get it later." To Carol I say, "So, what do you think? Do you want to stay in the program, try for another mission, or what? They told me at the end that I will be eligible only for short duration missions now, the same for you?"

"One at a time, chatty. No, I wasn't told that. But, no matter, I don't want to do another mission. It's too long, too alien, too much drama. It's draining. Besides, if I do decide to continue my career, my real love is astrophysics, and I don't have to sign up for any kind of mission to work in that field. Remember what you said about opting out?" She pauses as if to give me time to digest her thoughts. "Truthfully, I was hoping for a new focus for my life."

"And that would be?" I say, even though I dimly realize that there is something she's hinting at.

In response, Carol just looks at me, then turns to gaze out over the balcony railing at the view beyond. She waits long enough for me to figure it out on my own.

"But would that work? What if I… what if we forget about missions and the Academy? We could find positions somewhere, save up and have plenty of time together. To start a family I mean."

At that last statement Carol turns her gaze back to me and smiles. "Oh, Jason, that's what I would like. But how long before it's possible?"

"It's hard to say. We need to put down some goals, some numbers…"

"Oh dear, always the romantic," she chides softly. "I keep thinking about our time out there," she says, and I understand her meaning even before she continues, "at the bluffs, in the forest… It would be nice to find something like that. Don't get me wrong, I understand about economics, I know we can't afford a planetful of beautiful locations. But something… some small part of that would be delicious."

"There are nearby populated worlds. I know one that's

relatively undeveloped. If we could swing something there, I know you'd like it."

Her mood changes as she stands and leans with her hands against the railing, looking out. The sun is going down but is obscured by a band of clouds near the horizon. The clouds are themselves shades of gray, but the sun's rays cause their upper edges to shine bright white, yellow, and pink. "For now, let's look into the possibilities. We have a waiting period before active status resumes and we have to make a decision; let's use that time to see what's possible and what's not." She turns now and leans casually back against the railing. "We are both qualified for ground duty. That's always a possibility if we do stay with the Academy or one of the other departments."

"Yes, true, but those spots are hard to come by, and from what I hear we would have a hard time saving up anything at their level of compensation…"

"Ah, but I hear there's an opening for a new dean…"

———

Carol and I have made it official and have seriously begun a list of wants and needs. You know, a list with qualifiers like: must-have, would-like-to-have, could-take-it-or-leave-it, definitely-don't-want, and like that. For my part, my number one wish is for some way, ground based or not, that we can stay together and work towards our shared vision.

I learn more about Tom's last job—the testing job—from

talking to Mom and cousin Jared. He signed up to test an advanced version of the artificial skin, like we saw Gleshert use on the mission, but in an open space environment. Not sure what that means. The few messages that he sent relating directly to the testing seem to indicate a degree of success. It does nothing much to clarify his last message, sadly.

———

Jared is off and gone now. He left soon after the trial was over. Mom has decided to stay here at the apartment as long as she can manage it. We know that we are welcome here now, and after she's gone too. Mom makes a point of that. Well, it's on the table, but I know Carol and I both would like something out of the city; out of any city.

I find myself thinking a lot about the mission. Not so much about David, Brachus or his misadventures, or even most of the rest of the crew. I think about the people there mostly, and Dylan too. I think about the gorgeous planet they have to tame, to use, to develop. I think about their learning, step by step, how to grapple with their surroundings and each other. I wonder that they will have to stumble upon the same truths as every other civilization, and will have to make the same mistakes.

I wonder if they think about us and our interactions during our time there. Whether David's genetic meddling will pay off or not, who knows? The populations when we arrived, as David said himself, met or exceeded expectation. I can only

447

hope that we gave them something to think about—a standard toward which to strive. Was our intent understood? Did it spread like we hoped? Did they get the message that there's hope for a better life in the future? It would be nice to think that when we do return, we will be able to meet with them on equal terms and to welcome them into the wider universe of civilization.

Oh, an important note to follow up on my last entry. The delivery that arrived at Mom's for me was a crate that contained the remainder of my personal things from the ship. I went through them with Carol. However, the bulk of the crate's contents consisted of three unexpected items— metal cases with handles, dented, with red grit still visible in the seams and scratches, along with a dirty cloth bundle, wrapped up tight. Someone had attached a tag to one of the cases' handles which read:

Shipley: these were unlabeled but were uploaded during your last mission using your ID number and never picked up

I made sure Carol was with me when I opened them. We sat down in stunned silence as we let the reality of what we were looking at sink in. There were, as you may imagine, some long conversations about our next moves. In the end, I have to say that we implemented a satisfactory solution.

The contents of 'her' case were delivered to the Academy anonymously as found assets to be disposed of as they see fit. The rest, well...

We've both since retired and picked out a nice place to live, with plenty of room for family—hers, mine and ours. It's near the edge of a beautiful forest within walking distance, down the bluff, to the sand and the sea. We call it Amara.